—— "NYPD. Open up..." ——

Ever opens the door, but I can only see a sliver of her goddess figure because the chain is still on.

"Oh. Is something wrong, Officer?"

"As a matter of fact, there is." I tug my ever-present notebook and pen out of my back pocket, pretending to consult the first page, which sucks, since it means taking my eyes off her for a second. "We've gotten several complaints about the smell of chocolate coming from this apartment. You know anything about that?"

Ever bites her lip and throws a guilty glance over her shoulder. "Maybe. What's it going to take to make this go away?"

I lean forward, close enough to hear her breath go shallow through the crack. "What's it going to take?" I drop my eyes to her exposed stomach where a rhinestone sparkles from its place of honor in her belly button. "We can start with a thorough inspection of the premises."

T0050580

By Tessa Bailey

The Academy Series
DISORDERLY CONDUCT

Coming soon:
INDECENT EXPOSURE

Romancing the Clarksons
TOO HOT TO HANDLE • TOO WILD TO TAME
TOO HARD TO FORGET

Made in Jersey Series
CRASHED OUT • ROUGH RHYTHM
THROWN DOWN • WORKED UP • WOUND TIGHT

Broke and Beautiful Series
CHASE ME • NEED ME • MAKE ME

Crossing the Line Series
RISKING IT ALL • UP IN SMOKE
BOILING POINT • RAW REDEMPTION

Line of Duty Series
PROTECTING WHAT'S HIS
PROTECTING WHAT'S THEIRS (novella)
HIS RISK TO TAKE • OFFICER OFF LIMITS
ASKING FOR TROUBLE • STAKING HIS CLAIM

Serve Series
OWNED BY FATE • EXPOSED BY FATE • DRIVEN BY FATE

Standalone Books
UNFIXABLE
BAITING THE MAID OF HONOR • OFF BASE

ATTENTION: ORGANIZATIONS AND CORPORATIONS
HarperCollins books may be purchased for educational, business, or sales promotional use. For information, please e-mail the Special Markets Department at SPsales@harpercollins.com.

TESSA BAILEY

Disorderly
CONDUCT

THE ACADEMY

AVONBOOKS

An Imprint of HarperCollins*Publishers*

This is a work of fiction. Names, characters, places, and incidents are products of the author's imagination or are used fictitiously and are not to be construed as real. Any resemblance to actual events, locales, organizations, or persons, living or dead, is entirely coincidental.

Excerpt from *Indecent Exposure* copyright © 2018 by Tessa Bailey.

DISORDERLY CONDUCT. Copyright © 2017 by Tessa Bailey. All rights reserved. Printed in the United States of America. No part of this book may be used or reproduced in any manner whatsoever without written permission except in the case of brief quotations embodied in critical articles and reviews. For information, address HarperCollins Publishers, 195 Broadway, New York, NY 10007.

First Avon Books mass market printing: September 2017

Print Edition ISBN 978-0-06-246708-9
Digital Edition ISBN: 978-0-06-246709-6

Cover design and photo illustration by Nadine Badalaty
Cover photographs: © Sara Eirew (man); © xavierarnau / Getty Images (background); © IIIerlok_Xolms / Shutterstock (kiss)

Avon, Avon & logo, and Avon Books & logo are registered trademarks of HarperCollins Publishers in the United States of America and other countries.

HarperCollins is a registered trademark of HarperCollins Publishers in the United States of America and other countries.

FIRST EDITION

HB 08.22.2023

If you purchased this book without a cover, you should be aware that this book is stolen property. It was reported as "unsold and destroyed" to the publisher, and neither the author nor the publisher has received any payment for this "stripped book."

ACKNOWLEDGMENTS

I never thought I would have one of those dreams that inspires a book—but it actually happened! *Disorderly Conduct* started as a movie reel that played in my head while I was unconscious. A young man on his way to a lover's apartment, thinking their no-strings "arrangement" couldn't possibly get any better. Completely clueless that he's already in love—and about to get a hard lesson. In my dream, the young man was in a suit, so I fixed that tiny glitch when I woke up, putting him in a uniform instead. And thus, Charlie Burns was born.

So thank you, too much wine before bed, for giving me interesting dreams.

Thank you Nicole Fischer, my editor at Avon, for wanting this series, getting excited when I turn in my work, and typing loads of LOLs in the margins of the manuscript. You turn work into a total pleasure.

Thank you Patrick and Mackenzie, loves of my life, for supporting me every day.

Thank you Laura Bradford, my agent, for making this series a reality.

Thank you to the readers who I hope are about to fall in love with Charlie and Ever.

> "In all the wild world, there is no more
> desperate a creature than a human
> being on the verge of losing love."
> —ATTICUS

Disorderly
CONDUCT

CHAPTER 1
Charlie

*P*eople magazine isn't going to name me the Sexiest Man Alive any time soon, so I don't play the long game with girls. If I see one who interests me, I go in for the kill. Fast. Before some jerk who uses pomade or beard moisturizer gets there first.

Here is what I have going for me. One: My nose has been broken twice, I only have time to shave every other day and I'm strong as a bull. So if I'm walking down the street with a girl, no one is going to mess with her. Two: I'm capable as hell. I see a problem and it gets solved, because I don't mind hard work and sweat. It's a good thing, too, because I'm training to be a New York City police officer, and shit needing to be solved is part of the job description. Three: I don't go out with tons of girls. But I damn well know what to do when I get one beneath me.

That's not a boast. It's just me being grateful that I know how to pay attention.

And *damn*.

Speaking of grateful, the man upstairs must have been feeling sorry for us fellas down on Earth when he created the blonde who just walked into the Hairy Monk, the Lower East Side pub where I'm spending this rainy afternoon with my friends Jack and Danika. The nonalcoholic beer I'm holding remains suspended in my hand as the blonde peels back her hoody and shakes out her umbrella. I'm not ashamed to say her body caught my attention first. I'm a man in my sexual prime and by prime, I mean I'm horny most of the goddamn day. So the whole overalls that end in a skirt look? It's really working for me, because her legs are two sticks of dynamite and I'm more than willing to die in the explosion.

But it's her face that rocks me back on my booted heels.

Whoa. My stomach knots up. Which is unusual. I train at the police academy six days a week, and I eat like a pregnant horse. My stomach is made of iron. This girl's face, though . . . it's like I know her from somewhere, but there's no way we've ever met. Yeah, I would have remembered. Would have asked her out and possibly resorted to begging.

That's another thing about me. I'm not short on confidence.

Yeah, every guy in the place—including my pal, Jack—is checking her out, but I'm willing to bet no one has the balls to go talk to her. What *is* it with men making women do all the heavy lifting nowadays? Are they afraid of rejection? Worst case scenario, she tells me to fuck off, flashes a wedding ring or feigns deafness. In which case, I chalk it up to a lesson learned and walk away with my pride intact, knowing I had enough brass between my legs to take a shot.

"Don't even think about it," I say to Jack, finally sipping from my neglected beer. "She's mine. As far as you're concerned, she's invisible."

Jack smiles like a drunk pirate into his whiskey. To be fair, that's his default expression. Drunk, disorderly pirate. And yet women flock to him like he's giving away free Adele tickets. "One problem with that. I'm not invisible to *her*, Charlie boy."

"Good thing your ego is," Danika mutters, from eight inches down where she's sandwiched between us. Danika: small in stature. Large in attitude. "It's not a matter of who calls dibs. She could very well tell you *both* to fuck off."

I shake my head, still a little confused over the

whole stomach knot situation. The blonde is sitting beneath a bar light now and God. *God.* She's just been out there, roaming around the Earth this whole time? Her eyes are huge and full of humor. The good kind, like she'd blush over a dirty joke, then tack on an even filthier punch line. When the bartender asks what she'll have, she doesn't even look at the chalkboard . . . and then her incredible mouth moves and my fly almost unzips itself. "If she tells anyone to fuck off, it's going to be me."

Jack chuckles under his breath, which also makes him sound like he should be manning a ship with a skull-and-crossbones flag. "Now there's the can-do attitude they teach us at the academy."

My friend's sarcasm isn't lost on me. Everyone who comes into contact with Jack knows he can take or leave the academy. Whenever he makes his disdain known, I bite my tongue so I won't break into a motivational locker room–type speech. Becoming a cop is my sole purpose in life. I go to bed at night dreaming about the badge. About making my bureau chief father and lieutenant brother proud. It baffles me when my friend doesn't share my enthusiasm, but I'm learning to accept my freak-show overachiever status among our threesome of friends.

We're roommates, sharing a three-bedroom apartment a couple blocks away with Jack's childhood friend, and fellow academy attendee, Danika.

Danika is the reason Jack put his unmotivated ass through just enough college to enroll in the academy. And I'm pretty sure she'd scouted me out at orientation, pegging me as someone who would help motivate her pal, and the three of us have been inseparable ever since. Despite the fact that we're all opposites and drive one another crazy.

"You leave blondie on ice too long, someone else is going to get the honor of her fuck off," Jack says, signaling for another whiskey. "What's taking you so long?"

"Good question," I mutter, tapping my beer against my thigh. "Did I shave today?"

Danika lifts a dark brow. "You're asking us?"

"Thinking out loud. What am I wearing?"

"Look down and find out."

"I can't. She's looking right at me." And she is. The friend she arrived with is tapping away on her cell phone and gesturing, but blondie is watching me curiously through the crowd of Knicks fans, tapping a cocktail straw on the edge of her glass. The knots in my stomach now have knots. "If I do a clothing check, she'll know I'm wondering if I look decent enough to approach her. I'll lose all sense of mystery."

"You are eye fucking her across the bar. Mystery solved," Jack drawls, sipping his fresh drink. "Shit, Charlie boy. This might be the first time I've ever seen you . . ."

"Hesitant," Danika, the smartest among us, supplies. "He's right. Your caveman mentality is bent. Did you sleep on it funny last night?"

My scholarly roommate is right. And if I don't move soon, I'm never going to live this down. Glancing over at Jack, I can already see the wisecracks forming, preparing for delivery. What is it about this girl that makes me think twice about introducing myself?

Sure, I have *no* time for a relationship, now or ever. That fact is written in stone. If anything came out of approaching blondie, it would be a one-time thing, and I would make sure she knew that up front, out of respect. She might not be interested in casual, but I'm jumping the gun even having those concerns. We haven't even spoken yet. What is wrong with my man brain? And hell if she's not still watching me. I'm not sure either one of us has blinked in the last five minutes.

Everyone in the bar cheers, presumably because the Knicks scored, and I use the crowd's momentum to push forward through a sea of jerseys and half-drank pints. Something crazy happens, though, and it makes my lips curve into a smile.

Blondie jumps off her stool and comes to meet me halfway.

Ever

*O*h, *he'll do nicely.*

I have a sixth sense when it comes to unavailable men. It has been passed down through many generations of mistresses, going all the way back to my great-great-grandmother, Babs Carmichael. She created what I secretly refer to as the Mistress Manifesto, although the rules have never been written down on actual paper. *That* would be tacky. No, our means of survival are stored in the locked vault of my heart, same as they are for my mother.

Those rules are as follows:

1. *Remain independent.* This little gem is what has kept our lifestyle thriving for so long. We depend only on ourselves for that pretty green paper. No gifts. No personal information exchanged that could lead to messy entanglements. No holidays spent together, *especially* Christmas and/ or birthdays.
2. *Never let the arrangement last past one month.* We're not made of stone. Sure, we're using men to fulfill our needs, but even the staunchest of emotionally distant mistresses can fall prey to the right set

of dimples and sweet talk. One month is enough time to get a man out of your system without either party getting too comfortable. Or in too deep. One month means leaving the man before he leaves you.

3. *Choose only unavailable men.* This is the only rule I have modified slightly to fit . . . well, me. While my mother and her predecessors had no qualms making time with married men, I believe it's wrong. So my version of unavailable is men married to their jobs. In New York City, that is *not* hard to find. Walk down any sidewalk in any neighborhood, and you'll trip over a driven market analyst with too many dollar signs in his eyes to look for your secrets. I once had a fling with a food blogger who muttered about bottomless brunches and cocktail pairings while in the throes of passion.

Yeah, blog boy didn't make it anywhere near one month. Most of them don't.

And it has been *a while* since someone captured my interest at all. My roommate, Nina, and I have been getting our catering company—Hot Damn Caterers—off the ground, so I could blame my newfound career, but mostly, no one has tickled my mistress sense lately.

This guy walking toward me from the other side of the bar? He's making it hum. *Loud.*

What is it about him? He's not pretty or polished, like the men I normally gravitate toward. Men who obviously care a lot about their appearance are too self-absorbed to be absorbed by *me.* This one looks like he yanked on some jeans, threw a backward hat over his bedhead and chugged milk straight from the carton. Which is totally out of keeping with his ruthlessly fit physique. Dude's arms are like two torpedoes strapped to his torso, but he's not showcasing them at all, like most gym rats would do. No wedding ring. His eyes are blue. A beautiful, soul-sucking blue. And they're intent. Focused. Way too focused.

I stumble a little on my way to meet him half-way through the bar. Has my sixth sense grown faulty through disuse? A moment ago, his rest-less demeanor screamed unavailable. He'd been checking his watch, drinking an O'Doul's—nonalcoholic beer, if I'm not mistaken—like a clas-sic worker bee whose responsibilities await. Now? Now he looks ready to throw me over one of those muscle slab shoulders and carry me out of the bar.

Just as I begin to reverse directions and head back to Nina, Blue Eyes shakes his head at me. "No, no." He crooks a finger at me. "Finish what you started."

Whoa baby. That little quiver in my belly is bad

news. Being ordered around is not my jam, but I find myself edging closer, wanting to hear more of that scratchy baritone.

It can't hurt to see if he passes the mistress test. Can it?

"I'm Ever," I say, extending my hand. "I *never* start things I don't intend to finish."

"I want to believe that's a promise, but it sounds more like a warning." He takes my hand, and lightning shoots up to the curve of my neck. "Charlie."

Slippery heat crawls up my inner thighs. He still has my hand and it's so warm, his gaze so captivating and intelligent, I can't look away. Or walk away. Like I really should be doing. "Want to play a game, Charlie?"

"I don't know." He gives my hand a tight squeeze, then lets it go with something that looks like reluctance. "Are we competing or on the same team?"

"I . . ." How is this guy tripping me up? I always have the upper hand in conversations with men, but this feels almost like . . . an even playing field. "I've never thought about it in those terms."

"So you play this game a lot, huh?" He tucks his hands into the pockets of his worn jeans. "Since we're issuing warnings, you should know I don't like to lose. And if winning means you're not going to try to run away again, that goes triple."

Seeming to catch himself, his gaze cuts away and he clears his throat. "At least not today."

Okay, that was definitely code for *I don't do long term*, right? If his signals got any more conflicting, I'd get whiplash. The test would decipher his code, though. It was sure fire. "Are you ready?" He nods. "Where do you buy your socks?"

His mouth twitches, but he doesn't hesitate even a millisecond to answer. "Amazon."

Passed. That question is designed to weed out men in relationships and dudes who live with their moms. No man with a significant other or living in mom's basement buys his own socks. They just don't. "Prime member?"

"What am I, caveman? Of course."

God, he's tall. And warm. He's like a furnace. It's a physical strain to keep myself from rubbing my face on his butter-soft-looking T-shirt to heat the cold tip of my nose. Some crazy intuition says he would let me, chuckling deep in his belly the whole time.

Get a hold of yourself, woman. It's time for question two. He's got his arms crossed now, face all serious like he's taking the SATs, giving me the strong urge to giggle. "What is your favorite holiday?"

Question two sounds simple, right? It's anything but. If his answer is Christmas, he's the commitment type. Even if he doesn't realize it yet, he's going to find himself and a petite brunette in matching Frosty sweaters someday, drinking nog by the fire while his triplets rip open presents. If his answer is Valentine's Day, he's a goddamn filthy liar and doesn't deserve the pleasure of your time. If he says—

"New Year's," Charlie answers, smiling down at me. "Not New Year's Eve. I like the day after. It's like the whole city is sleeping. It's never quieter as those few hours after everyone finally passes out."

"You can walk down the middle of Broadway and—"

"Not see one yellow cab," he finishes for me, coming closer, including me in his warmth. "I know, right? It's the greatest."

"Yeah," I murmur, feeling more than a little dumbstruck. Around us, the bar goes wild for something on the television, but we just stand there, staring at one another. I know I'm supposed to run for my life right now, but I'm paralyzed. There is a *reason* for the Mistress Manifesto. It prevents us women from settling. From signing on for a lifetime of cumbersome routines and potential pain. My great-grandmother gave up her independence and moved to the suburbs only to be thrown over for a younger version of herself. My whole life, my mother has impressed on me that there are *no exceptions* when it comes to men. Relationships don't last, because men's affections are fleeting.

When we're in control of the game, we can't get played.

If Charlie passes the test, he won't be easy to shake when the one-month limit strikes. I know it for a fact. The longer we stand here, the closer he draws, the hungrier his expression. I *need* to scoot, but . . . "What do you do for a living?"

"Is this part of the game?" he rasps.

I shake my head.

"I just started at the police academy." His tone suggests we're discussing sexual positions, and my nerves stand up and cheer. "I'm going to be a cop."

The pride in his voice tells me a lot. "The best cop, huh?"

His blue eyes flash with determination. "Damn right, cutie."

There's my elusive answer. He's married to law enforcement. Thanking God my sixth sense hasn't completely gone to pasture, I now feel comfortable posing question three. "Which part of the movie *Titanic* did you cry over?"

He's not thrown off whatsoever by the randomness of the question. And I love that. "How do you know I cried at all?"

"Everyone cried."

Most men give me one of two answers. They either try to be funny, insisting they cried when Old Rose threw the Heart of the Ocean into the water, because it was such a waste of money. *Lame.* Or they lie and say they cried when Jack dies. No, they didn't.

Charlie doesn't take any time at all thinking of his answer. I can see he has it stored up, ready to go, but he's hesitating to spill. "What is it?"

He shifts the ball cap on his head, brim to the front, before turning it backward again. The subtlest of redness is visible at the top of his cheekbones. "When the old people are holding each other in the bed . . . all the water rushing around them. I might have gotten a *little* misty."

Fail.

FAIL.

My heart is going double time in my chest. I've never gotten that answer before, but it *has* to be wrong. Is he a relationship guy disguised as a casual fling? I can't figure him out. But I know a man who has a soft spot for an old, married couple isn't opposed to being the better half of one someday. Even if he doesn't know it yet. *I* know, though. So I have to walk away.

"Uh-oh," Charlie says quietly. "That wasn't the right answer, was it?"

"No." I start to back away. "You were supposed to say you cried when the captain went down with the ship. Alone."

"Cutie." The single word is low and urgent. "Come back here."

I'm in the middle of turning when he grasps my arm. He spins me back around, pulling me into his heat, molding the fronts of our bodies together. *Zing.* He's so hard and *inviting*, my knees go loose and I sag. My stuttered breaths boom in my head. I only glimpse the briefest hint of dread, mixed with desperation, on his face before his mouth lowers to mine. And then we're kissing. Oh, this is *kissing*. Like a Marine leaving behind his sweetheart on the tarmac. His fingers tunnel through my hair, his tongue awaits no invitation and we go for broke, right there in the middle of a bar full of buzzed twenty-somethings.

My underwear is soaked by the time we come up for our first breath. No lie, he's the most amazing kisser I've ever locked mouths with. Charlie yanks me up onto my toes, walks me backward until I hit the wall and we dive back in with even more enthusiasm than before. His erection is so thick and jutting, I have to remind myself it's not polite to climb men in public. He's making it so hard to resist, though, groaning every time our tongues slide together, his hands twisting in the material of my skirt. A male who needs to fuck and needs it now.

"Enough bullshit about right and wrong answers," he says huskily, right against my lips. "Just please, please, for the love of everything holy, let me take you somewhere, Ever."

Am I really considering taking this man home with me? After he failed the test? I can't escape the feeling that I'm venturing into dangerous territory, but his blue eyes, his hands, his . . . voice and personality are sucking me in and I can't back away. I'm powerless.

"I don't want anything serious, 'kay?"

His voice is rife with conviction when he says, "Me either."

We search each other's faces for long moments, looking for any traces of doubt. Finding none . . . or possibly refusing to see any . . . I let Charlie pull me toward the door.

CHAPTER 2
Charlie

E ver Carmichael is salvation.

I'm not *just* saying that because she calls me *big man* when we're fucking.

I'm already unbuttoning my uniform shirt, even though I haven't even reached her building's lobby yet. My cock is so stiff, I think I might black the fuck out before I get it inside her. Here's the thing, though. Ever will understand. She'll take one look at the tented fly of my standard issue, police academy pants and let her slinky, bad girl panties drop.

This *woman*. You just can't fathom the magic she wields.

I don't want anything serious, 'kay?

She said those words to me the rainy afternoon we met. At which point angels filled the bar and started singing. I've had women tell me before they didn't want entanglements or relationships, too. My long line of law-enforcement ancestry, however, has honed my ability to differentiate between truth and fiction. And Ever is the first woman who actually *meant* those words. Nothing. Serious.

I'm right across the street from her building now—a four-story tenement on the Lower East Side. She works nights running her start-up catering company and sleeps late, so at noon on my lunch break, she'll still be soft from bed. Freshly showered. I'm going to fuck her lights out, I swear to Christ. As soon as I walk in the door.

In the month since we met, the urgency to be inside Ever has only skyrocketed. The need to get my hands on her smooth skin, my tongue inside her bare pussy. You don't understand—I'm a *fiend* for this woman.

And guess what? That's perfectly fine, because I can have Ever any time I need her. Now, hear me out before calling me an arrogant prick—although I admit to being one on occasion. Ever can have *me*, too, when she needs me. This arrangement works both ways. After a Maroon 5 concert two weeks ago, she showed up at my apartment around midnight, high on Adam Levine—or whatever he's called—and we didn't even make it inside. I hiked up her tiny, leather skirt and gave it to her right there in the hallway. We weren't quiet about it, either, not that I heard the neighbors complaining.

My point being, this arrangement I've made with Ever is what most men don't dare dream about or even deserve at age twenty-three. For my species, it's usually a choice between empty hookups or committed relationships, complete with updating your Facebook, Twitter and Instagram bios, but *only* after deleting from all of the above any photographic evidence that you ever used your dick. Don't get me wrong. I'm all about commitment. Right now, though, my entire reserve of commitment juice is being poured into becoming a cop. A lieutenant, specifically, just like my older brother, Greer. And eventually a bureau chief like my father, his father before him . . . and back about four generations.

This thing with Ever? It's neither empty, nor committed. It's a fucking unicorn. It has made me a believer in life on other planets, Bigfoot and even the Jets winning the Super Bowl again someday. Apart from the Levine Incident, we haven't spent any time at my place, because Jack or Danika are usually home. Not to mention, I covet this little slice of heaven I've carved out, and I worry my roommates will make some crack to Ever about wedding bells—which is never happening—and blow the whole perfect situation to hell. Plus . . . they don't need to know a damn thing about Ever. She's mine. I'm hers. We're ours.

Unofficially, of course.

I'm halfway up the first flight of stairs now. Two more to go. There's no one around this time of day, so I give my king-sized erection a nice hard squeeze through the panel of my uniform pants, groaning under my breath when I let myself imagine Ever's hand replacing mine, somehow knowing better than I do how I like being touched. I only have an hour before the next training session begins up on East Twenty-First Street. If I want to graduate at the top of my program—which I will, come hell or high water—I need to not only show up on time, I need to be *early*. Which doesn't give me enough time with Ever, but frankly, I'm not sure an amount of time exists that would constitute the description *enough.*

I can see her door now. Just a thin piece of wood separating me from paradise. She's got a welcome mat that says "Come back with a warrant," which I've seen—and laughed about—before. But today it gives me an idea. Might as well kill two birds with one stone by practicing my cop approach and getting her panties wet at the same time. Coming to a stop outside her door, I'm like a jungle cat, balancing on the balls of my feet, swaying in slow motion, just waiting, waiting, for her to open that door so I can pounce. Just as I catch a whiff of chocolate and raspberry, I lift my fist and pound on the door.

"NYPD. Open *up*."

The blender that was whirring a moment before silences, and I hear her light tread traveling along the floorboards to reach me. Ever opens the door, but I can only see a sliver of her goddess figure because the chain is still on. "Oh. Is something wrong, Officer?"

"As a matter of fact, there is." I tug my ever-present notebook and pen out of my back pocket, pretending to consult the first page, which sucks, since it means taking my eyes off her for a second. "We've gotten several complaints about the smell of chocolate coming from this apartment. You know anything about that?"

Without missing a beat, Ever bites her lip and throws a guilty glance over her shoulder. "Maybe. Maybe not. What's it going to take to make this go away?"

I let my gaze wander down to where her thigh peeks out through the sliver of light and feel my dick protest this delay I've created. I wish I hadn't played this game, because I'm impatient for the door to open so I can get two handfuls of her ass. Short skirts. Does the girl own anything else? Forget I questioned that. What was I thinking starting this game of role-play when I'm short on time?

Ever knows I'm jonesing, too, because she's trying not to laugh at me.

Oh yeah, cutie? Two can play at this game.

I prop an arm against the door jamb and lean forward, close enough to hear her breath go shallow through the crack. "What's it going to take?" I drop my eyes to her exposed stomach where a rhinestone sparkles from its place of honor in her belly button. "We can start with a thorough inspection of the premises."

"Yeah?" She kind of breathes the word. "And if I don't cooperate?"

Pretty sure I'm dying. Or I'm already dead. "Then I'm afraid I'll have to use excessive force."

Oh, she loves hearing me say that. Did I fail to mention Ever likes it rough? She does. She likes it down and dirty. Sweating, swearing, filthy-talking, come-to-Jesus sex that leaves nail marks on my back.

"I have to admit . . ." Ever closes the door long enough to open the chain lock, then pushes it wide so I finally have my eyes on her. All of her. And it's just like that scene from *Weird Science*, when the ultimate woman—conjured up by two perverted males—is suddenly real, standing in front of them, fog twisting in the air around her. And yeah, I'm only *one* guy, but I'm easily horny enough for *two*. "I'm feeling a little uncooperative right now, Officer."

A unicorn, my friends. Nay, The Holy Grail. I've found her. She was right here in the Lower East Side this whole time I was growing up on the *Upper* East Side. But it doesn't matter. Because I've found her now. And nothing—*especially* some misguided desire for commitment plaguing the rest of humankind—could possibly fuck it up.

Ever

Charlie Burns, you dirty, dirty man.

Look at him. Sauntering into my apartment with that male stripper grin like he owns the place. He's already untucking his shirt, giving me an intentional peek at those do-me abs. This proprietary attitude is what I love about him, even though I should probably hate it. He was born to win. Someone told him on Day One: Post Womb, "Charlie, you can be any damn thing you want. It's your world."

He's done nothing but act accordingly.

It's what makes him perfect for me.

My mother taught me the same thing, although the sentiment was slightly different. On my sixth birthday, she took me to the mall to get my ears pierced. As I sat there crying—little ballerina slipper earrings that had seemed so harmless when I picked them out—now punctured through my lobes, my mother said, "Ever Carmichael, you can have anything you want in this world. But don't you dare believe a man when he says he can give it to you."

At the time, I never imagined how often men would make those claims when I got older. It doesn't hurt that I look like *that* girl. Oh, you know the one. She's dancing in the background while Calvin Harris spins records at a Vegas club opening. Drink in hand, not a care in the world, just working the ol' bump and grind. I managed to sneak through the assembly line with normal-sized tatas, but had no such luck avoiding a Playboy-bunny shade of blond. *That* girl.

Charlie is getting closer, but I'm backing toward the kitchen, because someone should have to make him work for *something*, right? He doesn't know which part of me to look at first. Tits? No. Legs? Hmm . . . no. Ahhh. It's an ass day. Should have known, considering it's a day that ends in *Y*. The way he spins me around is aggressive, leaving no more room for playfulness. He pushes me forward over the kitchen table, which is unstable to begin with, and the legs kick up a groaning protest. Or maybe that's Charlie. Yeah, it is. His calloused palms, roughened from constant training with firearms, are raking up my bottom, pushing apart the flesh, squeezing it back together.

"There's only one way these cheeks can get any sweeter." Out of the corner of my eye, I watch him dip a finger into my bowl of melted semisweet chocolate. When I feel him drawing a C on both sides of my bottom, I shake my head. Proprietary motherfucker. I love it. Especially when he scoops his hands beneath my knees, lifts with zero damn effort and props them on the table's edge, putting me in a very provocative position and Charlie mouth-level with his handiwork.

My pulse grows erratic under his inspection. What thong am I wearing? Blue? No, the red satin one. Nice. An appropriate choice to accompany the chocolate. It's like freaking Valentine's Day on my ass right now—and this is as close as we'll ever come to celebrating such a couple-esque holiday together.

Especially because our month is up. Today.

It has been exactly thirty days since we tumbled out of the bar together into the rain, beginning an affair that has gone by in the blink of an eye. I've managed to keep him at a distance, every way but sexually, but it gets harder every day. Thank God he is forever on the clock and racing back to the academy. His schedule means no cuddling, no pillow talk. And I don't yearn for those things at all.

I don't.

Ahhh. Wow.

I'm distracted from troubling doubts when Charlie peels down my thong. He gives my bottom a little slap that tells me without words what he wants. But I love when he commands me—perks of seeing a future cop—so I arch my back and give him a questioning look over my shoulder.

"Tilt your fucking hips and spread your thighs, Ever." He snaps my thong against the back of my thigh. "I skipped my lunch break for this, so give me something to eat."

That's what I'm talking about. I'm rewarded for following his directions when he spreads a line of chocolate through my dampening flesh and licks it up with his tongue, not slowly at all. Greedy. So greedy. I fall forward onto my elbows to give him more access, and he sinks his tongue into me with a growl. *Oh Godddd*. My mouth is open, sucking in oxygen, heartbeat pounding like the bass of a Nicki Minaj song in my ears. *"Charlie."*

Charlie's blunt fingertips massage the inside of one thigh, right below the juncture where his tongue slips up and back, like an erotic seesaw. He nudges my clit a few times until I slap the table . . . and he finally sucks the bud between his lips. Twice, three times. That's it for me, folks. I'm done. I'm *so* done. I've had the entire day to anticipate this, allowing myself to get worked up, and the fantasy doesn't even *compete* with reality.

The way he groans as if he's the one shuddering and sobbing through an orgasm with his bottom in the air elevates it to the next level. My arm flails out on its own, knocking the bowl of chocolate onto the floor and I don't care, *I don't care*, it's so good. I think I might be screaming that sentiment into the table's surface, because my throat feels scraped raw.

The flesh between my legs is still clenching when Charlie jerks me off the table, back against his chest. His mouth moves in my hair while he applies the condom, whispering disjointed, erotic promises. Then a chair scrapes across the floor and he sits, taking me with him. "You're going to lap dance me, cutie." His fist moves beneath my backside, positioning his erection and—

"Charlie." He's inside me. Thick and solid. "Oh my God. *Big man.*"

Confident hands grip my knees and drag them wide, levering me down even farther. "Move, Ever. I'm sick. I'm sick from needing this. Needing *you*," Charlie rasps against the side of my neck, baring his teeth and pressing close. "Move up and down on it. All over it. Make me better."

Yes yes yes. I love this. I love being the only thing who can heal him. The promise of being deliverance to such a driven, self-assured guy is what keeps me answering my phone when he calls.

That's all it *can* be. Mutual satisfaction and nothing more. I have no choice but to enjoy, to give and take, because the feel of him is nothing short of incredible.

Big hands glide up my legs and grip my hips as I start to move. Lean forward, hold the table's edge and start to dance. My head falls forward and I can see him entering me, his demanding erection extending from ruddy, rugged, non-manscaped male—completely unrepentant in his masculinity—and the sight turns me on like a 10,000-watt lightbulb. I lift my head and glance over my shoulder, finding Charlie's mouth open on a silent moan, eyes rolled back in his head. As though he hasn't had sex in five years. As if we haven't been attacking each other like animals for four solid weeks.

"Harder," Charlie grits past stiff, sweat-dappled lips. "Oh fuck. *Please*, Ever, harder. Stop pretending you want it any other way."

My eyelids flutter under the heat of being called out. Seen through. It should scare me—maybe it does a little—but I shove the unwanted emotion to the sidelines and ride Charlie's lap. Knowing he wanted this particular view for a reason—it's an ass day—I loosen my hips and let just my backside bounce up and down, my flesh glancing off his muscular thighs with a *smack*.

"Dammit," Charlie grates, lifting me with a violent upthrust. "You have me so fucking close. Get the hell back here."

He hooks his right hand around my throat, pulling me back so I'm flush with his chest, still moving, still climbing up and dropping down on his erection, my feet slipping on the floor to maintain purchase. It's a race, a frantic straining of bodies. The same point we reach every time. His shallow breathing has turned into all-out panting, grunting, filth. That hand around my throat is cutting off just enough oxygen to make it interesting, a little dangerous. His other hand finds my clit and steals what was left of the air. I can't breathe, I can't think. He's *owning* me.

"You won't take your sweet time opening the door tomorrow." The hand on my throat gives a quick squeeze, his hips undulating beneath mine. "Will you, cutie?"

My climax is even fiercer this time around. I turn my head, whimpering and moaning against Charlie's stubbled jaw, my legs stiffening, pressing me back against his lap, taking him so deep—*so deep*—that he follows me onto the other side. My name is growled over and over into my hair, his fingers still stroking between my legs as heat blooms where our bodies join, signaling his release. For a brief period of time, there is nothing else. A gilded space with no sound or responsibility. An experience singular to Charlie. To us.

My eyes fly open at the mental uttering of the word. Us. *Us?*

I'm off Charlie's lap like a shot.

I turn in a circle, as if I've forgotten I'm inside my own apartment. He's watching me from his sprawl on the chair with a half-grin, probably too deep in postorgasmic dude-glow to notice anything amiss. Okay. Okay, *good*. Because nothing *is* amiss. It was a stupid, one-off thought from which I've already completely recovered.

Charlie stands and swaggers toward me, sliding a palm over the curve of my backside before stooping down to tug up my thong, move my skirt back into place. "Damn, Ever," he whispers against my mouth, just before we both sink into a wet, languid kiss. *"Damn,"* he says again, before pulling away.

I give him a teasing peck on the cheek and shove him away. "I guess vocabulary isn't part of your academy training."

He reaches over and pinches my waist. "Smart ass."

"Much better."

Charlie fixes his clothing, watching me all the while. Closely. Like he's already a cop and I'm a suspect. Not wanting him to notice anything off about my behavior, I grab some paper towels and kneel to clean up the spilled chocolate. I'm not surprised when he hunkers down to help me. For all his arrogance and commitment-phobic ways, he was raised right. But what he asks next? That's new. "Anything you need done around the place? Creaky floorboards? Leaky pipes?"

"Leaky pipes. Really." I lift an eyebrow, trying to make light of the unexpected offer. "Too easy."

His laugh is as rich as the chocolate we're cleaning up. "Come on, Ever. I know you don't like gifts, but let me do *something* for you."

A fluttering occurs in the general direction of my chest. Oh. Ohhh no. This is bad. I'm not going to pretend I haven't gotten a little attached to Charlie. He makes me feel safe. We have fun, with the little time we allot ourselves. His lopsided smiles are the highlight of my day. But now he's starting to feel guilty about leaving after sex. Have I projected my sort of attached-ness and he's just responding out of decency? Legend has it, that's how the decline starts. Decency. Then decency turns to responsibility. Also known as The Mistress Kiss of Death.

This is why the one-month rule exists. Leave them before they leave you.

There's nothing but earnestness in Charlie's blue eyes trying to see right through me. But I know the stories. When a mistress becomes an obligation, instead of an outlet, that's when the fun stops. That's when men stop calling you, stop wanting you, and find greener pastures. Being discarded is a mistress's ultimate fear, and I may not be a mistress in the traditional sense, but I'm no different.

My concerns are only valid with guys like Charlie. And I chose Charlie for a reason. He won't hold me back on my path to catering company glory. He won't hog tie me and drag me to the suburbs or slowly become a fixture on my couch. I'm aware that men exist in Manhattan whose faces don't transform into Edvard Munch's *The Scream* at the prospect of commitment. So the fact that Charlie—who has shared my distaste for couplehood on numerous occasions—is causing a flutter? That's alarming, to say the least.

One more time with Charlie. Then I'll end it.

"I have a super who fixes things," I murmur around a smile, gaining my feet. "Go ahead and catch the train. I'll see you next time."

"Okay." He's still watching me as he backs toward the door. "Ever?"

"Yeah?"

He looks puzzled for a split second, but he rakes a hand over his dark, police academy crew cut and continues toward the door. "Nothing. Just . . . see you next time."

When the door clicks shut behind him, it takes me a while to get moving again. Minutes. And when I finally kneel to finish cleaning up the chocolate, footsteps move outside the door toward the stairs, as if it takes Charlie a while to get moving, too.

CHAPTER 3
Charlie

I'm staring into my locker like it holds the meaning of life, instead of my smelly, black gym bag. We've just gone through hours of safe takedown procedures, including the arm bar hammerlock, my brother refusing to dismiss us until every recruit demonstrated the move to his satisfaction. Now the future protectors of the five boroughs are snapping towels at each other and deciding between Chinese or pizza for dinner, but I haven't even changed out of my sweat-soaked clothes yet.

I'm not even sure what the fuck has me so baffled, but I've been in this weird, functioning coma since leaving Ever's apartment. I don't remember walking to the train or riding it back uptown, although I managed to pull together for this afternoon's training session since my brother was running the drills. If I'd slacked off for a second, I would've been the recipient of one of Greer's long-winded lectures.

Speaking of being in a coma.

Okay, let's backtrack. Everything was fine when I walked into Ever's place, right? Baking as usual. Dressed like a certified knockout. The sex was phenomenal, no getting around it. I'm actually starting to worry that we'll never reach a plateau, and one day we'll just bang ourselves into another dimension. Sex dimension. Actually, I think I might have entertained myself to porn with that title, if I'm not mistaken.

Focus, shithead.

Right. Nothing was off with Ever until she climbed off my lap. My cock springs to life in my gym shorts remembering the way she stood up, thong around one ankle, her ass red from slapping against my thighs. *Christ-at-large.* I can't ask her to meet me twice in one day. Can I? This isn't the first time I've kicked around the idea. More like, the four thousandth time. Since this afternoon.

I can't shake this memory of how Ever looked at me today. When I asked her if I could fix something or help out. God, I think I might have actually spooked her. Look, I'm just as antirelationship as Ever, but that seems a little extreme. So this is where I'm getting caught up. Wanting to know why. And that's against the rules. There's no discussing pasts or futures. Just afternoon delight with an occasional Adam Levine meltdown. I don't want to know where Ever's fear of coupling up comes from, and she doesn't want me fixing busted pipes.

End of story. *Stop moping around like a fucking puppy.*

The academy requires every ounce of my focus if I'm going to meet expectations. There's no room for anything else. Not now. Not ever. Both men in my family are sans women. My mother left when I was in first grade, because she was treated as an afterthought in a house full of men with a sole ambition. She wasn't treated right, so she left. There is no chance of me doing better when reaching the highest possible peak of law enforcement is my goal. I don't remember a time in my life when accelerating to the top wasn't drilled into my head as the most important thing life had to offer.

Jack straddles the bench beside me, tipping a water bottle to his lips. I can smell the vodka it contains. Everyone in our row can smell it. But no one says boo to Jack unless they want a busted lip. Unless you're me and you've already taken the busted lip and given him one back. Like some asshole rite of passage that makes perfect sense unless you think about it too hard.

"What's going on with you, Burns? You only beat everyone's timed mile by a full minute today." Another tip of the water bottle. "Everyone thinks I'm dragging you down with me."

"Now, come on. That's bullshit." I finally drag my gym bag out of the locker. "I was at least a minute ten ahead of the next guy."

That earns me a shove in the ribs. Fair enough.

"I guess the part about you dragging me down is also bullshit." Since that was kind of a compliment, I peel the T-shirt over my head to avoid any bro-moment eye contact. "I would remind you that showing up without a hangover once in a while might shave a minute off your time, but that would be one less person making me look good."

Jack snorts. Awkward moment averted. Well, *mostly*. Because he knows I'm not completely joking. Jack was raised in an illegal brothel in Hell's Kitchen, where he learned quite a few handy tricks (just another reason I keep Ever away from my apartment). When his mother got too old to entertain, he got a job unloading cargo from ships on the West Side in order to support them. He understands hard work and could probably be a powerhouse if he put in some effort. I guess it's going to take more than the promise of law-enforcement glory to motivate him. Time will tell.

"Come *on*, Burns," Jack groans at the locker

room ceiling. "Give up the goods. Your brother's voice has taken away my will to live. I need something interesting to kick start my brain again."

I pull on a fresh T-shirt with the academy logo on the pocket. Jack smirks when he notices, but I ignore him. "It's probably nothing."

"You ever heard the expression don't bullshit a bullshitter?" Jack salutes me with his bottle. "Words to live by."

"Yeah? Here's two more words to live by. Fuck you," I mutter. But now I kind of want to talk about what happened this afternoon. Why? There's nothing to talk about. Is there? "I saw Ever today."

"The girl with the golden—"

"You don't want to finish that sentence."

"I was going to say, 'golden heart'," my pirate asshole friend finishes.

"Sure, you were." A locker slams extra-loudly behind us, and we both give the offender our best *what the hell* expression before going back to the conversation at hand. "She wasn't . . . Ever today. Something was different."

"I knew it." Jack's voice echoes off the lockers. "You have to hand it to the girl. She put on a good show, but they all break out their tap shoes eventually."

"What does that even mean?"

"It *means* she's doing the relationship dance."

My eyes narrow. "There *was* dancing . . ." Ah

God, now I'm thinking about her climbing off my lap again. *Don't even* think *about calling her twice in one day.* "But you're wrong. She's the one who made the rules. Nothing serious. Her exact words."

"Right." Jack throws both legs onto one side of the bench and stands, leaning against the locker beside mine. "I've heard tell of this strategy. She was lulling you into a false sense of security. Playing the long game." He shivers. "She sounds ruthless, man. Glad I'm not in your shoes."

All right. *This* is why I should limit my discussions with Jack to fantasy sports. "You're way off. I'm telling you, she's a fucking unicorn." I shrug. "She probably just had a bad day or something." My neck starts to itch at the idea of Ever being upset, but I scratch it and move on. I have to. There are boundaries between her and I. Crossing them would mean the end of this perfect thing we've got going.

A relationship isn't an option for me. I've seen my father and brother, watching me train from the wings when they think I'm not aware of their presence. Their speculation on my progress. I've got some intimidating shoes to fill, and nothing is going to hold me back or turn me into a disappointment. When my mother left, being the best became a must. Otherwise she left for nothing.

A badge is something you earn and keep. It

doesn't disappear when things get rough—no, it shines brighter. It's a sure thing. A *lasting* thing. The goal is to make sergeant within the first three years of graduation from the academy, then take the lieutenant exam. Pass it with flying colors, as I've been groomed to do. After that, there won't be time for anything but keeping the streets safe. Living up to my legacy. Making my small, but powerful family proud.

Have faith. Tomorrow everything will be back to the way it was. Ever will be waiting for me with a smile. I'll have my head back in the fucking game, training to fulfill my legacy with a clear mind, free of women and relationship worries. Everything will be exactly as it should be.

But when I get home later that night, I don't even remember the walk.

Ever

We have a job tonight. Not a huge one. But not a small one, either. *Nothing* is small to our business—Hot Damn Caterers—right now. My roommate, Nina, and I were clueless when we started building the company. The first thing we did was design business cards. Red ones with white script and saucy clip art. When they showed up in the mail, we set them on our kitchen table, realized we were twats for wasting precious money and split a bottle of rum.

When the hangover passed, we got our asses in gear.

Nina's grandfather owned a donut shop in Williamsburg, Brooklyn, for thirty years, but was forced to close its doors when wine bars and designer cupcake shops moved in to accommodate the younger scene. However, he was left with the deed to an off-site bakery where the donuts were actually produced. Small in size though it is, the space is valuable, convenient and was quite generously bestowed on Nina—a top-notch pastry chef in her own right—when she turned twenty-one.

So what do I have to offer this amateur operation? In the beginning . . . not a hell of a lot. I could cook a mean cannelloni—oh yes, I could—for one person. Maybe two. But apart from an associate's degree in women's studies from Borough of Manhattan Community College, I had no education of which to boast. Especially of the culinary variety. So I learned and I learned fast.

I took night classes on the cheap from culinary school students looking to fulfill teaching credits. I cooked, failed and tried again until I could be useful. Food became my escape, my focus—each time I opened the oven, I accomplished something new. Now, almost two years later, Nina and I hire college students with waitressing experience to carry my creations around on trays at events, which comes with its own brand of drama, but works out for the most part.

Owning a catering company wasn't a dream I had since childhood or even college. Manhattan is such a kaleidoscope of opportunities—fashion, finance, fedora sales—that it took me a while to catch up with the rest of my eager beaver generation and decide on one path. Once I did, it was as though culinary arts had been waiting patiently for me to discover it, before leaping into my arms like a long-lost friend.

Bottom line is, Hot Damn Caterers is something I'm proud of. Something unexpected and wonderful. It requires all of my energy, and I'm happy to give it. I've actually *built* something out of nothing. I never thought I'd be able to say that.

Lately, though? I've been experiencing this sort of . . . anticlimax. Not sure how else to explain the feeling of bursting at the seams to share a triumph with someone, looking around and finding myself alone. Nina is great. Nay, the greatest. I couldn't ask for a better friend or business partner. Nina has a boyfriend, though, and I can't even remember the last time she slept at the apartment. We see each other at the Williamsburg kitchen occasionally when Nina needs help with a large baking order, but I've taken on the administrative side of Hot Damn and that work is done *here*, in the apartment. Where the only person to celebrate a new contract with is the dust bunny beneath my bed.

There have been these moments recently with Charlie when I had the urge to tell him a story about the prior evening's catering job. Or throw him into a chair and force my newest savory puff pastries down his throat so he can give me star ratings. Isn't that ridiculous? Yes, it is! It's ridiculous. The beauty of our nonrelationship is the lack of goo. We are *antigoo*. Charlie couldn't be happier with the arrangement, either. He blazes a trail out of here that still smokes an hour later. The closest he's come to tasting my cooking was licking chocolate off my ass yesterday.

It's probably a phase. I'm twenty-two. Everyone I pass on the street is coupled up or dating online. It's only natural that I should get the false sense something is missing. The phase will pass. Will it start when I break things off with Charlie? Over time, I think it might. Why that scares me even more, I'm not sure.

I'm piping cream cheese into these neat little phyllo dough puffs when I get a knock at the door. Huh. Nobody buzzed from downstairs. It's too early for Charlie to show, and he never stops by without texting first. Another one of our unofficial rules. And it can't be Nina, unless she lost her keys. Although, she'd be shouting Brooklynese at me through the door by now. Weird.

Piping bag in hand, I pad toward the door in my socks and check the peep-hole. A version of me, about twenty years older, stares back from the hallway. "Mother?"

"The one and only."

I force myself to stop gaping and unlock the door, although I use the piping bag hand, which results in cream cheese squirting all over the ground. "Shit." I'm in a flustered limbo, stuck between opening the damn door and trying to clean up the lake of cheese before my mother comes in and thinks I'm a slob. "Uhhh. Hold on."

I use my shirt to clean up the cheese. Hold your applause, ladies and gentlemen.

When my mother walks into the apartment, she looks like a hummingbird deciding on which flower to land. Or maybe an adult version of the hokey pokey. She sets one foot in the kitchen, cocks a hip, backs out. Turns in a circle on the way into my living room, perches on the couch arm, stands again. Then she reaches out with toned, tastefully tanned arms. "Baby girl."

"Hi." I walk into her embrace, inhaling the familiar scent of Dolce & Gabbana Velvet Sublime. I step back, giving her outfit the same once over she's giving mine. "You look amazing. What brings you to my neighborhood?"

"Oh, you know. This and that."

This is when things get strange. My mother, who never settles, never stops chattering, gossiping or running her fingers over everything in the vicinity . . . she just winds down. And flops— *flops*—onto my couch. I've never seen her execute a move that fell short of elegant, but she's literally slumping into the pillows, hand to her forehead. *Someone has died.* That's the first conclusion I land on, but immediately dismiss it as absurd. We *have* no people. My father was never in the picture, my grandmother made for greener pastures a decade ago. There's no one.

Unless. "Oh, God. Did Hula Hoop die?"

"*No,*" she cries, her spine shooting straight. "Why would you say that?"

Okay, so her half-blind poodle is still up and running. "I don't know. You seem distraught."

She holds up a hand as she visibly calms herself down. "Hula is fine. She's downstairs waiting in my Uber."

"I guess you're not planning on staying long." My throat aches as I say the words, but none of that comes across in my tone. The *no commitment* rule my mother taught me is a facet of our relationship, too. As a child, I remember her being somewhat warmer. Maternal with occasional flashes of bittersweet joy. She was the only Carmichael woman since my great-grandmother to disregard the three mistress rules—and she was rewarded with me in her belly. The summer she turned twenty-one, she interned at a retail buyer in the fashion district. She fell madly in love with her boss, only to arrive at work one day and find him in the back room with the lunch cart girl, rogering her against the copy machine.

The three rules cemented themselves once more for my mother after that. Not only did she come back from maternity leave and bust her ass until she usurped my father from his position as manager, she moved to a much higher level within the company, fired his ass and never relied on or trusted another man again. They are nothing more than one month's worth of free entertainment to her and the more unavailable, the better.

Unfortunately, while my mother was out kicking ass and taking names, she wasn't home very often as I grew up, leaving me with babysitters or interns. Whenever we spoke, it was almost always about the dangers of trusting the opposite sex. How to be independent. How to avoid entanglements.

"Are you headed out of town?" She still works for the same company in merchandising, sending her across the pond pretty frequently. "I lost track of the date . . . is it Paris fashion week or—"

"I've come here with something to say." She stands and clicks over to the window on impractical high heels. "Something very important, Ever."

At the rare use of my name, I fall back into my chair. Everything about this situation is rare, really. We don't have heart-to-hearts, my mother and I. She informs me via e-mail or text message if she's going out of town or relocating. That's about it. So there's a quickening in my pulse knowing she's thought of me, planned a conversation for us to have. Together. "What is it, Mother?"

"Until last night, I was seeing a man. Married, yes. I know you don't approve." Her slim shoulders lift and fall on a breath. "*He . . . ended things before the month was up. Decided to give things with his wife another try.*"

"Oh." I know better than to reach out and comfort her. Her associations with married men are a bone of contention between us, so I have to strike the right note of sympathy if I don't want to sound like, *them's the breaks when you creep on another woman's dude, Ma.* "I'm sorry."

She starts to wave off my apology with an impatient hand, but doesn't follow through, her hand just . . . dropping. "Last night was the first time since your father . . . that a man ended things first.

I've learned to choose my men very carefully, and I never failed to adhere to the one-month rule. But it had only been a week. A *week*." She meets my gaze, but it flits away before cementing. "For so long, these short associations have been a constant in my life. I was guaranteed one month with no strings. But last night . . . I realized there are no guarantees in the rules we live by. Not anymore. Not even the single month I've gotten so used to relying on." She smoothed a hand down her scarf. "It took being cut loose to realize something. The only thing I've guaranteed is my own loneliness."

Numbness moves straight down to my toes. "Mother. I'm . . . what are you saying?"

"I haven't been happy for a long time, Ever. After your father, I followed the rules because I was hurting. I needed to earn my self-respect back. Gain back the power I'd lost. And I don't know when following the rules stopped being . . . fulfilling. But it's been a while." My mother turns, and with sunshine streaming in on either side of her face, she looks almost divine. Divine but so incredibly sad. "I'm a lonely woman, Ever. I don't remember the last time I confided in another person. Or laughed. *Actually* laughed. And I think those opportunities with men have been right in front of me for the last twenty-three years, but I pushed them aside, because I was afraid of being hurt again."

You could have laughed with me. We could have laughed together.

Those words stick in my throat as my mother comes toward where I'm super-glued to the chair. Since walking into my apartment, she has aged a decade, I would swear to it. She's crumbling under the truth of her words, and it's a tragedy playing out, right here in my apartment. Seeing it, hearing it, makes my stomach twist into a pretzel. "Ever, I've steered you down my path, telling you to stay free and committed to no one. But there's still time to change." She kneels in front of me—such an uncharacteristic action for my unflappable mother—and tears push, hot and full, behind my eyelids. "Find someone to grow old with, Ever. A man who'll look you in the eye and respect you. A man who will care enough to argue with you. A man who can't think of a better place to be than with you. Get off this path. It only leads to meals for one and no one to laugh with, baby girl."

"But . . ." I haven't cried in so long, my garbled voice jolts me. "You said a woman doesn't need a committed man to make her happy. I can't . . . how can I change when it's all I've ever known?"

"Maybe it's okay to need someone, so long as they need you back just as much." My mother rises and lays a hand on my head. "Just promise me you'll try. *Really* try, Ever."

I've never been given the opportunity to make

my mother proud before. My whole life, I've been heeding her advice, but we've never bonded over it. Our emotions have never collided in any way. Now I'm in the center of the impact, seeing the strongest woman I know fall down on her proverbial knees. For me. She's humbling herself for *me*, so I don't face the loneliness she's experiencing. She's trusting me with her advice, with her hurt, and I'm not going to squander this chance.

As a young girl, I used to yearn for my mother to come home from work and talk to me. Talk to me about anything but avoiding being tied down. It's a long time coming, but her being here and opening up? I have a sense that it's her unique way of apologizing. For all those times she didn't hold me close. All those times she shut down conversations about boys, telling me to ignore them and stay smart. Be independent. She isn't the type to come right out and issue apologies, but actions speak louder than words. And she is physically here, trying to save me from her mistakes.

If easing my mother's concerns means dating— with the intent to become one-half of a relationship—so be it. I can do that for her. I can do that for *us*.

First step: end things with Charlie. My blood pumps heavily in my temples at the thought. I'm no longer abiding by the one-month rule, but that hardly matters now. He doesn't *want* a serious relationship. Our whole association is founded on that fact. So . . . in order to move forward, giving up Charlie is a must. No big deal, right? Why am I thinking about it so hard?

Maybe because . . . lately, I've been wishing he wouldn't run out so fast.

There. I admitted it. I've been secretly hoping he'll ask to try one of my brownies. And feeling disappointed when he doesn't text about something besides hooking up.

If I can feel the beginnings of more with Charlie . . . maybe there's someone else out there who could inspire the same feelings. Sure, I'm skeptical, but I need to find out. Not to mention, she could be right. Letting go of my resolve to be alone could be the first step toward shaking what's got me in a funk lately.

"Ever?"

I look up to find my mother paused at the door, hand on the knob. "Yes, Mother. I'll try my best."

CHAPTER 4
Charlie

All right. My head is back on straight. Whatever weirdness I vibed from Ever was a hallucination. Just like that time I drank too many Red Bulls at a Miike Snow concert and swore I was levitating. I'm going to have proof on my side in mere minutes, because I'm climbing Ever's stairs, my chest expanding as I suck in the citrus aromas dangling in the air like ripe fruit. She's going to answer the door, we're going to screw like a meteor is headed for Earth, and this weird, shaky feeling in my stomach will bounce.

So why does my hand pause on the way to knocking? I can hear her soft humming through the door, the gentle scrapes of kitchen utensils. Homey sounds I'm not accustomed to. Ones I don't normally absorb. And I shouldn't. I don't have *time*.

When my brother, Greer, was a recruit, he slept in the locker room between sessions. When he'd found the NYPD drills to be unchallenging, he'd designed new ones. They're not going to name a sweaty gym mat after me unless I raise my game. A lot.

I will, too. As soon as I get Ever out of my system for the day, I'll be able to focus. Ignoring the way her hums seem to swim lazy laps in my stomach, I knock. Harder than usual. There won't be any games played today. No flirting through the door crack. I'm going to make short work of whatever sexy outfit she's concocted to make me insane, then ride her on my dick until she loses count of her orgasms.

She takes *way* too long to answer the door. The longer it takes, the more my chest feels like it's caving in. There's no more humming. It's complete silence, and I'm contemplating the merits of knocking again—or breaking down the door—when she finally opens.

Immediately, I know yesterday wasn't some fluke. Everything has changed.

"Hey, Ever."

"Charlie." She smiles, but it dips at the edges. "Hey."

In red jean shorts and a tight, white, see-through T-shirt, she looks phenomenal, but for the first time, my lust is cut with desperation.

There's nothing more dangerous. A no-fly zone. A vision of Ever wrapped in yellow caution tape flashes in my mind, but I shake the image loose and focus. I see the writing on the wall here. The fun is over. But I can't get my feet to move. Going into her apartment is the absolute worst idea, but I can't stop myself from making it, because goddammit. This is *Ever.* A unicorn. I'm not just going to walk away and be left wondering what got her horn stuck in the mud. That would be rude, wouldn't it? Not to mention unprofessional. Cops aren't supposed to leave stones unturned.

"Can I come in?"

She nods and steps back, clearly putting distance between our bodies when normally I would be ripping off those tiny shorts by now, my cock in her hands. Fuck, I'm so *hot* for her. No matter what's going on here, I don't think that will ever change.

That's definitely not panic making me winded and edgy. I'm just very aware that my schedule only gives me twenty minutes before I need to be back uptown.

"Would you like something to drink?"

Whoa. She's offering me refreshments? "Um . . . no, thanks. I chugged a Gatorade on the subway."

"Gatorade." There is none of the usual seduction in her walk as she moves to the kitchen, sliding orange debris from a cutting board into the trash can. "I guess my lavender-flavored water wouldn't have been a hit, huh?"

"Flowers in your water?" I shake my head. "Why?"

"The floral notes are supposed to be calming." She closes her eyes and laughs. "It tastes like shit. I don't get it, either. Pretty sure everyone just drinks it because they think they should. In high school, the peer pressure is over cigarettes. As grown-ups . . ." She flips on the sink tap. "We're pressured to drink flower water and tolerate quinoa."

"Tell me quinoa hasn't invaded your repertoire."

"It's invaded everything," she whispers. "It's here *right now*."

Crazy as it sounds, this is the most conversation we've had since meeting in the bar that afternoon a month ago. Is this why I've had a ball of fire in my stomach since yesterday? Had staying just this side of personal started to bother me?

Nah. Couldn't be. We drew the line at personal for a reason. It's what made this arrangement so ideal. So . . .

"What's going on here, Ever?"

Slowly, she removes her hands from the sink and wipes them on a dishtowel, her eyes landing everywhere but me. "I have to end this, Charlie."

"Yeah. Believe it or not, I picked up on that." Although *hearing* it makes me feel like I've swallowed a glass full of rusty nails. We're a casual hookup. No pressure. Now she's ended it, so I should give her a kiss on the cheek and walk. Right? Yeah . . . "I want to know why, Ever." Sauntering toward the kitchen, I seesaw a hand between us. "I thought this thing we had going was pretty fucking perfect."

Her expression is one of shock. Really? I mean, she's acting like a man wouldn't be even remotely miffed over giving her up. This girl is dynamite, wrapped in *Please Santa, I've Been a Good Boy.* Hadn't someone told her that before? I *could* have, if my mouth hadn't been so busy elsewhere. Or if I hadn't been afraid she would read something into it.

"Charlie, I told you I didn't want anything serious. I'm tapping out." Her hands slip into the back pockets of her shorts. "It *was* perfect for a while. But I . . ."

Don't ask. "You what?"

Ever squares her shoulders. "I'm going to be straight with you." She blows out a breath and rolls her neck, like a boxer getting ready to enter the ring. "I've decided to give serious relationships a try."

Even as a two-by-four smacks into my middle, clarity descends. For once, Jack had been right. She was doing the relationship dance. I'd walked right into the trap.

Ever

Y ou could have heard one of my mother's Hermès scarves drop.

I can't tell what Charlie is thinking, but I assume there's horror involved. *Take a fucking number, bro.* I'm not exactly turning pirouettes at the idea of throwing my hat into the bizarre Manhattan dating ring, either. But hours later I'm still thrown from my mother's visit. In addition to having my belief system turned upside down, the woman sort of put the fear of God into me.

The moment she'd left, I'd opened my Mac and created a dating profile on the site with the least obnoxious questions, DateMate.com. Already I had a few dudes interested. They all looked and sounded the very definition of assholes, but it was still early days. Maybe Nina's boyfriend knows someone who is looking to engage me in an awkward conversation where a bill arrives at the end.

Shoot me now.

It's extremely difficult to conjure faceless date candidates when Charlie is only a few yards away looking delicious. The crisp, navy uniform pants and gray T-shirt do endless favors for his body. Biceps, thighs and throat muscles vie for attention. His blue eyes are a little deeper set than usual, black rings beneath, like he didn't get a good night of sleep. Which makes me think of naps. How he would look with his shirt off, in some freshly laundered sweatpants, burying his face into a pillow. A pillow right next to mine. Really, really good. That's how he'd look.

I need to get rid of him before I attempt to find out.

"Look, it's a long story and I don't want to bore you," I say, trying to fill the wake of silence. "Suffice it to say, someone very close to me pulled a Ghost of Mistresses Future and showed me what life could be like if I didn't give relationships a fair shake." My throat starts to hurt, thinking of my mother's distress. "I don't want to be left thinking what if. What if I'd tried. So I'm going to armor up and enter the battle." Dismissing Charlie from my life is even harder than I'd thought it would be. "The least you can do is wish me luck. You'll . . . find someone else."

I have to be imagining the flash of hurt that crosses his face at those two final words, right?

Yeah, a moment later, he proves I had.

Charlie's eyebrows lift. "You really expect me to believe all that?" He advances, rapping his knuckles on my kitchen counter. "This is the part where I say, 'No, please, Ever, don't date someone else. Date me. I've seen the light.' Right?" He scoffs. "There's no way in hell, Ever. We've never lied to each other about what we wanted. I can't believe you of all people would pull this shit on me."

Uh. *Wow*. I've now had my hair blown back twice in one day by the two most unlikely candidates. Charlie thinks my brave foray into the dating scene is a ploy to land him as a full-time boyfriend? Hot acid razes the back of my neck, my vision crowding together. "You've got to be kidding me, Charlie."

"Kidding about what? Not wanting to officially date you or anyone else? I assure you I'm very serious. I would be serious about that if you were Kate Middleton." There's a touch of discomfort to his jerky movements, as though he wasn't all that sure about his argument, but he'd committed, so now it was ride or die. "We were up front from the beginning, Ever. I don't have time to cuddle on the couch with you and watch *Fashion Police*."

"Okay, first of all, I haven't watched *Fashion Police* since Joan Rivers died. It has lost its luster." I hold up my finger and allow that to sink in. "Second, I understand you, Charlie. I know you don't do serious. I never had these ambitions *myself* until this morning. I was trying to let you down gently with some goddamn lavender water and you're shitting *all over it*." I can't believe this. I'm having a break-up squabble. As if we've even been dating in the first place. "I don't want to date you. I don't want to *cuddle* you. And by the way, I must really be a truly evil mastermind to trick you into a relationship with a month of no-strings sex. What a *bitch* I am, right?"

Charlie holds up both hands and whistles, long and low. "All right. I'm backtracking. Tracking *way* back. This is why everything said in a locker room should stay in a locker room. I'm sorry. I jumped to an idiotic conclusion." He searches my face, but I have no idea what he's looking for. Lingering signs of deception? Maybe he's just trying to decipher the shade of red my cheeks have turned. Magenta? Crimson? "I forgot for a minute I was talking to a unicorn."

"What?" I have the sudden urge to throw my bowl of chocolate-orange mixture through a window. "And Kate Middleton? I'm like her exact opposite."

"I don't know. It just came out," Charlie mutters. "I mean, if I *had* to pick, it would be Pippa—"

"Please leave, Charlie." I'm definitely not jealous of the Duchess of Cambridge. Or her sister. This whole conversation needs to be filed away in my *things to cringe about at odd moments* folder. "I have a job tonight. And dating matches to go through."

Oh, real mature, Ever.

"Wait. Just wait. This is going way too fast." Charlie drags both hands over his close-cropped brown hair, then visibly centers himself with a deep breath. "Ever. You're making a mistake. No one has what we have." His throat flexes. "It's too rare to give up."

I ignore the distant voice in my head, shouting from the back of the class to agree with him. Against my will, memories rise from that afternoon in the bar. When we met and kissed. I must have imagined the relentless sense that something huge was happening. It must have been the stupid romance of the rain or a trick of light. All he *really* wanted was a hookup. That's still all he wants from me.

"I've made my mind up, Charlie."

He's in front of me before I can blink. Big, frustrated, confused, turned-on male. His eyebrows are knit tight, his breathing heavy at my lips. He presses me into the counter, his fingers digging into my waist before his right hand drops to hook beneath my knee. That thumb of his, the one that has brushed my nipples and strummed my clit countless times so skillfully, makes circles on the inside of my knee. And then out of nowhere, he jerks my knee up around his waist with a groan. My neck loses power, my head falling back. He's hard, the shape of him mouthwatering against my stomach. Pressing, pressing, *thrusting*. "*Unmake* your mind," Charlie rasps into my neck, a thread of desperation twining with seduction. "Ever . . . *please*. I wanted you to ride me today, cutie. That hot as fuck way you do it, all bouncing tits and shaking legs. Don't you want that? Don't you want to feel me crammed up into your wet pussy?"

Oh shit. Yeah. He knows all my weaknesses and when to exploit them. I'm feeling exploited enough right now to need an underwear change. It would be so easy to say, *yes, Charlie,* and let him round out my afternoon with another one of the best orgasms life has to offer, but I know I'd be disappointed in myself when he left.

Although, I would be so satisfied . . .

Eyes on the prize, Ever.

"Charlie, stop this." I push on his shoulders twice before he budges. He stumbles back, his features tight, swiping a hand over his mouth. "I like you," I breathe, horrified over the wobble in my voice. "I think you're great. But we're not in the same place anymore. I can't give my full effort to finding someone if I know you're going to show up and take me to bed. My . . ." Heart? No way. "My energy won't really be in it."

His hands are back in his hair, looking as if he might yank it out by the roots. "You're really doing this," he enunciates, going from shell-shocked to angry. "You're going to be one of those girls who drags her boyfriend shopping, parades him in front of her friends at brunch and ends up with joint custody of a yellow Lab when it all goes south six months later?"

"I don't know," I say honestly. "That sounds awful, but I won't know until I try, will I?"

Charlie opens and closes his mouth about eight times, but can't seem to decide on what to say. "We have the perfect thing going here." His finger stabs the air with a jerky movement. "You're going to realize it the first time some chump asks you to split the bill."

"At least there will be a bill to split." Shit. Why did I say that? I need him to leave now. All these suppressed desires for our nonrelationship picked a really inconvenient time to reveal themselves. "See you around, Charlie."

He plants both hands on his hips and looks down at the floor, staying that way for a few seconds, then moving toward the door. When he opens it and stalks out into the hallway, he doesn't look back. "See you around, Ever."

The door slams.

CHAPTER 5
Charlie

One week has passed since I walked out of Ever's apartment.

Life is good. *Great*, actually. I feel like I can take a deep breath for the first time in ages. Birds are chirping. I'm seeing everything through clear eyes. My world is full of color! *Exploding* with the light.

Just kidding. I want to die.

Jack told me to go out and find a new girl. Which went *really* well. I made it to my building's lobby before I got the urge to vomit. That's normal, right? Missing your nongirlfriend enough that you almost paint your shoes with stomach sauce? I mean, I barely know a damn thing about her. She's the hottest woman I've ever laid eyes on. That's a given. She's got a great sense of humor—

at least, that's what I've gleaned from our short banter sessions that preempt sex. Her culinary skills seem tight, though I've never actually tasted her food.

And that's it. I shouldn't be sitting on the last stool of a dive bar on Bowery—still in my training gear—trying to erase her voice from my head. Christ, she was *moaning* most of our acquaintance. So why can I only remember the times we actually talked? I keep playing that ridiculous conversation about lavender water over and over in my head, like it holds the secret to life. She was just so . . . unguarded in those moments. What else would she have said if we'd talked longer? Why had I shut her up with my mouth so many times?

"Another, please?" I ask the passing bartender. Without responding, he uncaps a Heineken and sets it in front of me. "Thanks."

All right. After this beer, I'm done. No more wallowing. No more obsessing over how well her turn on the dating scene is going. I don't want to know. Don't want to think about other hands settling on her hips. Or other ears listening to jokes about quinoa. Or maybe a guy getting to the bottom of what spooked her about relationships in the first place. I'd never gotten that far.

And I shouldn't have. I don't *want* a commitment. They eventually land you in dank, smelly-ass bars with a layer of dust on the whiskey bottles, don't they? Or pouring yourself twice as tenaciously into a job, the way my father did when Mom left.

Guilt twists in my belly, remembering the silence in my childhood house.

Yeah. No commitments for me. I just want my uncomplicated, nonrelationship with Ever back.

As if my words floated up to the atmosphere and danced right into God's ears, a girl clomps into the hazy bar. I recognize her right away, which is a relief. My training isn't going to waste. I'm *meant* to be a cop. Ask both members of my family.

Loosening the tightness from my throat, I watch Ever's roommate—Nina, I believe—hand a dollar to the bartender and ask for change to pay the parking meter outside. There's a restaurant supply place next door—see? More capable police work—and she's probably picking up kitchen equipment or catering gear. *Jesus*, is Ever with her? I almost jump off my stool and sprint out of the bar to go see, but manage to remain seated like a normal human.

Nina had been with Ever the day we met. Thanks to my Ever-induced tunnel vision, however, I didn't speak to her and I haven't seen her since. But I remember two observations about her from that day in the packed bar. She's a redhead and her hand gestures are dramatic. As her gaze cuts down toward me at the end of the bar, I see recognition dawn. Yeah, I doubt she would forget the guy who mauled her friend's face in a packed bar, right? Somehow, just having someone acquainted with Ever acknowledge me makes me less nauseous than I've been in a week. I lift my beer bottle in greeting and after accepting the coins from the bartender, she comes toward me.

"Hey," Nina says, a huge sigh pushing the words free. One of those conversation openings that alerts one party that the other party has been through some rough shit since waking up that morning. "I don't have a lot of time, but I guess if I get a parking ticket, you can get it dismissed."

I smile into a sip of beer. "Not until I graduate."

Nina falls down onto a stool, propping both elbows on the bar. "You know what?" She wiggles her fingers at the bartender. "Jameson, please. Neat."

"Shit. That bad?"

"The worst."

Join the club, I start to say. But it might get back to Ever that I'm miserable. I want her to think I'm living it up, right? No. *Shut up, Charlie.* God, I hate this version of myself. This version wants to ask Nina about Ever and her activities over the last week, but I can't do that. Women tell each other everything. But maybe I can come at it from a different angle. Nina and Ever work together, right? So . . . "Is this a work-related problem, or . . ."

"Man related."

Uh-oh. Abort mission. If there is one guarantee in this life and the next, it's that I will probably put my foot in my mouth. I have no experience with comforting words because I'm surrounded by men who've either sworn off women or go through them like water, never settling on one in particular. My roommate Danika doesn't count, because as far as I can tell, she operates like us dudes, emoting about as often as an eclipse takes place. "A man, huh?" I'm stuck. I have no choice. "You don't say."

"My boyfriend broke it off this morning." She screws up her face, nostrils flaring. "Through a direct message on Twitter."

Okay, I don't need experience with ending relationships to know *that* was fucked up. "No way."

"*Yes* way." The bartender sets the drink in front of Nina and she tosses it back in one go, following it with a satisfied *ahhhh* sound. "He's seeing someone from work. I've suspected for a while, but . . . I thought he was losing interest because I was working too much, so I tried to be there more." She shakes her head. "Turns out, he wanted me there less. Never. Gone. *Replaced*."

"He shouldn't have done that to you. It's not your fault, either, Nina. It's his." I pick up my bottle and gesture at nothing in particular. Because I'm not seeing anything but Ever. Haven't seen much else in a week. "Sometimes people, you know, they grow apart. One minute everything is fine—it's fine—and the next, you're being offered lavender water and blurting the names of the royal family."

"Why do I get the feeling we're not talking about me anymore?"

My sigh blows a napkin off the bar. "I'm sorry, Nina. I'm not usually this self-centered. At least, I don't think so."

She looks me over with sympathetic eyes. "I think day drinking in sweaty gym clothes earns you a pass. Don't take this the wrong way, but it does my heart good knowing there's at least one man with the capacity to be torn up over a girl." Her lips pinch together, fingers drumming on the bar. "I tried to be the bigger person. I tried to make it work. I went *camping* for that douchebag. In the end, I think I deserved some respect at the *very* least." She blows out a shaky breath. "Maybe this makes me sound like an evil villain, but I wish there was some way to make him suffer. *Payback*."

Man, the more this girl talks, the more anxious I grow to help. I might not be a relationship guy, but I sure as hell wouldn't two time someone, then cast her aside like she never mattered. What if someone did that to Ever?

My fists curl beneath the bar. It *could* very well happen to her if she throws herself to the sharks, couldn't it? Oh, shit. My esophagus is on fire, and there aren't enough Heinekens on the island of

Manhattan to douse it. I never paid attention to the cut throat singles scene before, but now I'm forced to think about Ever ending up heartbroken like Nina. Fact: There sure as fuck isn't a man in this city good enough for Ever. So the odds of her ending up with some ass face who doesn't appreciate everything she has to offer? Astronomically high.

Next month, it could be Ever getting a break-up DM on Twitter. What if it makes her *cry*? Jesus, am I having a panic attack? Sweat rolls down my spine as Nina watches me curiously, but my mouth is too dry to speak. Because now I'm picturing even worse scenarios. Growing up in a law enforcement environment means I've heard terrible stories. The ones that always punch me in the gut involve women getting hurt. Physically.

There are too many bad people out there. I can't chance Ever ending up with one. She might be smart as hell, but she barely reaches my shoulder. If someone took advantage of Ever or harmed her, I wouldn't be able to live with it.

"What if you could? Get payback on your ex?" I'm speaking before I realize it, my words sounding scraped and raw. An idea is forming, and my concern for Ever doesn't allow me to consider it might be a bad one. Or an intrusive one. "I'm not an officer yet, but I grew up with half the force."

I tilt my head at Nina. "Might be nice watching your ex go crazy on Twitter tomorrow because his car or bike got impounded, right?"

"*God* yeah. Can you even *impound* a bike—" She points a finger at me. "Wait a minute. I know when a man is up to something. This is about Ever." A beat passes. "Start talking, buddy."

Suddenly I'm being strangled by a giant. "Has she gone out with anyone yet?"

Nina rears back with a gasp, eyes wide. "I can't tell you that."

"Blink once for yes, twice for no."

"Charlie." She gives a grudging sigh, looking like she wants to smack me. I don't blame her. But I also want to hug her when she blinks twice.

Relief rushes through my veins like I've been hooked to an ice water IV. All right. No dates yet. What do I do with this information? What do I want more than anything?

To go back in time. To the days Ever and I greeted each other naked. When I could lose myself in the feel of her, making sure she got lost in me right back, with none of the entanglements. When I could have her all to myself while maintaining my star recruit position at the academy. Add in this protective drive to keep her safe from the Shitheads of Manhattan and my next move is a no brainer.

Ever just needs a gentle nudge back in my direction. If I can accomplish that—safely—she'll come back to me in no time.

I turn in my stool to face Nina, folding my hands together. My *let me level with you* pose. "Nina, I vow right here and now to make your ex's life a comedy of non-life-threatening tragedies, if you give me details about Ever's first date. *One*," I rush to add. "Just one and then I will leave you alone." I tilt my head and give her the eyes. Over the years, these blue eyes have gotten me out of detention, girl trouble and once bumped a *C* grade to an *A* in trigonometry. "I'm having a hard time moving on and . . ." So far, I'm not lying. "I think if I just have some concrete proof she's over me, maybe it'll be the kick in the ass I need." Okay, now I'm lying.

Nina squeezes her eyes shut and groans. "I'm being played and I know it."

I have this sudden vision of me, Ever and Nina hanging out together. Eating pizza out of a box while we watch a movie in their apartment. Maybe Nina has a new fella over, and we're checking him out for new boyfriend approval. Why am I thinking of this? "Just consider the possibilities," I murmur cajolingly. "It would be a shame if your ex received a delivery of roses to his apartment with a *thank you for last night* card. Especially if his new squeeze is over cooking risotto."

"You're the evil villain." A glint sparks in Nina's eyes. "I kind of like it."

"Do we have a deal?"

She scrutinizes me. "I'm either being an awful friend or a really good one here. I guess we'll find out." She sounds thoughtful. "Ever is going speed dating tonight. It's in that converted church on the Upper East Side. The one that used to be a club—"

"Then they made it a Thai fusion restaurant? Yeah, I know it." Christ, this news is like a blow to the ribs. I'd envisioned Ever on a date with *one* guy. Some ex-frat member shithead with a tiny dick and no game. Instead, she is literally throwing herself to a *room* full of them. *Not happening.* "Thanks for telling me."

Nina takes my Heineken and drains a few inches. "I told her it was a bad idea. Speed dating. It's a shit show." She plunks the bottle back down. "I mean, she got so many hits on DateMate. com this week, she probably set some kind of record—"

"Thanks for that."

"Bottom line, she definitely doesn't need to speed date." Nina sighs and hops off the stool, then pokes me in the shoulder. "Don't make me sorry, Charlie."

I hold up two fingers. "Scout's honor."

Nina snorts on her way out of the bar. The moment the door closes behind her, I'm all over this information like a detective interrogating a perpetrator. I call Jack. When he answers, there is a woman giggling in the background. I have no idea if she's real or if he answered the phone while watching porn. And I don't want to know. "Charlie boy. What it do?"

"I need a favor. You near the academy?"

Another giggle. "Does it sound like it?"

"No." I stand, pulling my wallet out of the back of my pants, riffling through it for enough to cover my drinks and throwing it on the bar. "Well, pull out and get there. Round up as many guys as you can. Tell them there's fifty bucks in it for each of them. I'll be there soon as I can."

CHAPTER 6

Ever

Oh my God, I'm so nervous. Dating is cannibalism. I'm sure of it and I'm not even in the building yet. There are people lined up waiting to get in, as if the original *Hamilton* cast reunited and they're doing one show only. Everyone is eyeballing each other up and down, appreciating or discarding. I have a serious urge to turn tail and make for the closest drinking establishment. Where people meet naturally and aren't trying to find their perfect match. They're just trying to find one that'll do for a good conversation and maybe a beer-flavored kiss or two.

All the women in line are dressed in business-casual attire, carefully concocted in an Ann Taylor LOFT dressing room. I'm wearing ripped jeans, a faded Wilco tank top and flip flops, because hello, it's hot as hell. I have no time for single button blazers in this weather. I smell like cinnamon and chocolate, though, so I have that going for me, right?

"Shit," I mutter, twisting my hair up so I can fan my neck. "This is going to be terrible, right?" I say to the girl in front of me, hoping for some commiseration.

"With that attitude, it will be," she answers without turning around.

Great.

I breathe in the humidity and blow it back out. An NYPD vehicle rolls by through evening traffic on Third Avenue, and there I go again. I'm thinking about Charlie. What if he swaggered past right now? What would I do? Probably something bad. *Very* bad. I haven't had sex in a week, which is by no means a long time. I've gone for stretches that lasted nearly a year. But when you've been getting it as good as Charlie gave it to me? A week is a century. A millennium. God, the way he used to go down on me, as if he'd been strategizing his tongue maneuvers all day . . . there's no way to recreate that kind of ingenuity with a vibrator. I've been trying all damn week.

So yeah, if he walked past me right now on the sidewalk, I would be tested. Especially if he was wearing those uniform pants that made his package look like a Christmas present wrapped in a zipper. If I texted him right now, he would meet me. He would give me the Adam Levine sex and ask me no questions, tell me no lies.

Unfortunately, I miss his laugh and those adorable eyebrow waggles more than anything. So there will be no texting, because in that direction lies ruin. He's probably already looking for someone to be his new acquaintance with benefits. Maybe he found her already.

That jarring thought forces my eye back on the prize. I'm here to give an effort. Like the girl in front of me. She obviously knows her shit.

Tomorrow morning, I might actually have a reason to call my mother. As long as I remember that, as long as I remember I might be doing something that could make her proud of me, or give us something in common, I can face anything.

Toward the front of the line, I hear a commotion and bend sideways to check it out. There is a group of young men my age in a tight-knit pack. Like me, they don't look like they belong in line, either. The advertisement for this speed dating event mentioned young professionals, and I'm willing to bet these guys do *not* fit the bill. They're all wearing aviators and chucks. Crew cuts and shaved heads. Serious expressions like they're on some important mission from Ray-Ban. Maybe one of their little sisters is speed dating tonight, and they've come to keep tabs. If that's the case, I'm rooting for them.

The line begins to move, and the Aviator Squad slowly elbows their way into the queue, glancing back over their shoulders, probably checking out the competition. Or merchandise, I amend, when a couple of them zero in on me. I frown at one who stares a little too long, and he smiles back, whispering something to his buddies.

What the hell is going on here?

I don't have much time to think about Aviator Squad again, because once we're inside, a harried woman ear tags us like cattle—in the form of a name tag—and gives the women table numbers. As I walk into the dimly lit room, I hear men complaining outside on the sidewalk through an open window. I can't make out their exact words, but once I take a seat and watch the men file into the room, the nature of their complaints becomes obvious. The dudes who were here first, patiently waiting for their turn to impress the womenfolk, were muscled out by the new, hot-shot arrivals, although a decent number of the original line dwellers have made it through.

Someone passes by and clunks a glass of house red on my two-seater table and I gulp a few sips, hoping to round the edges of my nerves as quickly as possible. And I *need* the rounded edges, because there is literally a giant digital timer in the corner of the room, glaring at me like an electric vampire. It's set to five minutes. Okay, I can do five minutes with each of these guys. No problem, right? I have to make small talk pretty frequently at catering events, especially if I need to step in and make tray passes, so this should be a walk in the park.

One of them could be great, Ever.

This is the part I need to understand. I'm not dating to get it over with, so I can go home and soak in a bath. I'm *really* looking for someone. I have to remember that when the urge to give a half-ass effort arises. An image of Charlie winking at me through the crack in my apartment door arises, accompanied by birds chirping, but I shove it away.

"Okay." The woman who name-tagged us stands in the center of the room, beneath a dusty chandelier. She's been doing this a while, and it holds no magic for her anymore—that much is clear. Absently, I wonder if she'd be open to jazzing these events up with some catering. It can't hurt to leave her a business card. "The gentlemen have been given an order of numbers that correspond with each table. They will follow the order and have five minutes to visit with each of you. The clock will automatically reset and begin after the allotted time passes. Does everyone understand?" A low murmur of voices. "Splendid. I'll be out back having a cigarette."

On the way out, the woman smacks the timer and it begins counting down. It's like someone stuck the room's energy in a light socket. As soon as the supervision disappears, the men crisscross and plant themselves at tables, reaching across to shake their first victim's hand. When no one sits at my table, my skin gets extra-tight. Oh God, my first experience dating and an error has occurred. I'm at the dud table.

But . . . no. Two men are arguing at the center of the room, quiet enough that I can't overhear. One of them is wearing aviators. The exchange of words lasts about thirty seconds before Aviators wins the battle and the other man storms from the room. When Aviators slides into the seat across from me, I'm highly suspicious, but I say nothing. I just sip my wine and wait.

"Hi, there," he said eventually. His confidence melts before my eyes, probably because he's not surrounded by his posse. "Ever." He reads the name off my tag. "That's a cool name."

"Thanks." I set down my glass and lean forward. *Trying. You must try.* "My mother told the nurse to write Esther on the birth certificate, but she was still floating down on pain meds, so it came out garbled."

He laughs before seeming to catch himself and sobering. Weird. "Uh. What do you do for a living?"

"I'm the co-owner of a catering company."

"Well, I love to eat. It's a match." Again, he visibly reins himself in. Which is the opposite of the point of this exercise, right? "I mean, that seems all right."

"Yeah . . ." I send the timer a discreet glance. "What about you?"

"Unemployed," he answers quickly. "I'm in the process of finding something, though. It's been difficult." He shoots the table beside us a discreet look. "I'm in a prison work release program, so my options aren't exactly incredible."

"Wow. I didn't expect you to say that." *Don't look now, folks, but tonight just got interesting.* "Do you mind me asking what you were in for?"

His fingers drum on the table. "I robbed a jewelry store. I bet that's a deal breaker, right?"

God, he looks almost hopeful. Which, ironically, almost makes me want to try harder. "Well, I don't know." I fall back in my seat, trying to picture this clean-cut guy in horizontal stripes. "If you tell me you were stealing an engagement ring for your sweetheart, I could be understanding. Or if you tied up the store owners and were really apologetic while you were doing it. Maybe held a paper cup of water to their lips?"

I don't realize he's still wearing his sunglasses

until his eyebrows lift behind them. "Man, I totally get it now."

"Get what?"

The buzzer goes off, but he doesn't move right away. Actually, he looks as though he wants to say more, but eventually he stands. And another set of aviators takes his place. "Hi, there."

Is that the standard issue, speed dating greeting?

"Hi," I say back, wondering when and if they are going to refill the wine. Five minutes isn't really enough time to learn the important things about someone, is it? I barely scratched the robber's surface and now he's talking to some other girl. Am I imagining it or is he still looking over at me? "Um. Are you also in the prison release work program?"

New guy chokes on a laugh. "Is that what he told you?"

"Yes," I say slowly. "You guys came together, so I just assumed . . ."

Aviators Number Two hooks an arm around the back of his seat. "That was a cover story."

Oh boy. "What is he covering up?"

"We're actually paranormal experts. We're casing this place for a future investigation." He tips his head back and scans the ceiling, apparently looking for Casper. "You might have seen us on YouTube. The Boo Squad? We get a lot of hits."

"Was one of them in the head?" Realizing I said

that out loud, I hold up a hand. "Look, I'm sorry. That was rude."

Was he fighting a smile?

"Honestly, though, I think paranormal expert sounds slightly better than ex-con. You might want to tell him to just be honest next time."

The buzzer goes off and I bury my face in a palm. This is getting ridiculous. I get the feeling these guys are just bullshitting everyone for a laugh, and the possibility prods my temper. As if strangers judging your personality isn't hard enough, now we're being mocked on top of everything else?

When a third guy sits down in a pair of aviators and says, "Hi, there," I just stare back. He coughs, shifting in his seat. "In the interest of being up-front and honest, I'm here to inquire about your renter's insurance needs."

"Oh, screw this." Humiliation and outrage building in my chest, I toss back the final sip of wine, grab my purse and gain my feet. Nina had warned me about speed dating, and she was right. She'd said it was equal to torture, but I doubt even my seasoned friend could have predicted this. I was probably being filmed for some Internet prank show the whole time, so I guess now I just sit back and wait for someone to send me the You-Tube link. *Unbelievable.*

As I leave the room, I swear I hear high fives

taking place behind my back. I whirl around and scan the room through narrowed eyes, but no one has moved.

Walking out onto Third Avenue, I feel like I've just escaped from an alternate universe. My skin is clammy and my heart rate is jumpy. There's a lump in my throat. In desperate need of a place to crawl and lick my wounds, I promptly head in the direction of a Guinness sign in the distance. The international bat signal for cold beer and good music. Anything to take my mind off my first failed attempt to meet someone and start something meaningful. Next time, I'll be smarter. And there *will* be a next time. The speed dating fiasco could deter me if I allow it to. Or I can internalize the embarrassment and let it make my resolve stronger.

Yes. That's what I'll do.

Chin raised, I weave through the evening sidewalk crowds. People are heading to hot yoga or piling into restaurants. Probably muttering prayers under their breath that the date they've arranged for the evening isn't a felon. Or someone *pretending* to be a felon. How strange. One day on the dating scene and I'm seeing the world through new eyes.

So when I spy Charlie buying a can of soda from a street vendor, it takes me a moment to believe he's really there. My feet falter on the hot concrete, goose bumps racing down my arms. A tiny man plays the harp with my intestines.

"Charlie?"

He turns, nearly knocking me over with those blue eyes. The glow from a restaurant sign lights them up brighter than a beach day sky. *Wow.* I'd forgotten how unique his appearance is compared to everyone else. Slightly crooked nose, that crease down the middle of his lower lip, all that energy. It crackles. There's only one Charlie Burns. Intense, charming, sexy and capable, all at once.

"Ever." The vendor nudges his elbow, reminding him to take the change, and he pockets it, turning back to me. Scanning my face. Stepping closer. So close, I suck in a lungful of hot, summer city air. "What are you doing this far uptown?" The corner of his mouth ticks up. "Not getting into trouble, I hope."

I have this destructive urge to tell him how hard tonight sucked. That he was right, and I already miss the uncomplicated nature of our daily booty call. I want to spill everything, right there on the sidewalk, while foot traffic bottlenecks around us. Instead, everything catches up with me at once, the way things often do after one glass of wine, before the numbing effect of number two. My mother ending up lonely and unfulfilled. How broken she'd looked. How humiliated I am over the last twenty minutes. I've never witnessed a loving, functioning relationship, and I have this fear that I've done uncomplicated so long, I'm not equipped for serious. And only Charlie understands. That has to be why I'm kind of paralyzed, standing there, no idea what to say or do. But hoping he hugs me.

Stupid, destructive hope.

Charlie

Shit. Have I done something awful?

Paying off my fellow recruits to sabotage Ever's speed dating session seemed like the perfect solution to my panic this afternoon. Actually, I was so sure the plan had been genius right up until two minutes ago, when she approached me on the sidewalk. But she looks . . . crushed. What the fuck did they say to her? I probably should have been a little more specific than, "Don't let anyone with a penis get within two feet of Ever."

Keeping her safe and ensuring her heart remains intact were my main reasons for wrecking her speed dates. Well. That and wanting her back to myself. But if what I've done upset her, I've failed. Hard. Some jerk-off *did* hurt her feelings—me.

She's standing right here in front of me, looking like magic in the fall of nighttime, in all her golden blonde mermaidness. Exactly as I had hoped. I didn't want her to be sad, though. God, no. I've never seen her anything but smiling and full of mischief. My guts feel like they're being mashed together between two Hulk fists.

"Are you okay?"

"Yeah. *Yeah.*" Her voice is scratchy and she laughs, like she's trying to hide it. She seems almost disappointed, but I can't pinpoint why. I hate this feeling that I'm somehow letting her down, just by standing there. There was one other time in my life a woman stood in front of me, expecting something I'd never been taught how to give. It's a helpless feeling. An inadequate feeling. I'm much more comfortable with people expecting success from me in school or professionally, so I've learned to stick with expectations I can meet. Right now, though, I'm sorely wishing I had more in my wheelhouse.

"I was just going to grab a drink, then head back downtown," Ever says, tucking a flying strand of blonde hair behind her ear. "How have you been?"

"Busy with the academy." Scheming with a bunch of knuckleheads to purposefully ruin your night, then pacing back and forth on this street corner like a lunatic, wanting to strangle anyone who traded two words with you. "Training. Studying for exams. You know how it goes."

She nods way too eagerly; her eyes are no longer meeting mine. "It was good to see you, Charlie.

I'm going to skate." The wind moves around me as she sails past, throwing me a wink. "Take care of yourself, big man."

That's it?

I'm so stunned at her abrupt exit, it takes me a moment to realize the full scope of what happened. I failed. The plan backfired. I upset Ever for nothing, which makes me a bastard *and* a sucker. The bastard part is worse, though. Way worse. I turn and watch her float down the sidewalk, remembering the way she'd seemed to be waiting for something from me. What the hell was it?

She's more determined to meet someone else than I originally thought. That much is clear. Actually, I'm pretty fucking embarrassed for assuming she'd want to resume our arrangement so easily. Maybe I've been spending too much time with Jack.

Regroup, man. Regroup.

Here is what I know. I don't like the crashing cymbals that grow louder in my head the farther away she gets. My palms are sweating, and I think I might swallow my tongue. I definitely don't like her walking away upset, especially when I'm the one who caused tonight's fuckery. And I'm *not* going to end up in bed with Ever tonight.

That last one is downright painful.

A man with a more righteous moral code might walk away at this point. Resolve not to cause any more destruction. Leave Ever to find her Frat Founder Romeo and fade into the sunset. Me? I don't have it in me to quit. What Ever and I had only comes around once in a lifetime, if you're lucky, and if I can just *show* her that, she'll come back to me. Hell, I'm saving us both. This is literally God's work I'm doing.

No more date sabotage, though. I hurt Ever tonight, whether or not it was intentional, and I cannot, *will* not, see her like that again. If she'd actually cried, I would be in a fetal position on the sidewalk right now. So causing her dates to fail is out.

So what is the next play? Go with Ever right now to get that drink?

It's a bad idea. I know it. She's vulnerable after a shit show *I* caused. Having a drink means conversation, means me cheering her up. It is crossing the line from hookup to . . . friend. No way am I going to end up in Ever's friendzone and be subjected to details about her dates—

Wait a minute.

Wait.

I have a new plan.

That old saying, *keep your friends close and your enemies closer,* takes on a whole new meaning. Right now, my enemies are everyone on the island of Manhattan with a cock, Internet access and enough money for happy hour. That is a lot of enemies. But if I know about these pricks in advance, I can monitor the situation from the inside, ensuring Ever stays safe and my sanity remains intact.

Maybe the friendzone wouldn't be such a bad place to be, if Ever confides in me about her failed dates . . . and I'm sitting pretty looking like the better option.

A voice in the back of my mind screeches like a creature from the underworld. *Bad idea, Charlie. Bad.* That voice has tried to reason with me many times before and failed. From a young age, I've been somewhat notorious for coming up with ill-advised plans. Faking two identities so I could give blood three times, just to afford tickets to a Foals concert. Buying a tuba from a pawn shop on the cheap, so I could get out of school early, posing as a band member on their way to a big game. Using my father's classic Chevy as collateral on a bet in high school. And losing. Thankfully, I'd doubled down and won it back before anyone was the wiser, but it had been touch and go for a while there.

I'd promised my father I would be more disciplined, more logical-minded, when I joined the academy. So far I haven't let him down. And I *won't.* But I need Ever. This idea of mine is an avenue to achieve that. So I take it.

"Ever," I call, right before she dips into the bar. She turns, blonde hair flying in eighty directions around her face. A pounding in my chest begins, so loud it drowns out traffic whizzing past on the avenue. "Wait up."

CHAPTER 7

Ever

C harlie is up to something.

That's my initial reaction when he follows me into the bar, but I feel bad almost immediately. He's been nothing but sweet and respectful to me since we met, hasn't he? Toward the end, he'd even seemed guilty when he had to leave immediately after we'd rocked each other's worlds. He would wear a badge someday, serve and protect the fine—and occasionally smelly—city of New York. I have no reason to suspect he'd follow me into the bar for nefarious purposes.

I mean, I *know* he wants to get laid. So do I.

But it's not going to happen, so I decide to play a game with myself. Once I make it clear as crystal I'm going home alone, we will see how long he sticks around. I'm a little irritated at myself for being so cynical, but after the speed dating debacle, I think I've earned the right.

Nestling into my skepticism is a lot easier than acknowledging the zing of excitement shooting through my veins. The relief over having eyes on Charlie. After spending a week convinced I wouldn't see him again, this is like finding out it's Saturday when you woke up thinking it was Monday.

We find a space at the end of the bar. Happy hour in this city is a free for all, and most of the younger Madison Avenue work crowd has migrated this-away to wet their whistle. A lot of unbuttoned button-downs and loosened ties, mingled with service industry peeps who just ended a day shift. That's the beauty of New York City. A garbage man can sit beside a billionaire at the bar, and for that window of time, they're equals. I've waitressed here and there myself to fill a few financial gullies while I put myself through junior college, so I've made a study of men on bar stools. Common ground conversations usually involve the best place to get pizza or heroes, classic rock or sports. This far north of Wall Street, the best way to get ignored at the bar would be to bring up politics or money.

I love the buzz of a busy, dimly lit bar. Being part of something, yet anonymous, all at the same time. It doesn't feel like the real world, which is how I found the courage to approach Charlie all those months ago while basketball and beer commercials raged on television. I shouldn't feel at all nostalgic that Charlie and I are back in that same atmosphere together, but as we squeeze into the tiny sliver of bar space, our eyes meet . . . and I have this wild notion he's feeling it, too.

My body likes being in close proximity with Charlie's very much. My nipples pinch to tight peaks, mere inches from his chest. Has he always been so broad shouldered? Has he always been so much taller than me? We've been horizontal for a good chunk of our acquaintance, so it must have slipped my notice.

"Um . . ." I search for the bartender, hoping he'll take our drink orders and break the silence, but he's tending to another group. "I guess we should just acknowledge this is awkward, right?" I murmur beside his ear. "And go from there."

Charlie's laugh puffs out and rolls down my neck. "Acknowledged." He props a foot on the step beneath the bar, putting me inside the cubby of his thigh. But he does it so casually, I can't decide if he's flirting or getting comfortable. Either way, I can feel his leg heat on my hip now, and that's *really* hard to ignore. "While we're putting everything on the table," he says, giving me *the eyes*, "I didn't want things to end. I still don't."

Disappointment is like staples sinking into

my skin. That was easy. I already won the game. "We're not going home together, Charlie. If that's why you followed me in here . . . I'm sorry. But I'm going to cut this short."

"I followed you in here because you looked upset. I didn't like it." A line flashes between his brows, as if he'd even surprised himself. "And I missed seeing you. I saw you every day for a month, Ever. Did you think it would be so easy to go from—from . . ." He waves a hand around. "Ever at full volume, to switching off the whole damn sound system?"

"I didn't think about it." I manage to push the words past tingling lips. Everything is tingling. "I-I'm sorry I didn't think about it."

God, he looks almost angry. I've never seen him anything but lovable, charming or horny. "Was it so easy for *you*?"

No. *No.* I can't say the word out loud, though, because we miss each other for different reasons. He misses the sure-thing hookup, and I've stopped pretending that there weren't moments where I wished for more between us. More he wasn't willing to give. Now we are in some kind of stare down in the middle of a stale dive bar, he is irritated with me and it makes no sense. Hadn't he helped me craft the no-drama rules of our arrangement? Thankfully, the bartender chooses that moment to finally make an appearance.

"What'll it be?"

"The IPA," we say at the same time.

"The summer one," I add, so I won't get some fanciful notion about our identical beer selection meaning something. "Is that fine for you?"

"Yeah." Charlie swipes a hand through his hair as the bartender walks away. "Look, let's just get the remaining awkward out of the way, all right?"

"You should always clear the air before drinking," I mumble.

"Agreed." Those blue eyes pin me where I stand. "Why'd you call it off? You said someone close to you pulled a Ghost of Mistresses Future. What did that mean?"

The bartender drops off our beers and waits. Gaze still glued to me, Charlie reaches into his front pocket to extricate his wallet . . . and I blow it. I look down, eager to see his hand in the vicinity of his lap. If that makes me a sick puppy, so be it. Whenever my imagination isn't providing, my go-to porn is men . . . handling their business solo-style. Charlie did it for me once. I almost broke his neck afterward, fingers clinging to his hair while he went down on me, I was so hot and bothered.

When I manage to drag my gaze upward, he knows exactly what I'm thinking, too. And my eyes don't need to travel south again to know how his body is expressing satisfaction. The guy could get hard in a sandstorm at knifepoint.

Charlie tosses some bills onto the bar. "Ever, I won't push again. I won't even bring up how . . . *compatible* we are. In bed. Or in the hallway. Or on the counter. Or—"

"I get the picture."

His eyes crinkle at the corners. "But if you ask for it, cutie?" He licks his lips, so they're wet when they graze my ear. "If you say, *fuck me, Charlie,* I will drop whatever I'm doing. I will *get* between those legs if I have to kill, steal or sacrifice to get there. And you'll be a sweating, moaning, crying tangle of sex in the sheets by the time it's over. I know you don't doubt me, because I've done it. I've *done* it." He steps back and winks at me. "Three words. I just needed you to know."

"Consider me warned." Son of an undertaker. I'm dead where I stand. No. *Pull it together, Ever.* If I can make it through to the other side of this gutter-mouthed seduction, I can make it through, like, jumping out of an airplane without a parachute. Or the opera. "That's good to know. And yes, you're very good at tangling me up into a sex puddle."

He salutes me with his beer. "Thank you for noticing."

"You're welcome." This is getting ridiculous, and if I don't put a kibosh on the sex talk, I'm going to keep thinking about sex. With Charlie. Or maybe just the cords of Charlie's neck, standing out when he'd tipped his head back and moaned my name, that hand stroking, stroking . . . "This is serious, Charlie," I blurt out. "I made a promise to my mother. She has never wanted anything from me. Anything. If you knew her, you would understand how difficult it was for her to confide in me. I can't let her down the first time she gets the courage, because maybe—maybe—she'll come to me again. For something else. Anything else. If I can manage not to screw this up." Not having voiced my determination out loud before now, my heart is racing like a window-unit air conditioner in August. My voice falls to a whisper. "So, please don't try to knock me off course, okay?"

Poor Charlie. His face is white by the time I finish speaking. This little unplanned meltdown of mine is exactly why he avoids commitments. I can hear the man alarms going off inside his head. *We didn't sign up for this, bro! Get out. Get out now.*

To say I'm shocked when he sets down his beer and pulls me into his arms is an understatement.

Charlie

Well, *that* was a kick in the ass.

Since the day Ever approached me in the bar, played her game, let me kiss her face off and said those magical words—*nothing serious, 'kay?*—

she's been a mystical being without flaws. I mean, a woman who looks like a sexed-up angel that cooks and doesn't do relationships? It was like God had scratched his chin and said, *You know what? It's time to remind men they're not worthy of the fairer sex.*

Ever clearly *isn't* perfect, though. Her breath is coming fast in the crook of my neck, and I can tell she didn't expect to pour all that out. I sure as hell didn't, either. But if she thinks I don't understand the pressures a parent can place on you, she's wrong. We have more than identical beer selection in common. I've been sleeping with a woman who had a lot to say, things I would have understood, if we'd been functional enough to communicate.

"Ever. Hey." I smooth her blonde hair back, thickness building in my throat. "I won't—"

I cut myself off. *I won't try to knock you off course.* That's what I was about to say. Only, it's not true. Christ, I already ruined her very first chance to meet someone else. I probably shook her confidence, accounting for the sadness she dragged up the sidewalk. Worse, I'm probably going to do it again. I've already determined there's no one good enough for Ever. So if she lets me into the sanctum of friendship, I won't be capable of stopping myself from dissuading her from every new man she considers dateable. I'm becoming her friend in the hopes of knocking every other dude out of the running and graduating to friend with benefits.

So I can slide in there real smooth. Like a snake.

"What?" She pulls away from me, her cheeks pink. "You won't . . . ?"

I could lie and follow through anyway. But there's no pretense in the way she's watching me, chewing on her lip. I can't be untruthful when she's looking at me like that, grateful for the comfort. Especially because there wouldn't be a need for comfort if it weren't for me. "I won't understand pressure placed on us by our parents, is that what you thought?" I pick up my beer and take a long pull. Washing down my evasiveness. "My father is a bureau chief in the department. I don't know if I mentioned that."

She shakes her head slowly, gaze thoughtful. "No."

Why would I? It's only something I carry around on my shoulders all day. "Yeah. And my brother, Greer, is a lieutenant. The blue blood in my family must continue flowing at all costs, so I understand. About needing to measure up to a parent's expectations." Following impulse, I lean in and kiss her forehead. "I live it, Ever."

She looks down and away, almost like she's shy over me laying a smacker on her head. Really? I've kissed her a *lot* lower. A forehead kiss shouldn't even rate, right? Either way, it's goddamn adorable. What other reactions would she have to things? What if I tickled her? "It's a family institution," she says finally. "So that's why you work so hard."

"Yeah." I laugh at the word, because I'm thinking of Ever squealing and trying to get away from me. "Every minute is spent studying, improving my drill times, perfecting my shooting accuracy. My father expects me to make sergeant as soon as possible after I leave the academy, then take the lieutenant's exam by the end of my third year on the force. There'll be no time to breathe even after I graduate."

"You'll do it." She lays a hand on my arm. "It'll be fine. It seems impossible now because you're in the middle of it, but in ten years you'll want to do it all over again."

Holy shit, that actually makes me feel better. What have I been missing out on here? Trying to talk to Jack or Greer about the pressure is like a comedy sketch. They just eye roll or needle me. Three sentences out of Ever's mouth, and I'm floating on a cloud. Later I'll remember all the times my father told me never to let a woman lull me into a false sense of security. I'll recall his lectures about not letting women close enough to make a man comfortable, then bail. But right now, I'm soaking up her empathy like a sponge. "Thanks."

Her smile turns my cloud pink. "Don't mention it."

"What or who is the Ghost of Mistresses Future?"

That smile of hers morphs into a laugh, and I feel it down to my toes. "My mother. Until last week, she only dated married men. As a rule."

My beer is permanently suspended in midair. "Get out of here." Without missing a beat, she slides off her stool, turns and heads for the door, but I grab her elbow and haul her back. "You really are a smart ass."

Ever looks down at my hand, which is still locked around her elbow. My thumb is brushing the inside of her arm, an unconscious gesture, and we separate like I burned her. "Um." Her fingers fidget with the fringed hole of her jeans. "My mother expected me to follow in her footsteps until recently."

"*Be a mistress?*" Yes, I shout those three words, like we've teleported to a Gwar concert. I give myself a pass, though, because I'm suddenly imagining slimy, businessman hands all over Ever, and I think I'm going to be sick. Or find the closest dickhead in a tie and strangle him with it. "But you didn't, right? Follow in her footsteps."

"In a way, I did." Her head tips forward, and she peers up at me through her eyelashes. "I knew when I first saw you, Charlie, you were married

to a job. Now I know that job is the academy."
She's starting to look as uncomfortable as I feel.
"You were checking your watch. Drinking nonalcoholic beer. You held yourself like . . . you were
being held up on your way to something more important. I—"

"That's why you met me halfway?" What is this
discomfort in my stomach? Am I offended for the
first time in my life? I'm going with offended. Because I can't admit I'm feeling cheapened and still
keep my man card. I'm not the only one feeling
cheap, though (if I was admitting it). I thought
this whole thing with Ever started because we
were drawn together. Two souls with the united
goal of remaining single. Noncommitment aside,
I do not like knowing she's been equating us to
something seedy. "This whole time you've been
thinking of yourself as my mistress? *Jesus*, Ever."

It was her turn to be annoyed, apparently. "If
you make me apologize for no-strings sex again,
lasers are going to *shoot* out of my eyes."

How *dare* she be so funny. "I'm not asking for an
apology," I mutter, mopping a ring of moisture off
the bar with a napkin. "I'm asking . . ."

"For what?"

I don't know. I'm just certain that, in addition to
getting Ever back into bed, I'm now determined as
fuck to make her feel like more than just a diver-
sion. A *mistress*. God, she is right, though. That's

how I treated her. My magnanimous gesture had been offering to fix any leaky pipes. I fail. I fail *so hard* at life.

I walked into the bar with a plan. To become Ever's friend, so I could maneuver her back in my direction without anyone being the wiser. Back to normal. I can see now that our past normal wouldn't work for current Ever and Charlie. Because . . . I like this girl. Her personality, her humor, the way she leveled with me without a film of bullshit on top. Friends with benefits might have been the original idea, but I want to put my money where my mouth is. Make it more than just polite words for a painless hookup.

"What do you want, Charlie?"

"I want to be your friend." I mean it, too. Wanting to sleep with her is a *humongous* given, but I want to know Ever better. I know about her mother's wish now, though. It's important to Ever that she fulfill it. I will solve that problem . . . I just have no fucking clue *how*. Yet.

My plan needs fine-tuning.

That's the thing about plans, though. Bad ones usually mean several equally shitty ideas will follow.

That voice is screeching in my head again, but I give it the mental finger and focus on Ever. "What do you say?" I held out my right hand. "Friends?"

Her right eyebrow dips and she gives me a once

over, like a human bar code scanner. Suspicious and beautiful and red-hot sex, inches away from me, and I'm trying to be her pal. God, please don't let me regret this.

When she slips her hand into mine and smiles, though, regret is the furthest thing from my mind. I just bought myself more time with Ever. I'm going to be her friend, protecting her from inside the friendzone, even if it kills me. Because when she gets tired of dating a parade of douchebags, I'll be there. The better option.

"Friends," she breathes.

CHAPTER 8
Charlie

The Internet is mocking me.

For the last hour, I've been pacing my room, eyeballing the DateMate.com homepage. Sign up? It asks me. So casual, like it's offering me a stick of gum. The blinking cursor might as well be a box tied to a string. Soon as I lunge for the waiting carrot, I'm going to be trapped.

Okay, it's time to weigh the pros and cons.

Con: If I sign up to the dating site, I'm going to find Ever's profile within minutes and drive myself fucking crazy. There will be pictures of her. Words typed by her fingers. And I will know what every other man is looking at when they click on her name. Hello, mind fuck.

Pro: I'm already fucking crazy, so what's a little more fuel on the fire?

I crack my knuckles and sit down in front of my laptop. It's easy enough to enter my name and e-mail address, then I'm taken to a short question-naire. I have so much resentment for this bullshit site that my inclination is to make my profile name Magilla Gorilla and mock the system like a good little troll. But my cop blood gets the better of me. I'm already doing something pretty unethical by checking up on Ever, might as well be honest as possible to balance the scales.

Name: Reve S. Guy

(Reve spelled backward is Ever. Ever S. Guy.)

Clever, right? No. Not really. Because seeing the words on the screen makes my windpipe feel strained. I hurry through the rest of the questions, inputting my actual age, location, favorite music—James Brown—and a long list of physical stats. For a profile picture, I hastily upload one of me in a Jets ball cap, the brim partially obscuring my face. But when I reach the question about my profession, I hesitate. Combined with all my other answers, someone would definitely know my real identity if I input police academy recruit. What's the closest possible answer without revealing my-self? Fire academy recruit? Fine. It'll do.

It's not like I plan on interacting with anyone.

Or I don't plan on interacting, until I see there's a catch. I can't just search for Ever. The only profiles I can view are my matches. A sea of smiling female faces greets me as I scroll down impatiently. Christ almighty, our society needs to find a better way to pair people. This is why—luckily—no one approached Ever in the bar the day we met, while I got my shit together. The Internet is making it too easy. Poor ladies. They should all delete their profiles in protest of modern men being so dickless and force us to do better. In real life.

My rambling inner monologue screeches to a halt when I get to the very bottom of the first page. And there she is. Ever.

They matched us.

I take back every bad thing I said about this website.

My nose is pressed to the screen, I realize, so I make myself back up. I have a finger hovering over the mouse, ready to click, and my pulse is booming. Did she really have to pick the sweetest photograph of all time to lead off with? No wonder she was setting a record for hits. Who could resist a girl hanging from a tree branch in a Wonder Woman T-shirt? Central Park is spread out behind her in the background, a blanket and Frisbee lying haphazardly off in the distance. Who was she with that day? Does she go to the park a lot?

Did I think she spent all her time waiting for me in her apartment? Yes. I kind of did. Because I'm a stupid, self-centered idiot.

I click. Right on top of her nose, pretending

I'm tapping it with my finger. After that, I'm just fucked. There are around nine more pictures of Ever in various scenes that I am definitely not a part of. Carrying trays in a giant kitchen, a white apron tied around her neck, determination in her hazel eyes. Huddled under a blanket on her couch, making a squish face and a peace sign. Total joy bursting from her in rainbow waves as a sea lion kisses her cheek, a sign for the Bronx Zoo in the background. She's so beautiful, I put a hand over the screen for a few seconds to collect myself, then drop it once again.

That's when I see the bikini shot.

And my cock sits up for a better look.

"No. No, no, no," I tell my dick. "Don't even think about it."

But seriously, the bikini is cotton candy pink, with flimsy, little ties on the sides. The fringe rests on her suntanned hips like a taunt. I'm supposed to just pretend I don't see this? The bottoms mold to the pussy I know is criminally tight and always, always so damn wet for me. Her pose is modest, her arms twisted in front of her to hide her tits, but the photo is still so sexy I want to die just knowing other men have seen it. Die.

My cock does not want to die, on the other hand. He's alive, well and thriving, thank you very much. My self-loathing isn't strong enough to keep from enlarging the picture, looking for the reflection of a man in her sunglasses. Nope, though, just Nina. Knowing Ever was with a man in that bikini might have killed my erection, but no way that's happening now.

"I'm sick." I reach into my sweatpants and give my cock a vicious tug. This is what it has come to. I'm beating off to Ever's dating profile. "Fuck, I'm sorry, cutie, I'm so sick. I just miss being inside you so bad."

I let my head fall back and picture myself coming up behind Ever while she's dressed in that bikini. *Put the phone down*, I would say to Nina. *No one sees her like this but me.* She would give me a mischievous look over her shoulder, then shake that tight ass against my lap.

"Fuck me," I breathe, pumping my fist harder, my gaze zeroing in on the tiny pink triangle between her thighs. "Oh fuck, rub your pussy all over me. Slide it all over me. Make me so hungry for it. Make me hold you down and spread your legs to get my mouth on it."

Every muscle in my neck, stomach and arms is strained beyond belief. I'm going to go off so hard. I might even come close to the kind of orgasm Ever gives me. Maybe. Maybe . . . here it comes . . . just another few jerks—

My laptop dings.

What the hell?

I sound like a racehorse after the Kentucky Derby, my cock is a throbbing monument jutting from my lap, my hand squeezed around the base. But I drop my junk like it's hot when I see Ever is messaging me. She's messaging me. Jesus Christ. Can she see me? Did she see me rubbing one out to her pink bikini picture?

Hi, I'm Ever ☺

That's it? That's all she's giving me to work with? I mean, I definitely shouldn't message her back. She doesn't know I'm Charlie. But ignoring her would be rude. Especially when the hard-on she inspired is lounging on my abs like a sunbather. I drum my fingers on my desk a few moments, trying to ignore the voice shouting in my head that answering is a terrible, no good, very bad idea. The desire to speak to Ever wins by a landslide.

Hey. How's your night going?

Pretty good. I love James Brown, too.

"You do?" I have this crushing urge to hug my laptop. Or pick it up and shake it. I'm not sure which. "What else don't I know about you, Ever?"

Do you play Frisbee in the park a lot?

Only twice. Once to find out I was terrible at it. And then one more time to confirm.

It's all in the wrist.

Oh no. You're supposed to state up front in your profile if you're a Frisbee enthusiast. You didn't read the fine print?

Frisbee enthusiasts need not obey your silly human rules.

You're an alien, too? I have the worst taste in men.

My smile collapses like it's a Vegas casino that's just been imploded. Worst taste in men. As in, me? Charlie? Or is she just kidding around? I'm scared to find out.

It hits me at once that Ever is flirting with a man she thinks is someone else. Charlie is barely an afterthought right now for her. I have no idea how long I stare at the winking cursor, trying to count how many things suck ass about the current situation. In the end, I run out of fingers. And my erection has left the building on top of everything else. Another message dings on the screen from Ever, shaking me out of my stupor.

> Hey, sorry if that was weird, bringing up other men. You're the first guy I've messaged and I think I might be worse at this than I am at Frisbee.

> No, you're great at this, actually.

My fingers are stiff as I type, but I can't deny wanting to reassure her. And no lie, I'm back to a semi-even keel knowing I'm the first dude she's messaged. That's not the kind of thing Ever would lie about. She's not a liar at all, being nothing but honest with me since the beginning. I'm the liar in this scenario, and I'm making it worse the longer I continue this conversation, but I can't seem to stop myself. I want to talk to her.

> I'm probably the one that's sucking at this. It's my first time, too. I'm more of a face to face person.

> Same. There's too much left to chance here. You could have a voice like Mike Tyson.

I snort laugh. Then I make a pretty unmanly whining noise. She makes sports references, too? Reve S. Guy is one lucky asshole.

> We should meet so I can lay your fears to rest.

The words have been typed before I realize my fingers are moving. What am I doing? What is wrong with me? I can't meet up with her. I'm Charlie, not Reve. I'm pretty sure a Halloween mask and a voice manipulator are out of the question when we meet in person. So what is my end game here?

If Ever has plans to go on a date with Reve, it might prevent her from making more dates. And if I plan the date with Reve far enough in the future, it will give Charlie time to slide back in to her number-one spot. It's such a dick move, though. Am I really capable of something like this?

God, she could have just as easily messaged someone else tonight. If I hadn't signed up, she would be chatting with them right now. It could be anyone on the other side of the screen. Someone who could break her heart . . . or prey on her. I hear those kinds of horror stories every day. A woman meets a man on the Internet, he lies about his background and intentions, then boom. He's a felon with warrants for credit card fraud and assault. Not Ever. Never Ever.

> Wow. This is easier than I thought. Um. I think we're supposed to be in this talking phase longer, but as long as we meet somewhere safe . . . okay. Let's do it.

I'm jealous of myself. How ridiculous. But seriously, she's not even going to ask me for a better picture? Or some proof of citizenship? Or a hair sample? I could be a serial killer.

I have two options here. One is to turn up to the date as Charlie. In which case, I'm pretty sure she'll castrate me, right there in the dining room. The second option is to lead her on until the date rolls around and cancel at the last minute. Or not show up at all. No way. I'm not going to hurt Ever's feelings like that. I still haven't recovered from the first time, when I fucked up her speed dating night and made her sad.

So here is what I'll do. I'll give myself until the date to get us back to our original arrangement. As Charlie. If I can't pull it off by next Friday . . . I'll show up to the date as myself and come clean.

It's risky. Really risky. But I don't see another way that doesn't cause Ever pain.

God help me if I blow this.

How does next Friday sound?

CHAPTER 9

Ever

I't's a job night and everything has been royally fucked from the word _go_.

There are several drawbacks to hiring students to walk around and offer hors d'oeuvres to guests. They court drama among themselves, they're always cranky and they're flakier than cereal. No matter how effusive they are about their work ethic and punctuality, it takes almost nothing to make them call in sick. A light drizzle, a fight with their significant other, a Netflix binge they didn't see coming. They never cancel in a timely manner, either. They wait until oven buzzers are going off and the pinchy-featured woman who hired you is checking her watch.

Problem is, Nina and I haven't established ourselves enough yet to hire a full-time staff. We don't have enough capital to pay waiters until *we* get paid. God forbid something goes wrong and people are shortchanged. So on a job night—like tonight—we often squint one eye and wait to take a punch.

This evening, Hot Damn Caterers has been hired by the Women's Art League of New York—and that is no small potatoes. There was a small write up recently about Nina taking over the family donut shop in Brooklyn and starting her own catering company in the space. Apparently, it had caught the right eye, because the Art League had contacted us directly, interested in using the services of a female-run company.

We've been testing recipes and fine-tuning the menu for a month. Fois gras crème brûlée, spiced lamb meatball and tuna tartar appetizers. Sangria-marinated filet mignon, pesto-pistachio gnocchi and pancetta-wrapped pork tenderloin entrées. Yeah, we've pulled out all the stops on this one. No way we're going to let them down, knowing how much business a successful event could lead to. Of course, when we'd stressed the importance of this event to our college crew, it had gone in one ear and out the other.

We are short a waiter, which doesn't seem like a huge deal. But it *is*. Catering companies with more financial security always play it safe and book extra help. Hot Damn doesn't have that kind of bankroll yet. Maybe we should have tapped another waiter despite the cost, though, because now we're stuck.

"Maybe I can multitask," I mumble to Nina out of the side of my mouth, conscious of the nervous Art League chairwoman pacing the kitchen, going over notecards. "Stock trays and plate food, then do a pass with it . . . lather, rinse, repeat." In front of me on the stove, four pans sizzle with different sauces and a huge pot of boiling pasta. We spent most of the afternoon prepping the food off-site in Williamsburg, but the Art League hasn't paid through the nose for trays of ziti on chafing racks. They expect gourmet, and they expect it hot and fresh, which is why we've been busting ass in the Art League basement for four hours without a break. The event begins in half an hour.

"No, we need you down here." Nina chews on the thumbnail of her free hand, the other holding a cell phone to her ear. "Damn. No one is answering. That's the fifth voicemail I've gotten."

"College students with plans on a Saturday night." I sample the sauce and decide more fresh ground pepper is needed. "Never would have guessed."

When Nina would usually toss back a smart-alec response, she laughs and pats me on the back. "Good one." Such compliments have been the theme of the week. Maybe her heart isn't in our on-going battle of wits right now because she'd ended things with her boyfriend? Whatever the reason, I hope she gets back on the insult horse soon—there's only so much positivity I can take.

"Crap," Nina grounds out. "Crap. Six voice-mails. That's it. Wad blown."

"Damn." Now I'm nervous. I was able to hold off the anxiety until the final safety was pulled on our parachute, but now the deficit is real. This is a huge opportunity for us, and we're missing a vital player. "Um . . . do we know anyone—"

"No. Jeremy's sister could have done in a pinch, but . . ." Nina shrugs off the mention of her ex-boyfriend's sister, her eyes clouding over.

I turn and plop a kiss on her shoulder. "Look, we'll just send up more trays with each pass and set them out, instead of walking through. If the food can't go to the guests, the guests must go to the food."

Nina throws a look over her shoulder and winces. "That's going to go down like a wet fart in a church."

"*Nina.*" I muffle a laugh with the back of my wrist. "Maybe we should tell our not-so-calm-and-collected client now and limit the fallout."

"I already know what's going to happen," Nina whispers, massaging her forehead. "We're not go-ing to get paid in full and we'll lose money, Ever.

We really can't afford that right now. We're going to be paupers bathing in city fountains."

My pulse drums hard on either side of my throat. Times like this, I'm tempted to fall into the trap of uncertainty. Was I crazy to think I could just morph into a businesswoman, like my mother? What do I know about running a company? I'm learning as I go, taking it one day at a time. But this is a *now* problem, so I battle the urge to buckle and breathe through my nose. Thinking . . . thinking . . .

Later tonight, I will look back at this moment and wonder if some sort of voodoo had come into play. Inside the pocket of my apron, my cell phone buzzes and I fumble my spoon into its holder so I can grab it.

Charlie, says the screen.

For a full month, Charlie contacted me for one reason only. Sex. So it's little wonder that seeing his name on my cell phone screen makes my vaginal muscles clench like I'm trying to crack a coconut. Charlie Burns: a walking, talking reminder to do your Kegels.

Only, we're friends now. Not hookup buddies. Three days ago, we shook hands over beer and everything. When he walked me to the train, he kept his paws and mouth to himself, which had to mean he was serious, right? When three days passed without so much as a text, I started to doubt. But it's possible I've been too rash. Ninety percent of the afternoons we were together, he wore his uniform. Maybe the academy really does keep him too busy for a relationship, just as I suspected when I first laid eyes on him. When he claims to have no time, maybe it's the truth, plain and simple.

"Charlie?"

"Ever." His voice slides into my ear and the bubbling sauces on the stove fade out, but continue to warm my arms. "What are you up to?"

"Working a job." I notice Nina watching me closely. Motioning for her to keep stirring, I take a few steps away. "You?"

"Watching the game with Jack. Or I was, before he passed out." A pause, wherein I can almost feel him kissing my neck, simply because that's what usually happens when small talk is out of the way. "I was going to see if we could hang out. Like friends do."

"Like friends do," I say back, catching my reflection in the stainless-steel refrigerator. I'm twisting side to side at the waist like a middle-schooler talking to a boy on the phone for the first time. Really, it's heinous. "Maybe a different night."

There is a picture of Charlie beside the word *persistent* in the dictionary, so I'm not surprised when he doesn't take no for an answer. "Not even for a drink afterward? What neighborhood are you in? I can come meet you."

"Believe me, a drink will be necessary, but I think it'll be a bottle of red wine passed between me and Nina in bed." I look back anxiously at my friend, who in turn stares at the pacing Art League chairwoman. "We've had a pretty big setback tonight, so we'll be licking our wounds." When he doesn't speak for a moment, I nudge him. "Charlie?"

His sigh is almost wistful. "Sorry, I got stuck on the part about you drinking wine in bed with another woman."

"Lecherous man."

"You brought it up." His smile beams through the phone, reminding me of the hug he gave me in the bar. How he'd smelled. How he'd seemed invincible, those steady breaths lifting his chest beneath my cheek. "What kind of setback?"

"One of our waiters cancelled—" I cut myself off as a thought occurs to me. Call me a skeptic, a realist or both. I'm not one hundred percent sure if Charlie really wants to *only* be my friend. Heck, I'm not sure if women and men can be friends *at all* without one of them wanting to knock boots, let alone when they've been at it for a month. Why not find out if he can put his money where his mouth is? "How are you with a tray? Think you could walk, smile and carry one at the same time?"

I hear a creak and envision him standing up from a chair. "You're really asking about my multitasking skills, Ever? Remember when my fingers were—"

"If you're about to reference something sexual," I interrupt, a hot flush engulfing me. "I remind you, Charlie, you promised you wouldn't bring up our past . . . endeavors."

His groan is pure male frustration. "Fair enough. But I insist on a caveat. Don't refer to our past *endeavors* with the name of a space shuttle."

My lips twitch. "Well, you *did* blast off."

"Oh, *now* who's bringing it up?"

When our laughs collide into the buzzing static, I realize hearing his voice has almost made me forget about the problem at hand. He has blanked my mind before, but not unless we were in the same room. Naked. "So, about that multitasking thing—"

"I'm in. Text me the address."

A flutter begins a few inches south of my throat. "Just like that?"

"Yeah, Ever." His voice could melt butter. "You're in trouble so I'm coming. I want to help. Are you going to feed me for my trouble?"

Excitement blows through me at the idea of him finally trying my food. I never really expected it to happen. If possible, I'm more nervous about Charlie trying my meatballs than tonight's guests. "I'm going to stuff you like a turkey."

"Again, with the sex talk. You need an intervention."

"*You—*"

My comeback is sliced in two when the chairwoman growls behind me. Loud enough to send me toward the ceiling. "The harpist cancelled." She turns in a circle. "This isn't happening."

"I don't suppose you can sing, too," I whisper into the phone.

"I know a magician," Charlie offers, obviously having heard the chairwoman's meltdown. "And I use that term loosely. His show stealer trick is making a woman's panties disappear."

"*You're* the magician?"

"No, but I appreciate the compliment. I think." An exasperated sigh, followed by the clanking of glass. Bottles? "Jack, get up. Time to break a leg."

"Sure, baby," comes the muffled reply. "Just let me rest another minute, and we'll go again."

"Jesus," Charlie says. "We'll be there as soon as we can. Hang tight."

This is going to be a triumph or a tragedy.

"Thanks, Charlie."

"Any time, Ever." More clanking bottles. "I mean it."

I hang up and text Charlie the location, smiling like an idiot. Having him as a friend might be more black and white than I thought. Ignoring that ripple in my bones every time he's around will get easier, won't it? Especially when I find somewhere to focus my romantic energy. Right? A new start is the remedy for what Charlie makes me feel. I'm still a tiny bit . . . stuck on him at the moment. It'll pass.

My voice sounds a touch scratchy when I call to Nina. "Problem solved."

CHAPTER 10
Charlie

I have this vision. I'm going to sweep into the catering hall, balance one tray on my head, two in
each hand and save the day. Ever will watch in
awe as I stick a cocktail sausage in every available
mouth, weeping into her apron as I pass. Since
joining the academy, I've been climbing ropes,
running miles in a flatout sprint and doing push-
ups until my arms give out. How hard can it be to
offer hors d'oeuvres on a tray to people? I haven't
been to an upscale function like this, but I know
people like free food. It's like airplane cuisine.
Even if you don't like it, you eat it.

Yeah, I'm not worried about the difficulty level of
dishing out grub. I'm more concerned about feeling guilty when I see Ever. Dropping to my knees
and confessing my alternate identity. Reve S. Guy.

I've been feeling like an awful shit for deceiving Ever on the dating site. So much so, it took me a couple days to call her, thinking she would hear the sins in my tone and cut me off at the knees. As soon as I heard her voice, though, I forgot about everything but my mission. God willing, she'll never have to know about my alter ego because we'll be back on and better than ever before next Friday. Ever and Charlie 2.0.

"I can't believe you woke me up," Jack complains, hanging off the subway pole, eyes still half-closed. "I was having the best dream."

I'm checking the overhead map and counting the stops until we arrive, so I'm only half-listening. "Let me guess, there were women involved."

"One woman." He yawns. "But she had three tits, so like, one and a half?"

Now he has my attention. "I don't know. Sounds distracting." I squint an eye, trying to picture a woman with a third breast. "Where is it? Right in the middle?"

"Where do you think it is? On her fucking forehead?"

"Who knows what your brain comes up with, man," I mutter, starting to get anxious over how long the ride is taking. Ever really sounded like she needed help, and it took me half an hour to get Jack semisober and presentable. I have a secret weapon, though, to make up for the delay. Danika is meeting us there to help out, giving Ever three for the price of one. If I was charging, which I'm not. Right now, I'm just trying to be the guy she calls when shit goes bad. Call me Mr. Fix It. At some point, she's going to realize I'm exactly what she needs and end the dating bullshit. The sooner the better. I've been tearing my hair out not being able to see her. Wondering if she's set any more world records for interest on DateMate.com, speculating on whether or not she's getting over me with every passing minute. Basically, I've engaged myself in mental warfare.

Distract yourself. "What was Danika doing when you called her?"

"Writing something, I think. On that laptop of hers." The train pulls to a stop, and Jack stumbles in the direction of the sliding metal doors. "Didn't really hear much past her calling me a son-of-a-bitch."

Sounds like Danika. She's Jack's oldest friend and my newest, but after months of sharing living space, I know her personality well. She and Jack grew up together in Hell's Kitchen. They have the kind of oldest friend loyalty toward one another that you can't understand unless you're one of them. Naturally, I'd wondered if there was more to their relationship than friendship, but no. They might as well be related by blood. Danika took her calling as Jack's friend seriously, bullying him out the door each morning, visibly determined to keep him on the straight and narrow.

As much as possible, anyway, when dealing with Jack.

Danika is hot in a sharp, intimidating, *I-will-literally-cut-off-your-balls* kind of way, but I've only ever seen her as my pal. And hell, a competitor. She keeps me on my toes during drills at the academy, pushing herself more than any of my fellow recruits.

I watch Jack narrowly miss running into a concrete pillar on the way to the escalator leading out of the train station. Maybe I need to start doing my part for Jack, too. I know he didn't have an ideal upbringing, but I've never asked him if his constant drinking is a way to forget something from the past. Sometimes I catch him with a far-off expression, and my intuition tells me he isn't just imbibing for a good time. After talking to Ever through the dating site and realizing she has this whole life I wasn't aware of, I've started to wonder what else I'm missing when it comes to the people around me.

Jack hiccups as we climb above ground, both of our cells beeping as we regain reception. "Incoming," Jack mutters, just as Danika marches toward us on the sidewalk, in combat boots and a smirk. "Hello, sweet honey child."

"You don't charm me, babe, I've known you too

long." She leans in and sniffs Jack's breath, shaking her head. "Fuck sake, Garrett. I can't leave you alone for a minute."

Danika turns accusing eyes on me and I'm no fool, so I reach for the sky. "He was in this condition when I found him, ma'am." It's not good enough, I know. There is genuine concern in her eyes and I shouldn't make a joke, but I'm still navigating the newness of becoming the third person in their friendship. I don't want to make light of Jack's drinking problem, but I don't want to overstep, either. "He just needs to get a second wind, right, man?"

"Right." Jack winks at Danika and fast as lightning, he lifts her off the ground into a bear hug. "Come on, Danny. I hate it when you're mad at me."

"Not mad. Worried," she says under her breath, but I catch it. Breaking free of Jack's hold, she takes off down the sidewalk. "Come on, assholes, I already found the place and we'll be lucky if there isn't a mutiny over crab cakes by now. I don't know how I let you talk me into this." We catch up with Danika, and she throws me the speculative female side eye. "If I wasn't dying to find out more about this girl who used to send you running every lunch break, I wouldn't even have pants on right now. Are you guys back on now, or what?"

Grateful she isn't holding Jack's condition against me, I throw an arm across her shoulders.

Jack does the same, so we're a connected unit walking down the sidewalk. "We're friends. Ever and I."

Danika snorts. "I know how this story ends."

I give her a confused look, as if I haven't considered every angle. "We end up back in bed together? Everyone lives happily ever after leading their own lives, making their own schedules, not meeting each other's parents and having a sex lifeline to call, whenever they want it? Sounds terrible."

Jack fist bumps me behind Danika's head. "I'm glad we're friends," he hiccups.

"For the record, Charlie, you're playing a dangerous game. We always find out what men are up to. It's inevitable," Danika says, then groans. "How did I end up being the voice of reason in this trio? I like to make trouble, too, you know."

"And we'll be there to bail you out when that happens," Jack drawls, ruffling her hair. "What am I supposed to do when we get there, again?" he calls to me. "Besides eat."

I check the address we're passing and note we're almost there. Up ahead, I can see a swanky brownstone all lit up and know Ever is inside. Swear to God, I can feel her, and I relax completely for the first time since we were together in the bar.

I've missed her. A lot.

Pushing aside the realization, I steer Jack and Danika toward the brownstone. "You're going to pop an Altoid and be your charming self. You bring your deck of cards?" He salutes me with his free hand. "Good. Your only other order of business is to stay twenty yards away from Ever at all times."

He nods in understanding. "How am I going to get the free food?"

"I'll bring you a plate."

We disconnect and climb the stairs. The door is open, and voices drone out through the crack. Knowing there is no way they'll hear a knock, I push open the door and glide inside like I own the place.

Cop walk. It gets you anywhere.

The place is jam-packed—and it's all women. They're dressed like they're at a country club wedding, in pantsuits and dresses I know are expensive by just looking at them. When I was young, a police dispatcher, Malia, used to babysit me and she'd watch old episodes of *Murder, She Wrote*, one right after the other. This event reminds me of something out of that show, and I make a mental note to check in on Malia soon.

Nina passes by with an empty tray and without breaking stride, grabs my arm and leads me toward a staircase on the opposite side of the vestibule. Danika follows me, but Jack is already wading into the hall full of women, slipping the deck of cards from his pocket and cocking his head, as if to say, *who's ready for some* actual *fun?*

Bringing Jack might have been a bad idea. He'd learned to entertain the johns in the brothel where his mother worked, while they waited for their appointment. He entertained the women, too, when they weren't occupied. But this isn't exactly his typical crowd.

My concern is replaced by . . . more concern when we walk into the kitchen and I spot Ever looking frantic. My steps falter along with the ticker in my chest, I think because until that moment, I'm not sure I *knew* Ever. And something inside me rebels over that fact. *This* is what she does? I pictured her drizzling strawberries with chocolate, dressed in a cute apron and nothing else. Instead, she's like a beautiful pinball bouncing back and forth between the stove and a stainless-steel table lined with trays. This is what she loves. What she loves is *hard*. We have this in common, same way we have pressure from our parents in common.

I hear a low whistle and glance over at Danika, finding her staring at my profile. "I take it back. I have no idea how this story ends." She nudges me. "Go to her, Lancelot."

I do. Because I don't have a choice. I'm going to make this night better for Ever, or I'll consider my whole life a failure. I make footprints in the layer of flour on the floor as I walk toward her. When I'm five feet away, she turns, a hunk of blonde hanging down in front of her right eye. "Can you pin my hair back? My hands are covered in . . . everything."

"I-I don't know. I've never done it before," I say honestly, looking down at my hands, all my fingers turning into thumbs. "Where is the pin?"

She cocks her hip at me. "Pocket."

Solid. I've only been here one minute and I'm already touching her, sliding my fingers into her pocket, all while staring at her mouth. That pouty, kiss factory I always have trouble leaving alone long enough to get our clothes off. There isn't a lot of time spent rejoicing over having my digits in Ever's pocket, though, because what the fuck is this plastic contraption I've just pulled out? It's got teeth and it looks like a clam. "Okay, I can do this," I mumble. "How do I do this?"

"Pinch the top together. There." She tilts her head. "Just get that one piece, stick it on top of my head and lock the little spikes around it."

Jesus, her hair is soft. I knew that, didn't I? Her ear is perfect, too, like a peach-colored shell or—

"Focus, Charlie."

"Sorry." I manage to secure the hair on top of her head and release the pent-up breath I didn't realize was being stored in my lungs. "There you go."

"Thank you." There's a streak of green sauce on her cheek, and she rubs it off on her shoulder.

"Hi."

"Hi." Her eyes dip to my mouth and I almost do it. I almost kiss her. But she looks past me before I potentially blow my first real chance to be her friend. "You were with Charlie the day we met, but we kind of . . ."

"Gave each other a tongue bath?" my smart-ass roommate supplies. "I'm Danika." She steps into my periphery, eyeballing the half-full tray Ever is working on. "Charlie and I are in the academy together. I have no romantic interest in him, should that be of any concern to you."

"Thanks, Danny," I say dryly.

Ever's gaze cuts sideways, but she doesn't give me any clue as to what she thinks of Danika's remark. *Dammit.* "Nice to meet you, Danika." She wiggles her food-covered fingers. "I would shake your hand . . ."

"No worries. Put us to work."

Ever shakes herself, as if she'd been plunged back into reality and reality is a kitchen full of boiling pots and oven timers going off. "Now *that* I can do."

For the next ten minutes, I feel like a spare tool. Actually, I would like to go back in time and slap the version of myself I'd been on the subway. I was not Ever's white knight charging in on a noble steed. Ever is her own knight. I'm the court jester.

She moves like nothing I've ever seen. While I didn't grow up with a woman in the kitchen, so I have nothing with which to compare Ever's style, I pick up on a few nuances as I watch her prepare the next round of hors d'oeuvres. Detective's eye and all that jazz. Her movements aren't . . . precise, exactly. They're somewhat stilted, like she's learning as she goes. She has notecards propped up in various spots on the counter and checks them frequently, her lips moving as she reads the words.

When I take my phone out and secretly film her, Danika shakes her head at me, then goes back to looking at Twitter on her own cell. I don't know why I'm filming Ever, but I know I want to watch this again later. Jesus, she's extraordinary. And I can tell by the nervous way she keeps wringing her hands in a dishrag, she doesn't know it.

"Okay," Ever calls over. "These are ready to go up."

Danika grabs a tray and heads confidently toward the staircase, same way she does everything. I start to pick up my own tray, but Ever stops me, laying a hand on my arm. "Wait." She picks up a little bundle of meat and shaved vegetables, holding it against my mouth. "Eat?"

The way she makes it a question sends a flame burning up my esophagus. Memories of her cooking every time I walked in the door of her apartment flip through my mind. The way she used to leave it all out on the counter while we got busy. And I wonder if that was her secret way of offering me some of her creations. I never took her up on it. "Lay it on me," I rasp.

I'll go to the grave swearing it's the best thing I've ever eaten. Food-wise. Ever's pussy beats it by a mile, but in terms of stuff I can chew, this meat and vegetable bundle is insane.

She rolls her shoulder. "What do you think?"

"I think I'm going to sneak about eight more on my way up the stairs." She beams at me, and I wish I'd said a higher number than eight. "Damn, Ever. You're great at this."

"Yeah?"

No one's told her. "Yes. Better than great." I notice that chunk of hair I clipped up early has come loose again, so I reach up and fix it carefully, feeling her eyes on me the whole time. I don't know what she's seeing, but it's probably confusion.

I thought being Ever's friend was going to be difficult.

Now I'm starting to wonder what took me so long.

CHAPTER 11
Ever

I 've finally sent out the final round of main courses and start to plate the dessert. In my book, this is the final stretch. The victory lap. Not a single plate has come back with a complaint, also known as I'm breaking out celebration tequila. Since I'm alone in the kitchen while Nina supervises upstairs, I salute myself with a shot and throw it back, eager to see what's going on in the ballroom. Maybe I can just take a quick peek, then wrangle Nina to help me plate the last wave of her famous mini chocolate lava cakes I just put in the oven.

It's not very often someone surprises me, but Charlie did tonight. Dammit, he really did. He has been back down to the kitchen several times, even helping me transfer food from pans to plate, garnishing, and yes, stealing bites when he thought I wasn't looking. Or maybe he knew. I couldn't tell.

He wanted to put his hands on me several times as we worked side by side. Just something I could feel. Maybe there's an intuition that comes from having someone inside you enough times you lose count. Little ghosts had moved over my hips, slid across my belly and kissed my neck in place of his touch, because I could sense him wanting it there. As a consequence, I'm turned on as hell right now. No lie. The metal of the prep table presses into my stomach and I close my eyes, picturing Charlie unzipping his pants behind me, bending me forward and lifting my skirt, all at once. Impatient hands, groans, table legs creaking.

Will there ever be a point when we can coexist in the same room and not think of going at it like animals in heat? I don't know. But our friendship is worth trying to reach that point, isn't it? Look how he'd dropped everything to come help me.

Promising myself extra attention tonight with my vibrator, I push away from the prep table and remove my apron, gliding toward the stairs. I've been setting aside little portions for Charlie and his two friends, leaving them warming in the oven. They really came through for us, and I'm not about to let that go unrewarded. When dessert service is over, I'm going to spoil them rotten.

When I reach the upstairs ballroom, I stop beside Nina where she stands at the room's edge. I can barely believe what I'm seeing. There is an extremely good-looking young man with his shirt off, arm wrestling the host, a lit cigar clamped between his teeth. I vaguely remember him being in the bar on the day Charlie and I met, but I'd been so focused on Charlie, this guy's attractiveness barely registered until now. But . . . wowza. He reminds me of an outlaw card shark raising hell in an Old West saloon. And Good-Looking is clearly pretending his arm-wrestling opponent has a hope in hell of winning, but that's not stopping the surrounding women from throwing money down on the table, shouting for their favorite.

"What the hell is going on?" I whisper to Nina.

"I don't know." She's in a trance. "It's all just happening."

"There are two . . . maybe three laws being broken here."

Danika spies me and makes her way over, twirling an empty tray on her palm. "Hey, Ever. Take a real good look at what you're getting into."

My mouth falls open, because I finally see Charlie. He is on the dance floor, surrounded by women old enough to be his grandmother. One is being spun and dipped, her expression the picture of delight, while everyone else sways and waits their turn. "There's a plate of food in the oven for you," I say to Danika, unable to take my attention off Charlie. "Go to town."

"Sweet."

My gaze locks with Charlie's across the room, and the most adorable thing in history happens. So adorable, my insides turn to melted caramel. Hair askew, collar crooked, he gives me a lop-sided grin, just as his dance partner lays a smacker on his cheek. He's actually sheepish as he scratches the back of his neck, like a naughty boy caught in the act of being too cute for humankind's own good.

Before I realize what I'm doing, I'm floating toward him.

He's not cute after that. Oh no. He's eye fucking me, that wicked tongue resting on his bottom lip like it's getting ready to do something dirty. The women surrounding him on the dance floor turn to follow Charlie's line of sight, and they could not be *more* excited by this development. They're clapping and asking if I'm his girlfriend. Right now, with a tidy little tequila buzz, I'm not even bothered by the question mark hanging over our heads. Yes, I'm a girl. Yes, I'm his friend.

We'll worry about the rest after I dance with him. There's a rare clarity that comes after one shot of tequila—not dissimilar to the one glass of wine clarity—and right now, I'm damn well going to dance with this beautiful man who saved my bacon tonight and has the nerve to be adorable on top of everything.

"Ladies," Charlie announces. "A round of applause for the beauty who masterminded, prepared and plated your meals this evening." I curtsey as they applaud, throwing the sweetest compliments my way. Compliments I wasn't expecting and make my throat constrict. Nervous under so many sets of eyes, I reach for Charlie's hand and he spins me around. "She's got moves, too, ladies. Is there *anything* she can't do?"

They're eating him up and I don't blame them. I wouldn't mind a bite myself. This is a new side to Charlie I've never seen before, and it's not helping my current determination to secure him in my mind as a friend, while searching elsewhere for something real and lasting. With someone who is actually interested in those two things.

Just as the song "My Type" by Saint Motel ripples through the speakers, Charlie pulls me against his chest, one hand flat on the small of my back, the other brushing something food-related off my cheek. "You were amazing tonight, you little knockout," he murmurs, bringing our foreheads together. "Dance with me."

Oh, my poor hormones. They've all fainted dead away. I should step back and get my mouth a friendly distance from Charlie's, but instead, I settle a hand on his tight butt, earning a resounding cheer from our audience. "You may have this dance, sir."

He pokes the inside of his cheek with that tongue, smiling even as the tips of his ears darken. "You're not the first to have a hand on my ass tonight."

I swallow a laugh as he started to sway me. "Oh no?"

Charlie shakes his head. "No, but you're the first one who might have to face the consequences."

He's an *excellent* dancer, which I totally didn't expect, making every move feel effortless. Fluid. We're edging out of the friendzone here. I know it's bad. Very bad. Because I liked Charlie too much when we were only a long-standing hookup. Now he's becoming more and there's a premonition blowing through my head, telling me I'm taking a wrong turn. "Just friends, Charlie."

His hand presses me close, and I confirm just how unfriendly he's feeling toward me at the moment. Like, about eight solid inches of unfriendly. And he knows exactly what to do with it. "We could be friends that make each other feel good, Ever."

"Is that why you came here tonight?"

"No." He looks down at me with a line between his eyebrows. "No, I came to help, but I've been watching you be incredible for *hours*. I see you. I smell you. I know what you feel like. You just got over your period, so I know you're extra-hot for it, don't I?" He lets out a breath against my temple. "I know what you need, cutie. I *know*."

Maybe that remark about my period shouldn't get me hotter, but oh boy, it does. I love that he paid attention. I love that he isn't squeamish or afraid to talk about it. A man, not a boy. "I'm not going to stop dating." There's a hitch in the fluidity of how he's moving me, dancing with me, but he recovers fast. "I'm sticking to my decision, Charlie, and . . ." My heart is way too much in play here, but I can't say that out loud. Or maybe I should. It would scare him away once and for all, and I could focus on the future. There's one problem, though. I'm not ready for him to go anywhere. "Thank you for the dance. Thank you for coming to help, but this is a bad idea," I whisper. "Just friends."

I catch a couple of disappointed faces as I leave Charlie's arms and jog back toward the kitchen, getting there just as the timer goes off for my chocolate lava cakes. I'm the only one in the kitchen and it's a good thing, because my knees are shaking. My palms are sweaty. But I'm not alone for long, everyone assembling downstairs to complete the dessert service. And when Charlie brushes behind me at the oven, his breath feathering along the back of my neck, I have a feeling tonight's battle with my libido is far from over. Because I'm battling Charlie's, too.

Charlie

D amn. I almost had her. She's close to caving. I can tell by the way she's watching me beneath her eyelashes, rubbing her palms down the sides of her skirt. Jack and Danika were sent home an hour ago, but I stayed behind to help Ever and Nina clean the kitchen. If I could just get alone with Ever, we could end the night with a new understanding. I know we could.

She keeps up her search for Prince Charming. I get her body in the meantime.

I'm totally cool with that.

Yeah right. I want to claw the fucking drywall down thinking about it. For a start.

At the moment, my only option is to make this agreement with Ever, then make sure she realizes Prince Charming is an illusion. I'm not just being selfish here. I truly believe she's on a doomed mission. She's going to get hurt or disappointed, and I want neither of those things for her. What we had together was fool proof, and she just needs a little nudge back into my corner.

It's like Nina knows exactly what I'm thinking because she's hovering around Ever like a mother hen, shooting daggers at me with her eyes. What *is* it with women? I want nothing more than to give her friend multiple orgasms, and she's looking at me like I'm Scar from *The Lion King* and I sent Simba into the stampede.

I'm holding out hope, though, because Nina keeps checking her ringing cell phone and sharing eye rolls with Ever. It must be her scumbag ex-boyfriend. But scumbag status notwithstanding, it's only a matter of time before she—

"I'm going to answer it," Nina says, sending me into mental fist pumps. "Otherwise, he's just going to keep calling."

Ever looks concerned as Nina heads upstairs, her annoyed greeting ringing down the stairwell, and I calculate I've got about fifteen minutes maximum to make magic happen. I finish mopping the final corner of the kitchen and wheel the yellow bucket out of the way, aware that Ever is sending me anxious looks, like she knows the two of us alone spells trouble. That theory is confirmed a moment later when I come up behind her at the oven and she skates away, humming way too casually, and vanishes into the storage closet with a stack of pots.

I really need to bring my A-game here. When the winning move strikes me like a bolt of lightning, my blood heats in anticipation. Ever has a weakness. I just need to exploit it. Good thing her weakness is one of my strengths.

Ever is almost out of the closet when I appear in the entry . . . and I kick the door shut and just keep walking, forcing her to back up. She realizes she's made an error—that much is clear. She starts to admonish me, all breathless-like. "Charlie *Burns*." But just as fast as she tries to play it tough, she drops the strategy in favor of looking for a weapon. A rolling pin is what she comes up with and we both laugh a little, because it's straight out of an old-timey cartoon. "What are you up to?"

"Just want to talk." My voice betrays my lie. "Friends talk, don't they, Ever?"

Throwing the F-word in her face was a mistake. Or was it? Because when she swings the rolling pin at my head, I stop her wrist in midair and use the opening to back her against the wall. "Your heart wasn't in that swing."

"You don't know a single thing about my heart."

I almost let go and walk straight out of the closet when she says that. Really, I do. Because she's right. Mostly. After watching her cook and listening to her reasons for braving the dating world—her mother—I think I know some things about her heart. Not all, but some. Truth is, I . . . want to know more, but I have to exercise caution. I can't know everything in her heart because that would make our relationship too serious. I don't want serious.

I don't want serious.

So why doesn't that little hitch in her voice send me barreling out of the closet? Am I a complete bastard?

Does Ever *want* me to know everything in her heart?

No way. No, she knows I'm not the man for that. But since I've started overthinking her words in my head, her body has turned pliant against mine, her tits resting on my chest, shifting side to side with enough subtlety that I might have missed it if I wasn't attuned to every fucking movement of her body. This is what she needs me for. Not some Prince Charming bullshit I could never pull off in a million years.

Why does it feel like I'm swallowing a handful of pennies?

"Charlie," she whimpers, bringing me roaring back to here and now. "I can't—"

"You know what I miss the most?" I curve my hands around her waist, sliding my thumbs inward to stroke her belly button. "That first lick of your bare pussy. It always let me know how much you'd been thinking of me. How hard you were going to let me fuck you." My thumbs dip into the elastic waistband of her skirt, down, down, until they're right at her panty line. "You were never less than soaked." A slow press of my thumbs has her knees dipping. "Willing to bet you're in that condition right about now."

"Well, if I wasn't . . ." Ever half breathes, half laughs with her eyes closed, "I am now."

Jesus, I miss her honesty. This is why I need her. No more games, just . . . *Ever*. If her eyes were open right now, she would witness the intensity of that wish all over my face, so it's a good thing she can't see. "I'm going to kneel now. You *know* what to do." I push my hand inside her panties and groan—so fucking loud—because her pussy fits my palm like we were matched up by God himself. "Quit playing keep-away with this pussy. Pull up that stupid, little skirt you wore to be professional and let me lick what you're trying to hide from my tongue."

It's the filth that makes her cave. I love saying these borderline disrespectful things to her and she loves hearing them, otherwise I wouldn't. Thank God she does, though, because by the time I'm done talking, she's arching her back on the wall, a moan building in her throat. "Charlie, please . . ."

Yeah, I'm not waiting around for Ever to change her mind. My knees hit the deck like someone is robbing me at gunpoint. "Shhh, I've got you." The sight of Ever sliding the tight, black material to her waist and revealing a thong I haven't seen before sends a ripple through my blood. It's arousal, it's jealousy, it's making me ache. "You didn't buy this because you started dating." I hook a finger in the gray lace and drag it down to her knees, the axis of my world skewing right, then left. "Did you, Ever?"

"No." Her reply emerges as choked as my question, her fingers already sliding into my hair, holding tight. Oh yeah, she *knows* I'm going for a ten on the cunnilingus rating scale. "I bought it for myself. And I w-wouldn't suggest mentioning my new lease on life right now, unless you want me to overthink this."

"Roger that." My hands are a blur as I rip the panties down to her ankles, shove them into my front pocket and surge forward. The scent of her—warm apples—wallops me in the senses and if we weren't on the clock, I would have taken a moment to bury my nose against her soft cunt. Inhale her. Maybe paint a mural in its honor. But my mouth is apparently controlling my brain, because the taste is what I'm most frantic for. Her hips are doing these sexy, little circles, but I need her *still*. I need her to understand I'm a fucking maniac that's gone over a week without her. No, she *took* herself away from me, and it's my mouth's job to remind her why that was a bad decision.

I'm breathing like a bull as I tunnel my tongue into the tops of her slick folds. Right at the top, where the center of the storm lives. Eyes closed in euphoria, I slide the tip of my tongue down through her lips, like I'm making a credit card transaction. One that definitely got approved— 'cause, damn, she goes wild. So fucking wild. I'm not talking screams or begging. No, this unicorn of a woman *climbs* me. She throws both of her thighs over my shoulders, giving me all her weight, which I gladly accept, using the wall to keep her leveraged. Then she does a little scooting shimmy to bring herself right up against my mouth, turning my cock into a goddamn crowbar.

"Charlie, please. I missed this so bad." In the middle of polishing up her clit, I glance up and find her half-delirious against the wall. *Jesus.* Until that moment, I hadn't realized how desperate for proof I've been. Proof that she's had a hard time separating from me. That it hasn't been one-sided. "You're so good. The way you . . ." She whimpers and yanks at my hair. "And that, too. That, too. Your *tongue.*"

This. *This* is the greatest show on Earth. The girl of my dreams telling me she missed me, telling me I'm good with my tongue. I've barely gotten started and she's already close to an orgasm. Those gorgeous little muscles on the inside of her thighs are contracting in my peripheral vision, and she's giving that sweet, sexy babble above me. Pride is like a ribbon threading in between my ribs, pulling tight. I'm tempted out of my mind to stand up, take out my dick and fuck the ever-loving shit out of her, but it would be too much, too soon. Not just for her. For me, I realize. I'm barely going to retain my sanity witnessing her attempts at dating. If I'm sleeping with her, I don't know how I'll handle it. I'll find a way, but . . . one day at a time.

My brain is a little tilted from thinking about Ever with someone else, so the strokes of my tongue get somewhat mean. Can't stop it. I shove her mind-blowing thighs wider and cram my tongue inside of her, deep. Deeper. Shoving her into the wall with my head, massaging her clit with my upper lip while I tongue-fuck her.

"Charlie. Jesus Christ." Here it comes. "Big man."

I growl at the nickname and there she goes. That slick heat shudders and tightens against my mouth and she's done. I replace my tongue with two fingers and worry her clit between my lips, just to give her a little extra and *fuck*, does she appreciate it. Yeah, Ever's weakness has always been my mouth between her legs, but this reaction is another level. I'm going to need a hair transplant, because I'm pretty sure she ripped some of it out and she's still twisting, twisting my strands in her fists. It's goddamn heaven. She can have my hair as long as I don't have to live without this pussy. Her come is dripping down my fingers as I milk them in and out, groaning at the wet sound it makes.

My connection to her needs is still lit up, still throbbing, and I know that although she came, she hasn't gotten that knockout punch yet. Probably because she's gone a long time without me. So I deliver. I want her to be sure I'll deliver every damn time, and then some.

I push my fingers in deep, deep enough that she gasps, and let the pad of my middle finger tickle her G-spot. "No one knows your pretty cunt better than I do. Isn't that right, Ever?" She's babbling again—shit, I *love* when she does that—but I think I catch an agreement. Yes, I'm using the C-word out loud now, and I know that's part of the extra push she needs. I'm her filth man, and she can't be bashful about wanting more from me, because I never stop being hungry for her. "I've got a map of you in my head. In my bones," I rasp. "*Look* at me."

Her head pitches forward, like her neck muscles have taken a vacation. Both of our gazes are obscured by heavy, lusty eyelids, but we're looking at one another when I begin flickering my tongue against her clit. Her G-spot is still being exploited by my middle finger, but this additional attention to her sensitized nerves is going to orgasm her again. I know this, because I'm a certified Ever Expert.

"Look at me. On my knees, lapping at you. Fingering you. I'd stay here all fucking night, soaking up this sweetness. You *know* I would." I'm so hoarse at this point from needing to fuck, needing to make her come, that my voice isn't mine. "Who do you call when you're the kind of keyed up no one else knows how to handle?"

Several shaking drags of air into her swollen lips. "Charlie . . ."

I know that wasn't an answer. It was the beginning of an admonishment. But I'm taking it as my answer, anyway. Moving my middle finger faster, I lean in and give her clit a light suck, followed by slow side to side rubs of my tongue—and obliterate her.

By the time she stops shuddering and clenching her thighs around my head, I'm in danger of pushing too far. Try explaining to your cock it can't have the woman that has been satisfying it beyond belief for a month. The jerk doesn't want to listen.

I come to my feet, using my body to keep Ever from sliding down the wall into a heap. Our foreheads pressed together, I breathe. Breathe. Ignoring the stubborn prick in my pants, I look at Ever's face, finding it flushed and soft. So much more than merely beautiful. Have I ever looked at her like this? Just . . . quietly looked? Before I know what I'm doing, my mouth is pressing kisses to her hairline, the curve of her cheekbones. One corner of her mouth lifts, her nose wrinkling, and I find myself smiling back. Affection hits me so hard in the stomach, I almost fall back down on my knees.

Whoa. *Whoa.*

I need to get out of here. Something is different. Something has changed . . . or at least is in danger of changing inside me. I haven't touched Ever like this in a while, so maybe I'm just really grateful. I don't know. Time to hit the bricks, though, right? Why am I having such a hard time letting her go and backing up? She feels really, really great all pliant like this. I don't think I've ever held her afterward.

Ever's eyes pop open and she's searching my face, and that's what propels me backward. I don't know what she's going to see, but I-I think it's too much.

"I have an early training session tomorrow morning."

She jerks off the wall, like she just had a bucket of water emptied over her head. "Oh. Oh, you— yeah." Her hands are clumsy as they drag her skirt back into place . . . and they reach out to me. She wants me to hug her again. Hold her. Jesus, what am I going to do? Even if I want nothing more than to wrap her up in a big, squeezing bear hug, I don't want her to get the wrong idea. What is the wrong idea, again? "My panties, Charlie."

Oh. Fuck.

My hesitation seems to have . . . embarrassed her? But I'm definitely the one who should be humiliated. Of course she didn't want a hug. I'm an idiot, and I need to go home before I ruin every inch of progress I've made toward becoming her go-to guy for . . . everything. Friendship, cater waitering, cunnilingus. All of the above. "Sorry." I hand her back the gray lace, kind of wishing I could keep it. "They look great on you, Ever."

She steps into the lace and wiggles the panties up her body, forcing me to battle the groan of all groans. "Thanks for—"

"Don't you dare thank me for that."

Color climbs her cheeks. "Then . . . thank you for helping out tonight." She tucks her hair behind an ear and moves past me, careful not to let our bodies touch. "I don't think we could have pulled it off without you guys."

I grab her elbow before she can leave the closet, knowing I somehow fucked up, but refusing to let my error ruin the fact that we're almost back. Ever and Charlie. Committed to being uncommitted. "Hey, Ever." I slide my hand down to her wrist, bringing her hand to my mouth for a kiss. "Still friends. Please?"

Her eyelashes sweep down to hide her eyes. "Still friends." She leans in and gives me a soft kiss on the cheek. "Good night, Charlie."

This time it was goodnight, not goodbye—and I'm damned thankful.

It's short-lived, though, because as soon as I step out into the rushing Manhattan evening, I have the overwhelming sensation I should be back inside, taking Ever home.

CHAPTER 12
Charlie

I've done so many push-ups today, my arms are aching with the strain. Soon as I hit one thousand, I'm going to run another couple miles, try to beat my best time. I'm holing up in my room tonight with study materials, because we have an exam coming up. I don't need a refresher. Hell, I knew everything in the handbook before I entered the academy, but if I don't distract myself, I'm going to call Ever again too soon. It has only been a couple days since the catering event, and new friends space out their interactions more, right?

Who the fuck knows? I just don't want to appear too eager. Meanwhile, I'm about as eager as sailors during Fleet Week. How is she? Is she working a job tonight? If not, what the hell is she getting up to without me? Central Park, the beach, watching movies? I got used to living in the dark about her everyday activities, but that's really not working for me anymore.

I've been tempted to message her on DateMate. As Reve. God knows I've been logging on to look at her photos often enough. They've become part of my routine. There's a picture of her balancing a plate of toast on her head that I like to eat breakfast with.

It's time to have my head checked.

Danika walks into the gym, kicking the edge of my floor mat. "Saw your not-girlfriend."

"What?" I go down on my chest, roll over and sit up, like an animal that's been offered a treat for performing. "Where?"

"At that tapas place near Union Square."

"Fuck." I come to my feet, just as Jack saunters in eating a burrito. "A date?"

"Who's on a date?" Jack asks around a mouthful. "I like dates."

Danika crosses her arms, clearly enjoying watching me squirm. "Ever. With some sexy financial type. Caught them through the window as they were sitting down."

"Oh shit," Jack says, turning on a heel and trying to leave the room. "I have an appointment."

"Wait. Just . . . wait," I call, halting him in his tracks. My heart and brain must have swapped places, but my heart feels twice as heavy and my head is beating. I thought Ever's upcoming rendezvous with Reve would prevent her from scheduling dates with other dudes. Didn't Ever and Reve have a connection? Apparently not enough of one to keep Ever cooling her heels. "Sexy financial type? Like . . . sexy how? How is he sexy?"

"Objection," Jack waves his burrito. "Irrelevant."

"You're on the law side of law and order, Jack," Danika says. "You realize that, right?"

"Stay on the subject." I sound like someone is using my stomach as a trampoline. "Ever. Date."

"A sexy date."

"Sexy how?"

Danika throws up her hands. "Kind of a Patrick Wilson type, I guess. Cufflinks. Starchy shirt. Fresh haircut."

Jack smirks. "You need a refresher course on what's sexy, honey."

Christ, I think I'm having a panic attack. The last time I experienced this severe nausea and racing, spiky pulse was when I found out Ever was going speed dating. I thought of her getting hurt or being sweet talked by a bunch of chumps and . . . I came up with the plan to sabotage the event. Can't do that again, though. It made Ever sad. Made her lose her sparkle, and even for a short span of time, that's unacceptable. I can't meddle again. Unless. . . .

"Did he seem maybe like an asshole?" There's no way to keep the hope out of my voice as I throw the question at Danika. "Like he could ghost her after one date. Or maybe he looked more like Patrick Bateman from *American Psycho*, instead of Patrick Wilson?"

Danika tilts her head, like she's on the verge of calling me an idiot. But whatever she finds in my expression seems to change her mind. "Yeah. It's possible I might have seen a splatter of blood on his collar."

"She has excellent vision," Jack supplies.

"Okay," I breathe, bracing my hands on my knees. My brain is barely capable of functioning because it's melting. Ever on a date. A real *date*. And I don't think I can physically let it happen. I completely underestimated my ability to watch her go on dates from the sidelines, just being her supportive friend. No. Fuck supportive. I'm going to be sick. "Please. I need your help. Both of you."

Jack elbows Danika in the side. "Run this kind of information by me *first* next time."

"No way. I was the voice of reason last time." She rubs her hands together. "Tonight, I'm up for a little nefariousness."

I'm already heading for the locker room. "Let's move."

Ever

I'm on a date. A *date* date. Like, a buzzer isn't going to make this guy switch tables in five minutes. Yesterday, while in the Laundromat folding my unmentionables, I'd felt someone's eyes on me and turned around to see Landon sending me side-eye peeks. Landon is in his early thirties. An investment banker with almost freakishly light-colored eyelashes. He'd been folding ten versions of the same shirt and for that very reason, Landon is *not* a man I would typically approach. He's a full-blown commitment guy, right down to being on a first-name basis with the Laundromat owner. I mean, we sat down ten minutes ago, and he's already showed me pictures of his niece on his phone. This is a man with family on the brain.

Maybe I should be easing into the whole idea of lifelong relationships, but I've never been the kind to dip my toe into the water. My friend wants to start a catering company? I become a cook. My mother spooks me about a lifetime of solitude? I ask a Wall Street–type out for tapas and beer.

Would she be proud of me, my mother, if she could see me right now? I'm smiling and saying all the right things. I think. One of us poses a question, the other answers. Then we pause to look down at our menus. That seems about normal. But it's impossible not to picture Charlie across from me. How easy *that* conversation would be. I wouldn't be racking my brain for topics, they would just appear.

Charlie and I hit the ground running at the outset. I might have given him my standard three-question mistress test, but no one had ever responded like him. Or made the test seem almost . . . obsolete. Like we were clicking on some unseen level that went beyond the test. Not just a physical click, either. But *that* part had definitely come after we left the bar, stronger than anything in my memory . . .

Charlie kicks my apartment door shut behind him, shaking the rain from his hair like a playful dog, sending droplets everywhere and making me laugh. But my amusement is cut off by his low growl, his slow approach, the chest he reveals by stripping off his shirt. Rain smacks off the windows of my pitch-black apartment, thunder booming, lightning slashing and illuminating for a second here. A second there.

There's something I'm supposed to do here. What is it? What—

"Ground rules," I eke out, my bottom hitting the windowsill in the living room. "W-we should probably talk about those."

A line appears between his eyes as he unbuckles his belt. "Agreed."

I've done this before, and the words are supposed to roll off my tongue. Charlie seems to have tied said tongue together, though, and his zipper coming down, his jeans sluffing onto my floor only makes it worse. His thighs. They're cut and thick and hairy. Are his thighs commanding the thunder? Calm down, girl. You got this. "No pasts, no futures." I hold my breath while he unsnaps my overalls and lifts my shirt, uncovering my strapless bra. "No gifts or birthday cards. Totally casual, no expectations."

His breathing has turned erratic, his palms lifting my breasts, massaging them. "Deal." My bra is unsnapped, dropped to the ground. "No dates or meeting the friends and family. Just us. Whenever we need it."

"Yes," I breathe, the back of my head bumping off the windowpane. "No need for all the pretend concern or asking about each other's day. Just . . . easy. Just like this, right?"

A pause. "Right." I didn't hear a note of doubt in his tone, did I? No. No, I'm projecting, because for the first time, I'm feeling a smidgen of it myself . . . it'll go away. It's just jitters over liking how he talks, how he moves, how he smiles and—I've never felt this weight deep down in my stomach before. This is a bad idea.

I haven't even mentioned my one-month rule. Am I going to?

Charlie slides the overalls down my hips, leaning in

to lock our mouths together, erasing my reservations a little more with each expert stroke. He hooks a finger in my panties, tugging the waistband down to reveal the most intimate part of me, where I've left it waxed and lotioned. For me, not because I'd planned to bring someone home. But I'm glad I made an effort. It's worth it a million times when he curses, low and rough, a vibration thrumming through his body and pushing out into the air separating us. "Jesus. I'm going to need this a lot, Ever." He shoves down his briefs and fists his heavy cock. "Be sure about this. Be sure you don't need . . . more than sex. Because I think you're fucking great, but I can't give you—"

"Shhh." I can feel his frown against my forehead, his conflict as he applies the condom, and I don't want his guilt. There's no need for it. He might be one of the good ones, but this noncommitment is exactly what he wants. What every man—and this woman—wants deep down, right? So I peel my panties the remaining distance down my legs, using a kiss to draw him forward while I wrap my legs around his hips. "I want you inside me," I whisper, my voice shaking. I'm shaking. "Charlie—"

With a surrendering groan, he slides his smooth tip through my wetness a few times and shoves deep, a choked sound rending the air. Was it me or him? I don't know. My sight winks out, my mouth dropping open. Oh God. Too good, too good, too . . . right.

Charlie groans my name and yanks me off the win-

dowsill, thrusting his hips up while I use his shoulders for leverage and slap, slap, slap my hips up and down. "Ever, this is bad. This is bad. Bad, bad." Lightning shoots through the room, and I see how tightly his eyes are closed, his expression of half-disbelief, half-pleasure. I ride harder, he pumps into me with more and more feverish intensity. "This isn't happening," he rasps. "You can't be happening."

We break at the same time and Charlie's knees hit the floor, but he manages to hold on to me as he moans like a wild animal. My arms are tempted to creep around his neck, my satisfied body wanting to get as close to its savior as possible, but I can't set that precedent. Ground rules. We have them. I helped set them.

Minutes later, we dress in silence. He stands at the door, staring at me with a crease between his eyebrows. But I send him a flirty wave, a signal for him to walk out the door. I feel more myself once he's out of sight. Mostly.

"Ever?" My date leans forward, a concerned look on his face. "Everything okay?"

"Yes!" Oh God, the waiter is at our table staring at me expectantly. What kind of restaurant are we in, again? Tapas. Number system. "I'll have . . . one, three and nine." I look down at my empty pint of beer. "And another one of these, thanks."

My date looks a little disapproving over me having a second drink before the food even arrives, but somehow I dig deep and find the determination to change his mind about me. To make this date go well. I owe it to myself. Owe it to my mother. What I had with Charlie was amazing while it lasted, but sending a man home with nothing more than a pinkie wave can't be my normal anymore. Not if I want to move forward and start living for the future my mother wants for me. The one she wishes *she'd* achieved and I now want. For me, the loneliness didn't even take decades to set in. Deep down, I'd already started feeling it that first time Charlie left my apartment.

"Um . . ." I shift in my seat, aware that the memory of Charlie has made my underwear damp and my chest feel hollow. *Focus on now, Ever.* "Where did you say your niece lives?"

And then the fire alarm goes off.

Water sputters from the ceiling sprinklers a split second later, and the entire restaurant erupts in shouts and squeals. Patrons are doused as they futilely attempt to cover their heads, jogging toward the exit. Waiters drop trays and follow. I'm pretty sure my jaw is in my lap, but I have an insane urge to laugh. This is a sign. It has to be.

I'm unsure whether it's a good or bad one until Landon shoots to his feet, his expression pinched. "What the *fuck*," he growls, snatching my napkin off the table to wipe his face, blot his shirt. "They have to be kidding me. Is there a manager around?" he shouts. "I'm not paying for these drinks."

Bad sign. For sure.

Guess I'll be finding a new Laundromat.

Charlie

Sometimes things seem like great idea, until you watch them unfold from a coffee-shop window across the street. Like, a restaurant being evacuated, hundreds of people spilling out onto the street. The kind of *illegal* things I'll be arresting people for someday. Like instigating a plan to have one friend distract a restaurant kitchen staff, while the other friend pulls the fire alarm. Those kinds of things.

I stop caring about ethics, though, when I see Ever follow some fuck wad in a tie out onto the sidewalk. The coffee I'm sipping turns to battery acid in my stomach, and I can't feel the chair underneath my ass. She doesn't look nervous or anything, which was my main concern. She's easily one of the driest customers outside the restaurant, thank God. If my actions got her sick, I'd have to enter the monastery and take a vow of silence as punishment. But all in all? She seems pretty amused by the whole circus.

My lips curve in pure appreciation of Ever and her sense of humor, but my smile plummets when

I see her date. Really? *That* guy? He's one snifter of brandy away from an old-fashioned gentleman's club. His back is so straight, he must have swallowed a flag pole. I could go all day. I hate his guts. He's my sworn enemy on sight.

Not that I'm complaining or anything, but Patrick Bateman seems more miffed over his shirt being ruined than he is over Ever being exposed to possible structure fire. If I was on a date with Ever and the fire alarm went off, I would carry her out of the place and administer CPR, whether she wanted it or not. Instead, Bateman is waving around a white cloth napkin and ranting at the spooked wait staff, while Ever slowly eases away, like she's thinking of ditching him. That's my girl.

Damn, she looks incredible tonight. Her hair is down and loose, she's wearing a mint-green sundress with some kind of pattern on it. Sandals with heels. Most of the time I've spent with her, she's been barefoot. Which would normally turn me on, but is only serving to jam a cleaver into my jugular right now.

Ever waits until her date's back is turned, then ducks behind a potted plant. Honest to God, I want to do a cartwheel right there in the coffee shop and buy everyone a round of espresso. While I won't go as far as to say my rash date crashing was justified—I'm not completely delusional . . . yet—I appear to have saved Ever from wasting her night on someone who didn't deserve her company.

Now if I can make it better, I've done my job.

I dip to the edge of the window and dial Ever's cell. When she sees who's calling, a hand comes up to cradle her throat, her mouth popping open.

Oh no. Oh, cutie. She misses me, too.

I almost sink down to the floor when she answers, because it's too much. Seeing her miss me and hearing her voice at the same time. She's never let me see anything like that on purpose, but I caught it. I caught her.

"Charlie?"

It takes me a moment to answer. "Hey, cutie. What are you up to tonight?" I hate myself in that moment for lying to her, but it's too late to turn back. "You working?"

"No . . ." She frowns, glancing up and down the street. "No, I'm just, um . . ."

She doesn't want me to know she was on a date. I'm not sure if that's good or bad. "Want to meet up? I was just heading out for a walk."

Her sigh slides into my ear. "Meet where?"

"The law-enforcement memorial on East Tenth?" I don't know why I suggest this specific spot. Maybe I'm still in panic mode over finding out she was on a date and the memorial tends to ground me. Maybe I just need to show her an important part of me. Something that will help her understand why I can't commit all the way. Why I can't be the guy taking her out to eat tapas and giving her CPR when an alarm goes off. "I, uh . . . figure it's a good midway point between us. Meet me there in half an hour?"

Please. *Please*, say yes. After seeing her, having her so near, I'm not sure I can survive another night without getting closer. "See you in a while."

When she hangs up, I expect a sense of victory, but I only feel anxious. Like I'm standing on shaky ground.

Ever

I'm sitting at the memorial when Charlie rounds the corner in the distance. I speed walked here in an attempt to dry off. At least I didn't get as soaked as my date, who frankly needed a good dousing after yelling at that group of innocent waiters, as if they had anything to do with the alarm going off and ruining his Gucci loafers. Honestly. Men like him are reserved for the date horror section of *Cosmo*.

Seeing Charlie in the flesh takes me back to the daydream I had in the restaurant, right before the alarm sounded. How hot it made me.

Did my memories set off the fire alarm?

A laugh bubbles up at the silly thought. Actually, *all* my bad vibes fade the closer Charlie comes, my muscles relaxing, head clearing. Even though he looks a little irritable himself.

"I thought I would beat you here." He looks around the small park in the center of which sits the marble statues and benches. "I didn't mean for you to sit here alone in the dark. It's dangerous."

I unzip my purse and present my pepper spray. "I had company."

He growls at me, sitting down beside me on the bench, our thighs flush. "Hey, cutie."

"Hey, yourself."

"You look gorgeous." Our shoulders brush. "New dress?"

Charlie would make a great boyfriend. Acknowledging that . . . sucks. For the first time, I let myself think of Charlie in ten years. Older, wiser. Wanting a place to call home. And I think he'll change his mind over time about relationships. I can't shake the impression that he's built for one, somewhere deep down. After all, he cried when the old couple in *Titanic* were about to bite it. He's just not ready for a commitment now. And not with me.

A spiky, slimy realization creeps under my armor. What if I'm just not the kind of girl you bring home? What if Charlie . . . knows it? Am I destined to be a mistress, no matter what?

"I borrowed it from Nina." I try to shake away the ugly thought, but it hits its mark. I could be the girl Charlie meets . . . on his way to meeting *the one*. He likes me, we're compatible in bed, but what if something about me is holding him back from taking the step I know he's meant for? Maybe he doesn't even realize he's hedging because of *me*, not himself. "Um . . ." I rise from the bench, feeling seasick and blindsided. "I-I saw the name Burns on here. Are you related?"

"Yeah." He's scrutinizing my face as he follows me over to the statue, a little frown playing on his features. "My great-grandfather was killed in the line of duty the year this was erected. To honor the fallen." He stoops and rubs a hand over a long list of names. "They add to it every time there's a police casualty."

Looking down at the top of Charlie's head, his hand poised on the marble, voice hushed with reverence, he looks like part of the memorial. Future touching past. I'm finally seeing what's important to him, instead of imagining it. He's *showing* me. Hot pressure pushes behind my eyes and I blink it back. "You're going to have a dangerous job."

Charlie stands. "The danger comes with the territory, yeah." He appears to be searching for words in the darkness. "But the job . . . it's neverending. You are the badge and if you do your job right, it can't be taken from you. It's permanent."

A hand lifts and runs through his hair. "Shit, I don't even know if that makes sense."

"It does." Although, I think if I knew more about Charlie, a clearer picture would be presenting itself right now. My throat aches with the possibility that I'll never get that clarity. The possibility that I *want* it, can't have it, is almost too much. "The job is you. You are the job. There's no one to let down but yourself."

His gaze cuts to mine, but it's clouded. "Yes. Once I get to the level where I'm expected to be, yes. It's just me after that."

I nod.

The breeze ruffles the trees around us, making his voice carry. "For every hundred cops you see on the street, there is one who works harder than all of them combined. They don't punch a clock, because they don't have one. The clock doesn't exist for them—only the safety of the city." His expression is a touch chagrined, but mostly it's pride on his face. "I know I sound like Dudley Do-Right over here, but my father pinned a badge on me the day I was born. I've got four generations of pressure on my shoulders. To be that one unseen officer who calls the shots for the hundred."

"It's not just the pressure, though." I clear the cobwebs from my throat. "You want it for yourself, too."

"Yeah." Appreciation shines in his eyes as he

looks at me, but it seems to crumble when he dips his head. "Yeah, most of the time." He's silent a moment. "It's a responsibility. I've seen how big an impact men like my father have. How a single call or hunch can prevent a disaster. Disasters for people like *you*, Ever. If I didn't know that kind of responsibility existed out there, waiting for me, maybe I wouldn't feel so obligated to give it everything. But I know. It's in my veins to be the one who . . ."

"Answers the call." It sounds like a catchy slogan, but it's the only accurate answer. Charlie is damn near stealing my breath away, so big and unyielding, backlit by the sacrifices of his ancestors. It's such a huge moment, such a gripping image, I can't swallow or move for fear of messing it up. "I'll feel safe, knowing you're there. Not punching the clock. I'll think of you and feel safe."

His voice is hoarse when he responds. "You're talking like you won't see me anymore."

Right here, in this moment, it feels like I won't. Or at least I'll never experience this much raw honesty from him again. Why is he giving it to me in the first place?

"I understand now that what we had wasn't enough for you." His words are stilted. "What I was giving you . . . an hour here and there . . . wasn't worthy. Of you." He shakes his head. "But it's only going to get more demanding. Sometimes

I only saw my father once a week growing up. I watched him sink into the job and never come back out. It's wrong to commit to anything . . . or anyone else. And give them half-measure. That's when they leave."

Leave? I want to question him, but I don't know if there's a point. He's telling me we can't be more than friends, as if I didn't already know. If I question him or ask for an explanation, I'll come across pathetic. "I don't need an explanation, Charlie."

He comes toward me, his blue eyes pleading. "There's no place for anything real, no matter how bad I want it, Ever."

My words are cut off by his mouth. We don't kiss. Our lips simply lock together and stay that way, the earth tipping sideways under my feet, pulse dancing. "You should demand explanations from me. From . . . everyone who gets to spend time in your company. You earn them just by being you." His lips slide between mine, a touch to the left, and the world tilts again. "I'm telling you that as someone lucky enough to be your friend. You deserve explanations whenever you want them."

I barely manage to keep my knees from buckling. "This doesn't feel very friendly."

"I'm keeping my tongue in my mouth." He gives a pained laugh, our foreheads bumping together. "That has to count for something."

"It does."

I don't know why, but he looks conflicted when he pulls back. "Let me walk you to get a cab, huh?" He holds out a hand and I take it, letting him walk me out of the park, up toward the avenue. It's the first time we've held hands . . . and I know it should be the last.

The deeper I fall into friendship with Charlie, the deeper I sink into the point of no return.

CHAPTER 13
Ever

E xercise is not my friend. It's probably my least favorite pastime, right below going to the DMV, but just above pedicures. I have extremely ticklish feet. Since I taste test every calorie-packed morsel I create for Hot Damn, however, I've been thrust into a world of spin classes and treadmills, at least three days a week. My biggest qualm with working out—apart from the way it makes you feel like dying—is the monotony. I've found a way to combat my routine from going stale by purchasing a pass from some online deal site. I paid a one-time fee, and I can do classes of my choosing all over the city. Happy wallet, happy Ever. Except for the actual exercise part.

I'm in particular need of exertion today, however, so I'm not cursing the instructor to hell. He's teach-

ing us the choreography to a Bruno Mars video—
yes, it's a real class—and I'm actually keeping up,
instead of pretending to need water breaks.

This need to burn energy is all Charlie's fault.

I haven't seen him in a couple days, although he
has been texting me steadily, when I least expect it.
Friendly texts. But there wasn't anything friendly
about the way he'd looked at me as I drove off in
the cab the other night. He'd been almost . . . torn.
That whole meeting at the memorial felt like a
dream now. We'd dropped pretense for a couple
seconds, Charlie giving me a deeper explanation
for not wanting a relationship, even though I'd
never asked. Never *would* have asked. But saying the words out loud had been proof we'd both
thought of the impossible possibility of being together, right?

As I side-lunge into a booty shake, I replay the
text-alogue we had this morning.

What are you eating for breakfast?

This is how you open a conversation?

You've ruined me for other people's food. I'm living
vicariously.

I definitely hadn't felt a deluge of pleasure over
that. Definitely not. I also hadn't lied about what

I was eating. Okay, I had. I'd been going to town on a bowl of Lucky Charms, but in the interest of living vicariously, I'd said, Belgian waffles with berries and cream.

Cruel girl. You going to make this torture up to me?

Nope.

Come on. I'm off today. Meet me for lunch.

Groaning into my Lucky Charms, I could just see him, all blue eyed and cajoling. If he'd been there in person, turning him down would have been impossible, so thank God for modern technology.

Sorry, Charlie. Can't today. I have plans.

Lies. When did I become a liar? I really didn't want to become one, so after I'd sent the text passing on lunch with Charlie, I'd signed on to DateMate with a head full of determination. Of course, not a single one of my matches gave off sparks, probably because I was still spooked over the Aviator Squad and Laundromat Landon. I toyed with the idea of messaging Reve S. Guy—weird-ass name, but a great sense of humor—and seeing if we could bump up our date, but I worried that might appear desperate. So I sent him a knock-knock joke instead. Just to prove to myself I'm trying to connect.

And I can admit to myself that I'm getting anxious. Anxious for a place to put these feelings Charlie stirred up inside me. Which makes lunches with him a bad idea. I don't like the unsettled feeling I get every time we part ways. Like I'm dying to see him again, even though I know I would feel . . . abandoned afterward.

There, I said it. Charlie makes me feel abandoned. And that shit really isn't going to fly with me. When we'd both wanted nothing to do with relationships, that sense of loss when he blew out of my apartment had been scary. Now, it was like a ghost that follows me around room to room, haunting me. I need to exorcise it.

Plans? Charlie had texted back.

As in, *what are they?*

I haven't answered. Which is the right decision. Mostly because we don't have another catering job until Wednesday night, and I don't *really* have any plans. If I relayed that to Charlie, he would persuade me into lunch. Just a friendly little lunch with a man whose smiling face comes to me in dreams, whose voice whispers in my ear even when he's not around. The guy who'd stood stock still on the sidewalk and watched my cab disappear out of sight in the darkness.

Right. Maybe there was another workout class

across town I could take after this. Anything to keep me away from my cell phone and answering that single-worded text that wouldn't stop popping wheelies in my mind.

By the time class ends, I know the dance moves to "Uptown Funk" and my head is somewhat clear of Charlie-related thoughts. I'm going to round out the afternoon by showering, throwing on fresh clothes and checking out the farmer's market in Union Square. Maybe it will inspire a new recipe or two, and I can try them out for Nina tonight. We've been spending more time together now that she is boyfriend-free, and I'm really enjoying the company. Silence lately only reminds me of my mother. How often had she been without a shoulder to lean on, thinking it was exactly what she wanted, but not really believing it?

After showering, drying my hair and throwing on a red sundress, I call my mother and leave her a voicemail. I don't ask her to call me back, because she rarely returns phone calls, instead letting her know I'll be stopping by for a visit this week. After business hours, of course. As I walk out of my building, empty tote bag in hand, I rethink the message I left, hoping I sounded upbeat enough. If I'd betrayed one hint of sympathy over her confession last time we were together, she probably wouldn't be as open this time around. And I'm really hoping she is.

I turn in the direction of Union Square—

Charlie is walking toward me, coming from the direction of the train.

"Hey, cutie."

The most annoying part of his showing up unannounced? I'm not annoyed *at all*. I'm relieved. And my second reaction is all-out joy. Just a giant, glowing burst of it. *Don't show it. Don't let him know.* "Charlie. Hey."

"I know you have plans." He holds up both hands, palms out, except there is a bag dangling from his right thumb. "I'm not intruding. I was just hoping to catch you, before you went out."

His crispy aftershave hits me and my tummy takes a dive. And the rest of him keeps it plummeting. Worn-in jeans, boots, a faded navy T-shirt that makes his eyes a blinding blue. Honest to God, he looks better every time I see him. I'm starting to think I'm the victim of a conspiracy. "Well, you caught me."

"Yeah." He gives me a once over, his gaze lingering at my low neckline. "I have late classes tonight, so this was my only chance." He drops his hands, but jiggles the bag he's holding. "You know when you have a gift for someone, it burns a hole in your pocket until you hand it over?"

"That's for me?" Charlie nods and the sidewalk turns into ocean waves under my feet. "Oh." I love presents. *Everyone* loves presents. I've just never accepted them from men, because it was against the rules. No gifts was one of mine and Charlie's ground rules, too, but technically that was *before* we stopped hooking up and became friends. So it's okay to accept, right? Man, this situation is confusing.

"Don't think about it too hard. Please?" He's watching me with a hopeful expression. One that makes my palms sweat, my mouth dry right up. Cautiously, he hands me the bag and we step into the shadow of my building, allowing cranky Villagers to pass on the sidewalk. There is so much tissue paper in the bag, and none of it was placed there skillfully. It's a manmade mess. "Go ahead and laugh."

"Somewhere in Connecticut, Martha Stewart is rocking in a corner."

"Smart ass," Charlie murmurs, propping an elbow on the building. "We wrapped presents in newspaper growing up, and it worked just fine."

"It would have worked fine for me, too—" I stop talking when I finally reach the actual gift and remove it from the bag, a couple pieces of tissue paper flying away on the wind. It takes me a moment to realize what I'm holding, but when I do, my heart jerks and stutters, like a stalling car engine. I'm holding a metal tree, welded to a stand, with big branches poking out in different directions. At the end of each branch, there is a little spiral. "It's for holding my notecards when I cook."

"Yeah." He looks relieved that I figured it out, but he's trying to hide it by gesturing and not meeting my eyes. "I noticed you had them all over the counter that night in the kitchen . . . they kept falling down."

"Charlie." I press the notecard tree to my chest. I'm horrified to feel little pinpricks at the backs of my eyelids, but there's no help for it. I can't recall a time someone has bought me a gift this thoughtful. "I'm going to use this all the time. It's perfect."

"Yeah?"

"*Yes*. Thank you."

He's suddenly serious. "I found it because you needed it, and I thought you should have it. Your job is hard, and I hope this makes it easier." We're standing closer now. Who moved? "But I also wanted you to know it hasn't stopped bothering me. How you thought of yourself as some kind of mistress. I should have been a better friend. I can be."

There it was. The F-word. And yet it wasn't nearly enough to ruin the gift. Or the moment. "Do you want to come to the farmer's market with me?"

His shoulders lose tension, but his eyes stay sharp. "I thought you had plans."

"I'm making dinner for Nina later. That's the

plan." I shouldn't be telling him this. I know. But the way he's looking at me is so earnest. And I'm holding his thoughtful gift in my hands, and I don't want him to leave just yet. "I'll just run this upstairs and be back down. I-If you *want* to go—"

"I'm going."

CHAPTER 14
Charlie

The Union Square farmer's market has changed. I have fuzzy memories of my mother bringing me here when I was a child, before she split, but they don't match up with the huge production I'm walking into with Ever. There are so many stands set up, I can't see the end of them. As with every major park in the city, there are sightseers and slow movers, so the market is twice as packed as it needs to be. Normally, an overcrowded sea of people makes me extra vigilant, because my father and Greer have trained me to be suspicious and careful.

Every ounce of my vigilance, however, is being occupied. It's a good thing I came with Ever to the market, because unlike the times my mother brought me here? There are no little old ladies selling carrots from their gardens. No, it's like bridges and tunnels of Manhattan vomited a bunch of oversized, bearded farmers into Union fucking Square and every one of them knows Ever by name. Not to mention, they all have food in common with her, which is brilliant. Just brilliant.

Oh, they don't like seeing me there with her, either.

Good.

Because I'm in a perfect mood to dissuade every single one of them from sniffing around Ever. She sent Reve a knock-knock joke this morning, through the dating site.

What did the alien say to the garden? Take me to your weeder.

Sure, the joke was cute as hell like everything else she does, but I could read between the lines. Could see our text conversation made her even more determined to move on. I'd already had her present sitting on my desk, but the gut-sick intuition that she was fighting to put me behind her got me moving even faster.

Her message to *Reve* also served as a reminder to *Charlie.* I have less than a week to convince Ever that her dating mission is ill-fated. Less than a week to prove that this better, friendlier version of what we had before can make her happy. Sure, it's not the kind of commitment she *thinks* she wants.

But I know it's better than opening herself up to strangers who could cause her pain.

We stop at a booth beneath a big sign proclaiming the best produce in Vermont. "What do you have today, Oscar?"

Oscar. Fuck this guy.

"Hey there, Ever." His hairy-knuckled hand digs through a bunch of greenery. "We've got some Swiss chard. Some baby bok choy."

"Ooh. I'll take some bok choy, if you please." She hands over her tote bag and tugs some bills from some magical, secret pocket on her dress. "How's your day going so far?"

"Great. Thanks for asking." Oscar the Friendly Knuckle Dragger is quickly becoming Oscar the Grouch. Probably because while Ever has been counting out her bills, I've been giving him a *don't even think about it* look over her shoulder. "You brought a friend today."

"Yes." She turns those sparkling eyes on me. "This is Charlie. If you have any problems with vegetable thieves, he's your man."

"Nice to meet you," I say, guiding Ever away with a hand on her hip. Low enough to warn off Oscar. High enough not to raise Ever's suspicion. Not that I don't throw Knuckle Dragger the side eye for good measure. "What else is on your list?" I ask Ever, when we're out of ear shot.

"I don't have one." She lifts her shoulders and lets them drop. "I'm winging it."

"Such a wild woman." I scan the booths. "My mom used to buy the pulpy apple juice. We hated it, but she kept bringing it home." A dull ache forms behind my jugular. One I've lived with so long, I'm not even sure what it means anymore. "It was just one of the things we complained about." After a minute, I realize Ever is looking at me funny. "What?"

"Nothing." She looks down quickly, adjusting the straps of her bag. "You've just never mentioned your mother before. I wasn't sure she was in the picture."

"No, she's been gone since I was six." Feeling jumpy, I take Ever's hand and head for a fresh-baked-pie booth. "I don't know where she went."

We stop at the back of the pie line, and Ever speaks in a low voice. "Your father doesn't know?"

"She asked him not to look." I don't know why I'm having such a hard time explaining the damn situation. It's not like I haven't had almost two decades to acclimate to having no mother around. There isn't some big drama surrounding what happened. People grow up in single-family homes all the time, right? "Look, she didn't have anything to stick around for. If you want the truth, we were awful to her. She cooked and cleaned and took my brother and me everywhere . . . and we just made more messes and fought all the time."

Ever's forehead creases. "Of course you did, Charlie. You were six."

"Yeah, well, I still *knew* better." The sun seems hotter and more intense than it had when we arrived. "My father told me that . . . I should have *known* better."

The tote bag drops off Ever's shoulder, but she just leaves it dangling near her ankle. "Hold up." She chews her bottom lip and studies me. "Was he implying that if you'd acted better, your mother *wouldn't* have left?"

"Yes." Why is she acting as though this is some huge revelation? I can remember my mother slamming cabinets and weeping over the sink while Greer and I acted like dickheads. I remember giving her some shoddy Mother's Day card I'd made in school and nothing else, even after everything she did for me. Of course she'd blown the Burns Popsicle Stand as quickly as humanly possible. Why wouldn't she? But the way Ever is staring at me, as though she's holding her breath? It is one of those moments where you realize you've been pronouncing a word wrong your entire life, except this is trying to hit me much harder. "She had to get away from me, from us, she said. I heard her talking to my father . . . and he let her go. He understood."

"No. Oh no, Charlie." Ever pulls me out of line, leading me to a pathway beneath a fall of trees. I can't account for the numbness as she wraps her arms around me, but her fingers messing with the ends of my hair makes me feel better. Makes me feel anchored in the present again. She presses her ear to my chest for a while, before glancing up at me. "I have no experience with kids, but I know from the Internet that parenting is hard. For everyone. And you don't just get to walk out and never look back. *You* wouldn't do that. I wouldn't, either. That was wrong of her, Charlie. Wrong, wrong, wrong. And nothing about it was your fault." Her breath expels in a rush. "I'd like to smash something so hard right now."

Is she right? She seems so sure. My heartbeat sounds like it's being amplified through a loud speaker. I need something to drown it out. The way Ever makes me feel is the only thing that can do that. "Will you kiss me instead of smashing something?"

Ever doesn't just kiss me . . . she cares for me. I stand up the entire time it happens, but mentally I watch it happen from flat on my ass. Her lips tug on my bottom one as she makes a sad noise. Maybe it's crazy, but that little noise of hers kicks something free inside of me and then, I'm sad, too. I can't remember being sad before. Not like this. I can't control it and don't know the source. It drags me down and stabs me between the shoulder blades, but Ever doesn't leave me there to flounder. She props me up, stroking my face and kissing me. Right there in the park, the way couples do.

"Not your fault," she murmurs against my mouth. "Not one bit."

Here's the problem, though. I don't know if I believe her. As bad as I want to swim into the cool lake of comfort Ever is beginning to repre-sent, I've lived with this certainty too long that I wasn't enough. Or worse, I was *too* much. For so long, these memories of loss and guilt and shame were suppressed. Now they're riding in with guns blazing and I'm totally unarmed. My father was there when it all went down. Ever wasn't. She can't know it wasn't my fault. Not when I remem-ber so differently.

Oh *God*, I will avoid having something and los-ing it—again—at all costs. So why am I clinging to Ever like a drunk with his last forty-ounce? She'd been the initiator, but the engine of despera-tion inside me is in overdrive, and I'm practically mauling her mouth in public, yanking her onto tiptoes so I can get her from every angle, even un-derneath.

"Charlie." Her whisper is shaky and I want to

feel that tremor, so I kiss her with suction, drag-ging, *dragging*, her into my lungs, until she twists free. "*Charlie.*"

Breathe. Breathe. "I'm sorry."

I don't even know what I'm apologizing for. Or to whom. I'm caught up in a confusing slide show of past and present, and Ever's eyes are the only concrete things I can grasp. I woke up this morn-ing with renewed determination to get Ever back the way I had her before. The world made sense. Now I'm veering into a place I don't recognize.

My goal was to be Ever's friend with benefits. To lure her back to the perfection we had together, while allowing myself to get safely closer to her. To understand her better. Am I fooling myself into thinking that's realistic? I'm pretty sure friends aren't supposed to make you feel as though you're drowning without them around. What happens if we get even closer, then she cuts me off? The burn of being cut off from someone I loved is so unnaturally fresh right now, and it hasn't been in so long. I should walk away now. Leave Ever to find someone who doesn't resent her for having the ability to leave.

I resent her for having the ability to leave?

Has that insecurity been shoved down so deep, I couldn't even see it?

I feel unclean, just knowing it exists. That some-one could hold anything against this amazing, optimistic girl. Especially something out of her power. I should go. I shouldn't play any more games with her. But when she holds out her hand and says, "Come on. We'll buy a pie and go home. I have some vanilla ice cream in the fridge." I thread our fingers together and promise myself a little more time.

CHAPTER 15
Ever

Charlie looks as if he's just disembarked that creepy ride at Willy Wonka's factory. His eyes are glazed as we walk into my apartment, his step lacking its usual confidence. God knows I'm the furthest thing from maternal, but I have this impulse to bundle him into bed, wrap him in my comforter and guard him from the world with a metal bat. I do none of those things, though, because I'm not sure what he's thinking. I'm not even sure he wants to be here.

The sun is beginning to grow subdued. Not quite afternoon, not quite evening, and it gives the apartment a golden vibe. When Nina and I first moved in, we hung crystals in the window and they're showing off their effects now, painting the wall in dancing prisms. I watch Charlie out of the corner of my eye as I unpack my goodies, stowing them away in the fridge for later, save the strawberry rhubarb pie, which I leave on the counter.

I'm still coming down off our kiss in the park. I have this distinct impression Charlie has no idea that we kissed for nearly an hour. His gaze was almost startled when I finally broke away, as if we'd only just begun. I spent the quiet walk home stuck in this weird limbo between arousal and outrage. Who would let a child think his mother left because of him? Even if by some crazy long shot it were true, which it couldn't be, wouldn't a parent go to extra lengths to assure him otherwise?

Across the room, Charlie falls into a sitting position on the couch, hands clasped between his knees. Did I push too far when we talked about his mother? His shoulders are rigid. He wants to leave, I think. I don't know. But something tells me if I let him walk out the door like this, I won't see him again for a long time.

I'm pretty freaking far from okay with that. And no, I don't want to examine why. Not when I'm more worried about his current state of mind than anything else.

"Do you want that piece of pie?"

"What?" His head comes up slowly. "Oh, sure."

I take two plates out of the cabinet and remove a knife from the drawer. Just as I'm preparing to slice the first piece of pie, I hear a familiar ding across the room. The knife in my hand drops. The sound that is bleeping from my still-open laptop is the signal that I've received a message on the dating website. My pulse purrs a little louder, but I pick up the knife again, intending to continue cutting, as though nothing is amiss. And nothing is amiss, *right*? I mean, just because I spent an hour making out with Charlie in Union Square Park doesn't mean he'll be weird about matches coming in while we eat pie together.

Do I *want* him to be weird about it?

Charlie's gaze is already zeroed in on the laptop . . . and he stands. The second he moves in the direction of the device, I drop the knife and jog out of the kitchen, intending to beat him there. And I lose.

He slides into the rolling chair at my Ikea desk and rubs his index finger across the control pad, bringing the screen to life. Behold, in all its glory, the match site of mundane questions and inopportune dinging.

"Charlie, that's private."

Yeah, he's ignoring me. Gliding a finger along the pad and tapping over the red bubble that decrees I have fourteen new notifications. "In high demand, aren't you?"

The hair on the back of my neck prickles at his tone. It's half-detached, half- . . . on the verge. Of what, I'm not sure. "You don't really want to look at this, do you?" I strive for casual, attempting to pick up the laptop. But he intercepts my wrist and pulls me down on his lap, wrapping a fore-arm around my waist. "It's none of your business, Charlie."

"Oh come on," he says with a flat laugh. "Let me see a few of the contenders."

I try to stand, but he tightens his hold. "No. Don't look."

"I want to help, Ever." His voice is hard. Not Charlie-like at all. "I'm a guy, which gives me a first-hand perspective on the bullshit they're spewing. I can weed out some of the bad ones for you." He gives a rude snort. "Although, that might narrow the field down to zero."

Oh, screw this. He isn't going to sit here, in my apartment, and make this undertaking of mine sound stupid. I won't let him. "Leave it alone. I don't need any help."

"You're getting it anyway." He clicks on the red bubble and I close my eyes, rage simmering like hot oil beneath my skin. I hate this. *Hate* it. He's still raw from talking about his mother in the park—I see that—and if we're really attempt-ing friendship, I should probably be more under-standing. But I'm raw, too, goddammit. My lips are still swollen from the over-the-top passionate way he'd kissed me before deflating into Phantom

Charlie . . . and we are now browsing my dating matches together?

When I feel his body stiffen beneath me, my eyes fly open and I only get a glimpse of the cursor hovering over a vaguely familiar face before my hand flies up and slams the laptop shut. I'm done with this.

I shove to my feet and round on him. "Time to go, Burns." I wedge the laptop beneath my arm, my spine vibrating with a surge of adrenaline. "I'm sorry you're having a bad day, but it's not exactly coming up roses for me, either. Get. *Out.*"

His smirk doesn't completely disguise his surprise. "What about the pie?"

Oh, the nerve. "Take it to go, homie."

The bravado on his face thins as he stands, eyebrows dipping. "I really did want to help, Ever."

"No, you didn't. You wanted to laugh at me." My voice is just this side of hysterical, so I force my shoulders to relax. "Believe me, you've made it clear you find this hilarious. Me looking for the one."

"The one," he says tonelessly. "Is that what you're calling him?"

"I don't know. Maybe. Are you going to make fun of that, too?" I set the laptop back down harder than I should have, and give him a pointed look. "I don't need anyone's help weeding out bullshit. I can do that myself."

He takes a step closer. "You have, haven't you?"

"Haven't I what?"

"Weeded out the bullshit." The blue of his eyes is sharp enough to slice the atmosphere in two. "You've set up a date. *Haven't you?*"

"Yeah. I *have*." My voice is like a whip cracking in the bright room. "This Friday. He's training to be a firefighter. Any other questions?"

"Yeah, *about a million* that you definitely didn't ask him." He's shouting at me. Charlie? Is *shouting* at me? There is a restraint to his posture, almost like he can't help but reassure me I'm safe, but that's where his caution ends. His nostrils flare, and the muscles beneath his T-shirt are more present than before. Flexing, tightening. He's downright furious at me. "Does he have a record? Why did he break up with his last girlfriend? Is he a safe driver?" Charlie advances and I back up, circling the couch backward to avoid him. "Does he know you move like a nervous fairy when you cook? Or that your real smiles are the ones that look kind of grudging?" He rakes a hand through his hair, leaving it looking a little wild. "I'm just trying to be a good *friend*, Ever, and make sure you go out with someone who deserves you."

"I think y-you should leave," I whisper, because I'm shaken. So shaken. When did he notice those things about me? Why do they make him angry? "Charlie—"

"You're right. I should go." But he's still coming, still moving toward me. I run into a kitchen stool and send it skidding, my back coming up against the kitchen counter. When he reaches me, my pulse is rioting and it goes crazier when he closes that final gap and drops his forehead into the crook of my neck. "I'm sorry." His breath is coming out in great, shuddering rushes. "It was a lot today . . . what we talked about. Christ, I'm being such an asshole and you don't deserve it. You never could. I'm *sorry*."

"Okay, Charlie," I manage to say, my arms aching to go around him. "It's all right."

"We never talked about it afterward. My brother, father and I. We still haven't."

Understanding more about mute parenting style than he realizes, I reach up, wrapping him in an embrace. A tight one. He moves so fast to hug me back, another stool is sent crashing down, jarred by his hip. There's something about the knocking over of furniture and the way he's breathing so heavily, holding me so close. It ramps the mood back up to when we were making out in the park, the planet ceasing to spin while we devastated one another with lips and tongues, hands and groans and teeth. I was wet the instant we began, and my panties still hold the uncomfortable weight of that arousal. Now his breath is blowing down the back of my top, his erection nudging my belly button and I'm lost. I've been dropped down in the middle of a maze with only one sure path out.

Maybe Charlie is robbing me of sanity, because this feels almost forbidden. This relationship is supposed to be platonic. I'm meant to be dating, looking for someone to share my days and evenings with. Is this cheating . . . on myself? I don't know, but letting Charlie overwhelm me is bad, very bad. God help me, though, the bad is what's getting me off. It's my mistress blood, I think. Letting a man have me while I'm in the market for another. Giving myself over to a man who isn't even available. *Bad*, Ever. I'm ashamed of myself and yet, that's the very reason I'm unfastening his belt.

There's a deep yearning carved inside me that begs to relieve Charlie. Comfort him with my body. It's biological. It's undeniable.

"I need you so bad, Ever. *Ever.*" His mouth is racing all over my face, his tongue dipping into the hollow of my throat. Those hands start in my hair, scrape down my back and grope my ass. He's nasty about it, too, pulling my cheeks apart, shaking them, sliding three fingers right down the middle. He keeps going until he's cupping that soaked part of me through the material of my dress. "Are you letting me? Please say you'll let me."

His question doesn't require a verbal answer. Instead, I push his jeans down to midthigh, followed by his briefs . . . and there isn't a woman with a pulse who could stop once she saw his erection. It's thick and painful looking, prominent veins and a wet head, bobbing against a lickable six-pack. If the kissing hadn't gotten me so horny, I would kneel and suck for everything I'm worth, but getting him inside me is my world right now. My galaxy. His dilated pupils and frantic hands tell me Charlie is starved for it, too. He unties my halter dress and it slides down my body, like a curtain dropping, leaving me in nothing but drenched, gray cotton panties. At least that's what I'm wearing until I shimmy them down my legs, giving Charlie's dick a teasing lick while I'm down there.

We dive back into a kiss, and it's a race to get him planted between my legs. I hear the crinkle of a condom wrapper and Charlie's long, drawn-out grunt as he rolls it on. A hard slap on my ass is the only signal I need to climb aboard—and I do. I throw up my right leg, he catches it under a hooked arm. And then he guides himself to my entrance with the other hand, all while looking me straight in the eye, beneath hooded lids, drawing rough-edged kisses from my abused mouth.

"No one moves like us, Ever. No one talks to each other without words like us. Don't you *know* that?" He grits his teeth, thrusts his hips and . . . *sweet Christ*, he's inside me to the hilt. My other leg shoots up and clenches around his hips, giving him my full weight, and it doesn't faze him at all. He's too busy moaning with his head thrown back, the tendons of his neck stark and sexy and male. "I've been dying for you. *Dying.* You don't know what it's been like."

"Yes, I do."

His fingers dig into the flesh of my ass, lifting me, grinding me down on his rigid flesh. My clit drags in a delicious path against the slick base of his erection, back up, back down. "You know how hard it's been? Tell me how you know." His forehead pushes into mine, his teeth bared. "Tell me."

My heels find purchase on his tight ass and we hit an incredible rhythm. I writhe to the tip of his hardness, Charlie gives an upthrust, and at the same time, I roll my hips and drop hard. We're melded together, a sweaty tangle supported on two legs, and it's like a naughty fantasy in the flesh. It never stops being that way with Charlie. "You used to come around lunchtime every day . . . and now you don't, so I—"

I break off when Charlie strides toward the living room. Hope catches in my throat when I think he's going to keep walking. Straight into my bedroom, where he's never been before, but he doesn't. Instead, he drops onto his knees on the couch, impaling me even more fully on his thickness. I'm still screaming from the impact when he turns us around and drops down on top of me, bearing down between my legs. "What do you do at lunchtime, huh?" His inches slide out and slam back in. "Do you lick your fingers and slide them into your pussy, Ever? Yeah, I think you do. I think it's so hot and sweet and tight, even you can't resist touching it."

"The sink," I manage, reaching down to palm my breasts. "You pushed me over the kitchen sink once and . . . I loved it." His gaze is riveted to my hands, so I pinch my nipples for him, clenching the inner walls of my center at the same time, my femininity rejoicing in his string of rasped curse words. "I close my eyes and pretend you're behind me and I touch. I touch myself until it's all over."

God, Charlie goes wild, hearing that. My knees are yanked up near my elbows, and with my head having landed on a pillow, I have a first row seat to watching his ass pump. Those muscles flexing, those cheeks going loose, then bunching on a thrust. I could climax if I watch his hips and buttocks work overtime long enough, but the result of that hard labor has my stomach twisting, my nerves firing, distracting me and forcing my eyes closed so I could embrace the build-up. So good. *So good.*

Charlie is close to hitting his peak—he's chanting my name in that hoarse voice—but he doesn't ride it out. He slows down, pressing our mouths together, and gives me great, rolling slides that hit me so deep, I forget to breathe. "I want a picture of us together." Those blue eyes drill into mine. "One where my hands are on you. Touching your hips, your belly. Your face. Need something to look at when I'm not here to remember. Remember I got to feel you. When you're not under me, I swear I fucking dreamed it all."

"Charlie . . ." I whisper, shaken, pulling him down for a kiss. It's not just a kiss, though. It feels different. Like the never-ending one back in the park, it's like we're imploring one another, no idea what we're actually seeking. What does it say about me that I break away, desperate to get us back on footing I recognize? A place where I'll still be standing when he leaves after we're done. "What would you do with the picture?"

I expect him to say something filthy and he does. "Stroke myself off like an inmate who got his dirty hands on a *Maxim*. Don't act like you don't know, Ever." But I don't expect the blow that follows, so I'm not prepared. I'm without armor. "Or I might just stare at it and wondered what the fuck is wrong with me. That I'd stand there, let you tell me you're going to date other men and not *beg* you to reconsider." He burrows his face into my neck and rides me hard. Harder than before. "What the fuck is *wrong* with me, Ever?"

My arms band around the breadth of his back,

my ankles cross just above those rolling hips. His breath is jagged, his drives relentless . . . and there's no place to hide from the orgasm that grabs me around the throat. It consumes my body, throwing my back into an arch, turning my eyes blind. "Charlie, Charlie, Charlie."

My sight returns just enough to watch his jaw lose power, mouth dropping open as he climaxes, his erection straining inside me, hips jerking with powerful spasms. "Oh Christ. Ever. You're so god-damn tight. So tight, squeezing me like that. You turn me fucking crazy. Coming so good inside you. You make me come so good."

I'm depleted of all strength by the time Charlie finishes completely, his weight dropping down on me like a quilt made of sweaty man meat. But the cloud of euphoria is fast to dissipate. A sob tries to climb the inside of my throat, but I trap it. Examine it for meaning. I've never cried after sex before. Never even close.

Because it has never meant anything. Or I've never allowed myself to admit the times with Charlie were *beginning* to mean something, even as far back as when we started meeting. This time, there's no pretending, though. My feelings for him have catapulted from questionable to *stop fooling yourself, idiot*. Which is why I've allowed this charade of friendship to continue past the point it was wise. And now, I'll be the walking wounded when he bounces with a wink out my front door. Because he doesn't want something meaningful with me. This is what he wants. Couch sex. Kitchen counter sex. Even venturing into my room is too personal for him.

As if he can sense the direction of my thoughts, Charlie's head comes up and he's scrutinizing me. Just a gorgeous, scruffy, baffled, beautiful boy. "What is it?"

His body is too welcome against mine. Too warm and solid. I have to get away before he *takes* himself away, leaving me feeling like his relief button. Swallowing nails, I scoot out from beneath him and stand, going in search of my dress. "That shouldn't have happened."

Charlie stands, already giving me a warning look. "Ever."

"I mean it." I pull up my dress and tie it with shaking fingers. "Please, Charlie, I really need you to leave this time."

"Not until you explain why you're freaking out." He looks down at the couch, his face the picture of male bafflement. "What happened between then and now?"

I gather my hair in a bun. Realizing I have no rubber band, I let it drop. Deep breaths. This isn't like me. I don't lose my cool and do postorgasm meltdowns. If I can just keep my thoughts from blowing around for one second, maybe I can make him understand. We owe each other understanding, don't we? "I like you. I really do. But I don't think we make good friends. Not right now." I toe my panties, kick them up and shove the material into my pocket. Just for something to do with my hands. "We're going to fall into the same pattern we were in before. If I let that happen, I'll never focus on what I want."

"What *you* want? Or what your mother wants?" While I reel, he finishes zipping his pants and takes a long breath. "Look, I've put some thought into this. If you want me to go with you to meet your mother, I will. You can call me your boyfriend and put her mind at ease. Whatever you want. I know it's important not to let her down, and you don't have to."

My mouth and mind sputter in tandem. Oh wow. Oh, this is *beyond*. "Fake it? You're asking me to *fake* having a boyfriend, instead of looking for the real thing? Why would I do that, Charlie? Why?" He doesn't answer, his jaw stiff, but I can see he wants to take back the offer. He's maybe even a little ashamed to have made it. "This is about what *I* want. Not just my mother." I caved for his needs, even when I knew it was a bad idea, driving home how weak I am when it comes to Charlie. That weakness is only going to be exploited further if we keep seeing each other under the guise of friendship. I always thought the mistress gene ended with me, even though I was playing by the fundamentals. It's inside me, though, to be the woman Charlie seeks out for relief, and he's banking on it. Isn't he? Did he ever want to be my friend in the first place? Or were we on a single lane highway leading to here? I don't want to be the place where he comes to scratch an itch, then walk away scot free. I don't want to be that for anyone anymore. "This isn't only for my mother. I-I don't like the feeling I get when you leave now. It's not fun anymore."

His face loses some color. "What feeling?"

"A used one." The words catch in my throat, and when Charlie staggers back, like he's been struck, it takes me a moment to gather my courage and continue. "Maybe we were using each other in the beginning, but the balance is off now. And it *hurts*." I force my shoulders back. "So I'm asking you to leave. Stop texting, please. Stop calling and respect my decision." How can I feel my heart racing when my chest seems empty? "I'm going to miss you, but I'd rather miss you than start to hate you."

"Ever," he breathes, his blue eyes tormented. "No. I can do better."

Even now, I want to give him that chance, but I bite down on the temptation and shake my head. Secretly, I think I wanted more than friendship from Charlie this whole time, but I'm done waiting around for him to want it, too. Hell, I could be waiting forever. "Go, Charlie."

He stares at me for torturous moments, looking haunted, but eventually he falls toward the door, opening it. Thinking he's leaving and it's safe to let my strength drain out, I sag against the counter, but Charlie stops at the last minute. He pulls out his cell phone and takes a picture of me, the click sounding unnatural in the silence, then goes.

CHAPTER 16
Charlie

Fuck, I'm hungover. Did someone use my head to play horseshoes last night? I am never attempting to match Jack shot for shot again. I'm going to die. I *want* to die. As soon as I left Ever's apartment last night, I called Jack and met him at a bar. Shock of all shocks, he was already inside one in his old Hell's Kitchen neighborhood. What time did we leave that dive? How did I get home? Why is "Landslide" by Fleetwood Mac stuck in my head?

No clue.

I only know one thing: Drills start in fifteen minutes and the second I start running, I'm going to throw up. It's just going to happen. It's going to be disgusting. I'm probably going to get some fucked up nickname like Pukey, which will follow me around until I retire from the force four decades from now.

Somehow I've managed to dress myself in my uniform, which was a challenge in itself, let alone drilling at eight in the morning, with none other than Greer holding the whistle.

All of this is cool, though, because I *want* to die. I do. This is just my version of suicide by cop. I can't think about the words Ever said to me without wanting to rip my hair out by the roots, hence the fifth of whiskey I put away last night. *Why did I take that picture of her?* I seem to recall asking myself that same question around one o'clock in the morning, while holding out my phone to a bleary-eyed bartender. It's not a *bad* picture. I don't think Ever is capable of spawning anything bad whatsoever. It's not pixelated or off center. No, it just happens to be a perfect depiction of loneliness.

She looked so lonely watching me leave.

Is that the first time? Or has she always watched me go with that same half-brave, half-dejected expression on her face? I managed to drown those horrifying possibilities in a vat of liquor last night, but I can't ignore them now. I made her feel used. I hurt her. How was I so fucking unaware?

Because sure as shit, I was aware of meddling in her life. Screwing with her plans. Showing up at her building with the full intent to take her to bed if she gave me the slightest encouragement. I'm only ignorant when it comes to *other* people's needs and feelings. Ever was right to throw me out. For the second time. She might love the sex—God knows we both do—but she sees me for the selfish prick I am.

She recognizes damage I can cause to people who have the potential to love me.

All the recruits have made their way from the locker room into the gymnasium now. Well. Except for Jack. Danika isn't speaking to me after encouraging Jack to drink last night—which I deserve—so I'm sitting alone, up against the wall farthest from the platform where Greer will stand in mere moments, ready to make his younger brother's life hell. As if it wasn't already.

With brimstone curling in my nose, I spot someone across the gymnasium floor and my spine straightens. The agonizing throb in my temples ratchets up until I swear, blood swims in my vision. *That little fucker.* In the mental four-alarm-fire I've been in since leaving Ever looking so sad, holding the counter for support, I forgot all about my fellow recruit who never takes off his god-damn aviator glasses. He's one of the jackasses I sent to go ruin Ever's speed dating event, so imagine my surprise when the dickhead showed up as one of her matches on DateMate yesterday.

Yeah, he'd gone and found her somehow among the dozens of dating sites. I don't believe in coincidences.

I'm on my feet before my brain has given a formal command, probably because it's on a ten-second whiskey delay. And yeah, even through the rage, I'm aware I'm about to make a huge mistake. Do I give a shit? Nope. I need someone to give me a nice, hard right cross, because this hangover feels like a nail gun to the skull, and it's still the *least* I have coming. I want to hurt. I want to bleed. I want to stop thinking.

About Ever. Her scent, her hands, her eyes, the way she kissed me with so much. So much. About everything that came rushing back in the park yesterday, before she saved me, then cut me loose again. I'm floating somewhere in space with nowhere to land, and I need outer pain to distract me from the inner.

"Hey, you. Ass Face." I slice through my enemy's posse of mouth breathers, delivering a two-handed slam to his chest, flattening him up against the cinderblock wall. "You ever try talking to my girl again, I will take those stupid glasses and ram them down your throat. Are you hearing me?"

He's nervous. He should be. I've busted my ass to earn every single recruit's respect by working twice as hard, so they wouldn't think I was riding on my family's coattails. I'm not someone to be taken lightly. Unfortunately, males aren't known for making the best decisions when their friends are around. "If she's your girl, why was she speed dating?"

There's a chorus of *ohhhs* behind me like we're starring in some corny eighties movie, which pisses me off almost as much as the comment. Of course, "It's complicated," is the only response I have to that, which I deliver through clenched teeth. "You're going to go home to your mom's basement tonight and delete whatever lame-dick message you sent her," I enunciate. "Or we're going to have a problem."

"I'm not deleting shit," Ass Face spits, his face growing redder, thanks to my forearm wedging against his jugular. "Just because you couldn't hold on to that hot piece of ass doesn't mean I shouldn't have a chance at tapping it."

That's all folks.

I don't even see red. Oh no. I'm blind. I can't see a goddamn thing. It's like someone stuffed pillows into my ears and kept shoving, trying to squeeze the juice out of my brain. My fists are moving before I register the action, connecting with flesh and bone. There's a crunch under my fist and it's *so far* from satisfying, I have to keep going. Swinging again. And with that second right hook, everything changes from slow, underwater movements to rapid, hyperspeed chaos. The fucker who dared to call my Ever a name is on the ground, I'm straddling his neck and beating the hell out of him. I can't stop. I can't even feel the third or fourth hit. I don't feel anything but a repeated shattering inside my ribcage.

I couldn't hold on to her.

I can't hold on to anything.

"Charlie!" It's Jack's voice, among the chorus of others. Several sets of hands are attempting to haul me off my bloody opponent, but none of them are successful. There's a bonfire in my throat, and the smoke is billowing into my noise, behind my eyes. I'm screaming through clenched teeth and—

My back hits the mat. Jack is blocking out the gymnasium lights above me, and I let him. I don't have a choice. My breath is rattling in and out so fast, my adrenaline like a fire hose blast, I don't feel the pain radiating from behind my eye socket at first. But it roars in, and that's when red finally seeps into my vision, liquid and sticky.

"Stay down, Charlie," Jack shouts at me. "You got your hits in, man. It's over." Behind my best friend, someone complains. I think I hear the word *psycho*. But the nasal sound cuts off when Jack throws a look over his shoulder. "Hey. Keep your mouth shut. You really don't want me coming over there." He focuses back on me. "You could have told me there was going to be a scrap this morning. I might have shown up on time."

Danika's face appears to Jack's right, but she isn't looking at me. No. I know that expression. It's the one people get when my brother is coming. "Gird your loins," she mutters, backing up, along with Jack. "Incoming."

No way in hell I'm going to face Greer on my back, so I push into a sitting position, fall forward onto my knees and stand, swaying a little. The whiskey in my stomach protests, sloshing around like water in a barrel. My hands fly up to keep my head from breaking apart into fragments, but I still have the urge to shout. *He insulted my girl. My girl doesn't want me anymore. My fault. All my fault.*

Frustration and helplessness is like a fucking noose tightening around my neck, and when I catch my first glimpse of Greer's stonewall, unimpressed, void of an expression, the noose snaps and I surge forward, catching him square in the chest with a push. Clearly not expecting the attack, my brother falls back a few steps, looking at me like I've lost my mind. Maybe I have. The gasps behind me should have reiterated how stupid a move I just made, but instead they make me laugh. I'm laughing, there's blood running down my face and my brother is livid.

Good. *Good.* Finally there's some proof he isn't a

fucking robot like my father. Like they expect *me* to be. *Good*.

"My office, Burns. Immediately. No one move until I return," Greer says, his tone packed with frost. He slants a glance at the punk I just knocked around, his face betraying disgust. Probably because the guy is still lying on the ground, being supported by his dick wad cronies. "Jesus Christ, recruit. Clean yourself up."

In a familiar move that reminds me of our father, Greer pivots on a heel and strides toward the back offices. I'm still stuck in such a state of rebellion, I consider not following, until Jack gives me a shove between the shoulder blades. "Get to stepping, man. You can't avoid the devil forever."

Grinding my back teeth, I follow my brother through the parted sea of stunned faces. Maybe it's useless, but I think of Ever. How she held me in the park yesterday. I wish she were here right now. I'd walk right into her and bury my bloody face in her neck, and I bet she wouldn't even flinch.

It's these thoughts that have my heart in my throat when I walk into Greer's gray-walled, frill-free office and close the door. He's stationed permanently at the 9th Precinct, but this characterless box serves as his office twice per week, when he graces the academy with his presence. Greer used to trade off the responsibility with his old partner. Until just over two years ago when the other officer was gunned down after a two-hour hostage stand-off in Alphabet City. My brother was difficult to communicate with *before* the tragedy. Now? It's damn near impossible. I don't fault him for dealing with things his own way. I can't imagine the mental shit he's stewing in, especially because he was present when his partner died. But today, I can't find it in me to respect the trench-deep boundaries we've drawn. I've been doing it so long.

"Just checking, did you actually *push* me out there?" Greer starts, his jaw brittle. "Or was I dreaming?" Falling into the chair facing his desk, I don't offer an answer and he doesn't expect one. "You're supposed to be setting an example, Charlie."

"Can I have the waste basket? I'm probably going to hurl."

A sound of repulsion follows my request, but he kicks the plastic trashcan into the space between my sprawled legs. "Is this Jack Garrett's influence?"

"No," I ground out. "I make my own decisions. And I decided to get drunk. Leave Jack out of it."

Greer is so stiff and formal as he paces, hands clasped behind his back, I wish I'd pushed him a little harder. Maybe razzed him a couple times in the liver. "You realize I have to suspend you for this."

"Yeah." I pull the basket closer just in time. The contents of my breakfast and last night's drinking binge come up. When I fall back into the chair, swiping a hand over my mouth, acid clings to the insides of my throat and I don't feel even remotely better. "It was worth getting suspended over. I'd do it again. What do you think of that, Greer? Have you ever felt strongly enough—about *any-thing* in your life—to put your perfect record in jeopardy?"

"Never."

A laugh tumbles out of me. "Of course not." I'm exhausted. I've lost Ever. I'm hollow. The throbbing behind my eye is getting worse by the minute. Which must account for the next question that comes out of my mouth. "Why did Mom leave?"

The silence is so loud. "Excuse me?"

I look at Greer. My polished, perfect-haircut-wearing, starched-uniform-owning brother from the same mother. And I think I see a hint of vulnerability pass across his features. My brother, my father and I don't talk about my mother. We never have. "Why did she leave? You're older than me. You would know better than I do."

"I don't, actually." The vulnerability is gone, replaced by antipathy, before I can blink an eye. "What the hell is this, Charlie? You potentially screw up your future because of something a million years in the past?"

I take a deep breath, remembering how final the clicking of a door can sound. Especially when everyone just carries on like nothing happened and it's still ringing in your ears. Any other day, I would be mortified by showing my brother a weakness. Tomorrow I will be, I know. But today, I'm depleted of anything other than confusion. Loneliness. "Wasn't that long ago, Greer. Doesn't feel like it."

His fist pounds down on the desk and I flinch, but only because it turns up the volume on my headache to full blast. "You pull your head out of your ass right the fuck now, do you hear me?" His eyes launch flamethrowers of outrage at me. "You don't have the luxury of dwelling on this. Dwelling on *anything*. You take the shit life shovels at you and move on." He stabs a finger in the air. "Do you want to be a cop?"

"Yeah." I do. I want to be a great one. But it's only starting to hit home the sacrifice it takes. It's not just long hours training or acing exams. It's . . . life. "Does it always mean leaving everything and everyone else behind? Does it always have to be the most important thing?"

"Yes. It does mean that. If you want to be the best. You earn the most respect when nothing gets in the way of your job." His shrug is smooth, his eyes evasive. "My guess is our mother didn't understand that. We'll never know. But I'll tell you one thing, you're probably putting more thought into this than she did."

A sharp pain goes straight through me, like a bullet. Then it's gone. Ever's face shimmers in the air in front of me, fresh and smiling. Is she my sacrifice? Have I already sacrificed her?

"I'm giving you a two-day suspension, then you're going to come back and remind everyone why they'll never be any higher than second place." Greer grabs me by the shoulder and shakes me. "Do you understand me?"

"Yeah," I say, watching my vision of Ever float away. "First place."

What choice do I have?

CHAPTER 17

Ever

My mother is wearing sweatpants. Not the cute kind, either. These are End-of-Times sweatpants. They are stained and loose and covered in lint. The kind you don't wear unless it's laundry day and there's no chance of human interaction. Not even with the mailman or the food delivery guy. My mother is rocking them hard, paired with gold-studded Chanel flats. Today marks the first time in my life I've felt overdressed around my mother, and I'm wearing jean shorts.

I haven't seen Charlie since Saturday. This morning, while sitting on a bench in Washington Square Park—a pit stop I made on the way back from buying ingredients for brie cheese and mushroom crepes—I considered texting Charlie. I was anxious after how he'd opened up to me about his mother. Maybe it was a mistake to drop him so hard when he was clearly having a difficult moment. Sure, I'd been having a tough one, too, but that didn't stem the flow of guilt.

Recognizing the fact that I was about to cave, I'd dropped the bags of ingredients off at the apartment, left Nina a note that I would be back soon and took the train to Columbus Circle. My mother owns a two-bedroom condo in a high-rise—not quite a park view, but still swank—and close enough to the Garment District where she works. I needed to remind myself why broadening my horizons was so important. My mother's initial visit had shaken me up in the first place, so here I am again.

Drinking grape Fanta and eating Chinese takeout on a dinner tray. I'm not fancy by any stretch, but the last time I visited my mother, we'd been served by a maid. Coupled with the sweatpants, I'm wondering if her epiphany has led to a full-on lifestyle makeover. Her energy is almost relaxed, compared to the nonstop hummingbird movements I associated with her for so long.

"So have you met anyone yet?"

Yeah. A stubborn, gorgeous, anticommitment police academy recruit who talks to me with his heart in his eyes, but will never, ever, hand it over. "Uh, no one special just yet." Her shoulders deflate, so I rush to add, "I met some nice boys in sunglasses while speed dating. And I'm seeing a fire academy recruit on Friday night."

"Oh." She perks up. "Firemen don't make great money, but we all have to start somewhere." She salutes me with grape soda. "Consider it practice."

"Practice." I nod, unable to think of a better response. "Okay."

I confirmed my plans with Reve last night through the dating site. He only gave a short response to my knock-knock joke, so I'd almost been nervous to try again. But when he'd cited a heavy work schedule and assured me he'd be at our date, I decided not to take his abruptness personally. Some time had passed since we'd arranged the date, so maybe the magic was dwindling without any actual face-to-face interaction? I wasn't sure, but all the mysteries would be solved on Friday night.

The silence stretches between my mother and I. All I can hear are the bubbles popping and fizzing in my soda. Out in the hallway, I hear an apartment door slam and musical laughter as neighbors pass her condo. She shoots me a glance from beneath naked eyelashes, and I scold myself for not visiting sooner. Coming home to an empty apartment and hearing lives being lived on every side of her must be awful. Especially in light of her realization that flying solo isn't all it's cracked up to be.

I set down my drink because my arm simply can't support it anymore. "Mother, I know it's hard learning to live without the three rules, but you don't have to sit here alone. You can go out and make friends. Or even meet someone who's single—"

Her scoff cuts me off. "And what would I tell them? I've spent the last twenty-odd years carrying on with various married men?" She gives me a pointed look, but it's laced with sadness. "I doubt people will be very receptive."

"You won't know until you try."

"Maybe it's not even about my past," she blurts. "I don't . . . really know how to *talk* to anyone. All my life, most of my conversations outside of work revolved around sex. Where to meet. How to be discreet. And don't get me wrong, I enjoyed some of it, even if I have regrets now." Her laugh is watery. "I wouldn't know where to start if I walked into a bar or met someone for dinner." She sighs. "I'd probably ask my date to wear a wedding ring for old time's sake."

Even though I'm shaking my head, we both laugh and something melts inside me. I've been waiting for this warmth for a really long time and it doesn't disappoint, rolling over me like a honey glaze. "When I went speed dating, I chugged a glass of wine, I was so nervous. And you know what, it was awful. I didn't even make it through to the end."

My mother sits forward. "But you're so . . . industrious. Brave. Out on your own and running your own company." She shakes her head. "I might have climbed the corporate ladder, but creating something uniquely mine? I never had it in me to do that."

"Yes, you did," I rush to say through the overwhelming shock of having her pride bestowed on me. "When I think I can't handle a situation, I just ask myself what you would do. And the answer is always, kick ass and take names."

There's a sheen in her eyes. "Really?"

"Yes."

My open adulation has caused her to retreat into herself, becoming more recognizable as my aloof mother, nudging aside the earnest woman I saw breaking through. For now. Never expecting us to make any progress, though, I'm . . . content. I don't need to push for another Hallmark moment just yet. Maybe it's just enough to know there is potential for more. "How about this? You go out and give the over-forties single scene a try and . . . I'll go out tonight and try, too. With twenty-somethings, obviously. Bumping into you might be awkward." That earns me a laugh. "We don't have to tell one another how it went. Or what happened. It'll be kind of like a mistress honor system."

She snorts, then covers her nose, as if she can't believe that sound emerged. "I don't know . . ."

"Wear that green dress. The loose one with pockets you wore that time we met for dinner in Chelsea." I snap a wonton in half and pop it into my mouth. "You look smoking hot in it, but also approachable."

"Leave fashion to the expert, daughter." Her expression is stern, but she softens it with a wink. "Fine. What's the worst that could happen, right? I just end up back here watching *The Dog Whisperer*."

"That's the spirit, Mother."

She collects my glass, traipsing off to the kitchen, and I know that's my signal to leave, but I can't help but smile at her retreating back. I don't feel so alone anymore, heading out into the sea of faces, pulses and personalities. Dating. I expected to come to visit my mother this afternoon and be jolted into a renewed determination by her loneliness. But it's *more* than that. For the first time, I can see my future self in my mother, and I want to be the brave person she believes me to be. Maybe the trick is to start believing it myself.

On the walk to the train, I hit speed dial on Nina's number. "Hey, you." She grumbles at me on the other end of the line. "If you're still sleeping and it's past noon, this girl's night is even more vital than I thought."

"Girl's night?"

"Yeah." I smile and pick up the pace, refusing—*refusing*—to think of Charlie. Or miss him. Not even a smidgen. "You have seven hours to get ready. Think you can manage it?"

I can almost see her chewing on her lip. "It's a Tuesday night. Is there even anything going on?"

"Did you forget your zip code?" I see the steps up ahead and move into a trot, noticing passengers disembarking, meaning a train in the station. "I'll be home within the hour. Shower up. We'll go get pedicures and do pregame drinks at Lorelei."

"What's gotten into you?" Nina asks with a smile in her voice.

"I don't know." I swallow the lump that's been living in my throat since Charlie walked out of the apartment, taking a picture of me along with him. "Hope."

"I can't even handle you this corny."

My laugh echoes down the train station stairwell. "Shut up and get your ass in the shower."

THERE IS A stride I hit around eleven o'clock on a night out. Not dissimilar to the one glass of wine high. Or the post-tequila shot euphoria. Once eleven o'clock comes and goes, I can taste the following day—it's only an hour away—and there's no turning back. Might as well stay out all damn night.

My quest for the ultimate night is particularly rewarding this time around because Nina is on the same page. We're right on one another's level, finishing each other's sentences, ordering rounds of vodka tonics without confirming if the other wants more. It's a given. It's one of those nights.

Our outfits are freaking amazing, too. In fact, the more we drink, the better we look. Nina is wearing a fringed and beaded vest she found at a local consignment shop, paired with leather leggings. When she walked out of her bedroom earlier, we had to take a moment, she looked so dope. I've gone more of a traditionally trashy route in red pumps, red lipstick and a black shift dress that hits me midthigh. Okay, high-thigh. The more I drink, the higher the hem seems to look.

This is a great night. The greatest.

Where are we?

Oh. Some DJ Nina swears is world-famous tweeted he was doing a surprise set at Webster Hall, so we're half jogging, half stumbling arm in arm in that direction. We're one block away, and it appears we're not the only ones who fielded the tweet. Oh no. There's police trying to corral everyone onto the sidewalk as Nina and I hop into line. It's already moving and we high five, miss and connect on the second try.

"Is my makeup smeared?"

Nina squints at me through one eye. "Yeah, a little, but it looks on purpose."

"Nice." A policeman approaches, ordering us to move closer to the building. He looks thrilled beyond words to be herding a throng of twenty-somethings on short notice on a Tuesday night. "Hello, Officer." In my current state of loving the world in general, I smile and give him a thumbs-up. "You're doing a great job."

"Thanks," comes his dry response. "My night is complete."

"I used to date a cop." These moments come part and parcel with post-eleven o'clock nights out, especially when you've been pregaming since seven. I'm rambling, I know I'm being that drunk girl, but the words won't stay inside. I was the happiest I've ever been one minute ago, now one little reminder of Charlie and I'm swallowing rocks. "Only we weren't really dating. And he isn't a cop yet. So I guess none of the things I said are true." Nina is a good friend, so she's pulling on my arm, begging me to shut up. "His name is Charlie Burns. Good old Charlie *freaking* Burns."

The cop is very interested in us all of a sudden. "No shit?" He looks like a cat who caught the canary. "Yo, Burns!"

I go very still, my pulse jackhammering in my skull. "Charlie is here?"

"Next best thing," Canary Catcher answers, shrugging, just as another cop approaches. And holy hell. It's like looking right at Charlie. If he aged half a decade, grew a lot more hostile and hated everything in sight. My gaze dips to his badge. *Burns.* This is Charlie's brother. I don't even know his first name. I should. I should know the name of the brother of the man I miss like crazy. Right? "This girl here says she dated Charlie." Canary Catcher again. "Only they didn't *really* date. It's a long story, I'm guessing. Aren't you glad you came down to help us grunts out tonight?" He claps Charlie's brother on the back and walks away. "Have fun."

Elder Burns tries to burn a hole through me with his laser-like focus. "You dated my brother?"

The way he asks, you would think I was being questioned about stolen jewels. "Should I call a lawyer?"

He doesn't like my sarcasm. "*When* did you date my brother?"

"We didn't technically date." I look to Nina for help, but she's staring ahead at something in line, leaving me out to dry. "But the last time I saw him was a few days ago." I swallow hard. "Is he . . . doing all right?"

A long pause. "Why wouldn't he be?"

"I-I don't know." I sound so pathetically sad. My buzz is flatlining. I need to get away from Elder Burns and circle back to the drawing board of getting over Charlie. Running into his brother has set me back a good hundred years. Or that's how it feels right now with vodka humming in my blood. "If you see him, just . . . tell him I've been using the notecard tree he gave me. It's really handy."

If I ever form a band, I'm going to name it Drunk Masochist.

"This is my brother, Charlie Burns, we're talking about." Was that a question? I have no idea. "You dated, but not really, up until a few days ago. He gave you a gift. And now you're not seeing him anymore."

"You're making it sound like *I'm* at fault here."

He gives this annoying neck tweak. "Are you?" When my mouth drops open, he holds up a hand. "Not involved. I'm not getting involved." His cheek ticks. "It's just the timing . . ."

Nina grabs my hand and pulls me forward, along with the line, which is moving again and growing rowdier by the second. Elder Burns frowns at me as I walk away. I assume the conversation is over, but he curses and breaks into a stride to catch up.

"Listen, this isn't a good scene," he barks at me over the surrounding laughter and screams. "Why don't you head on home . . . ?"

"Ever. And we'll be fine . . . ?"

He sighs, like I just asked him for a loan. "Greer."

I pat his arm. "Good night and good luck, Greer."

We turn the corner into the venue and it's so loud, my molars clamp down. People are pushing their way through the narrow staircase into the downstairs performance space, harried personnel trying to guide the crowd. Once we get downstairs, though, everyone spreads out as much as possible, the music kicking off almost immediately. Nina takes off her shoes and shoves them into her purse, then leads me out to the dance floor. I'm still replaying the conversation with Charlie's brother, reveling in how he'd sounded so amazed that Charlie had dated someone, let alone bought them a gift. Maybe I *was* a little special to him, even if he never said it out loud.

I push aside the useless, leading thoughts with massive determination.

There are boys everywhere. They're a little too hipster for my taste, but I promised myself I would try. I promised my mother. So when a pair of bearded bros move into our circle and start dancing with us, I don't excuse myself to use the bathroom or head to the bar, like I would do normally to avoid any kind of meaningful interaction. I throw my hands up in the air, close my eyes and let myself have fun. Even if there's a significant part of myself that never really allows it. A part that keeps dragging me back to the boy with blue eyes who told me he could do better as a friend, if I let him. The boy who kissed me in the park like our lives depended on it.

Half an hour has passed when a prickle blows across my shoulders. I stop dancing to scan the crowd. Am I crazy . . . or do I feel Charlie here? No. I just spoke to his brother outside, which has to account for this odd premonition. Someone takes my hand—one of the guys we've been dancing with—and I jerk it away. I've been maintaining a careful distance from everyone of the opposite sex, dancing but not touching, and I command myself to stop holding back. Stop. But the feeling of being watched won't go away.

I'm distracted when Nina gets way too close to her dance partner. Hands on the booty close. Which is nothing like Nina. This is newly single Nina, yes, but it's out of character for her, making me worry. Her motives become clear a moment later when I see her ex-boyfriend dancing with another girl about twenty heads away, his thunderous gaze steady on Nina.

"Hey," I lean in and shout so Nina can hear me. "I see what you're doing there, friend-o. I have the full scope of the situ-sitch-situation." Okay, maybe I didn't sober completely. "Do you want to leave?"

"Leave?" She gives me a full, over the shoulder eyebrow raise. "I'm having fun, aren't you?"

"Yeah." I am enjoying the music and the guy I'm dancing with is funny enough, in a watered-down Paul Rudd kind of way. So, yes. *Yes*, this is what people equate to a good time. Plus tonight is Nina's first night out since the breakup, and I owe it to her to hang out as long as possible. "Okay, let me know if you change your mind."

She doesn't answer, and my dance partner catches my wrist, spinning me. Once again I encounter the tingle on the back of my neck, but command myself to ignore it.

CHAPTER 18
— Charlie —

So this is what hell looks like.

Drinking warm beer while my girl dances with an Urban Outfitters model. Yeah, I'm jealous. I'm jealous as fuck. Ever looks like everyone's secret jackoff fantasy. She's literally not even wearing pants. And then she went ahead and stuck some red high heels on, *just in case* anyone needed extra convincing her legs are two miles long. On top of that sexy little outfit, she's moving her tight ass like someone might rob it, if she stops.

Today was my first day back after being suspended, and the drills kicked my ass. I kicked theirs, too, meaning I was dead asleep when the text message from Greer hit my phone a while ago. *Ever at Webster Hall. Bad scene.* I almost broke my neck diving out of bed and pulling on the closest pair of jeans. Of course, my motherfucker of a brother didn't answer his phone when I called for more details, but I can see with my own eyes now he'd been right. The place is filled well past capacity, meaning the fire marshal is likely due to arrive any minute. Bodies are crammed in tight at the bar, on the dance floor, along the walls. If there's an emergency, hell will break loose.

So my jealousy is secondary to Ever's safety, even if it *is* an evil, spinning ball of shit banging around in my stomach. Truthfully, the green-eyed monster would be seven times uglier if I thought *for a second* that Ever could be into the guy attempting to dance with her. But every time Bearded Wonder tries to pull her close, she slips away like an elusive kitty cat, tucking hair behind her ear. A nervous gesture that forces me to pound the beer I'm drinking—temperature be damned—because she used to make that same hair-tuck gesture with me. Usually when I was on my way out the door after we'd had sex, and we were working through the goodbye portion. She'd been *unsure* and I hadn't even seen it. I'd just bailed.

Someone jostles my shoulder and beer sloshes out onto my shoe, but I barely notice. I'm watching Ever toss that mane of blonde hair around, hips moving in quick circles, the way she used to move them on top of me. *Fuck.* Bearded Wonder can't keep up, so he's literally just standing there like a garden rake, stroking that shit growing from his chin, and watching the show close up. Jesus Christ, I can't witness it anymore. He needs to stop ogling my girl, and for the love of everything holy, someone needs to give her a decent dance.

Dropping my half-empty plastic cup on the sliver of available bar, anticipation kicks in my gut. Just knowing she's going to give me those eyes, even if she doesn't let me touch her, is enough. I'm just relieved I'll be within reaching distance of her if something goes down.

I'm still a good twenty yards away when Ever stops dancing and turns, our gazes locking through the crowd. As though she sensed me. That awareness sends my blood running south, but I hold on to my inhibitions. I'm not here to take Ever home, much as I'm dying to. She drew the boundary line and I'm not crossing it. I've looked at her hurt expression too many times on my phone to put it there again.

Hey, cutie, I mouth, throwing in a wink. Her expression is a little dazed and I can see she's tied one on. There are black streaks extending out from the sides of her eyes, making her even more cat-like than before. So drunk and adorable and hot, I don't know why everyone in the fucking room isn't staring. Maybe they are, but I can't look away from her long enough to find out. She sways a little, and my hand shoots out to catch her elbow. Shit. If I thought I was feeling protective watching her from afar, it doesn't compare to the increased weight of it now. I'm going to make sure she gets home all right. I'm like an ancient knight that's been given a quest, and I either succeed or accept certain death.

She winks back at me, but that one eye stays closed *way* too long. "Hey, Charlie," she calls over the noise. "I met your brother."

"Yeah, I heard. My condolences." Bearded Wonder edges closer, as if he's going to reclaim Ever, and the look I give him is designed to cause an exploding pancreas. "You're done here, bro. That was pathetic."

Further proving his unworthiness of Ever, Bearded Wonder's shoulders sag. He gives Ever's legs one more longing look and gets swallowed up by the still-growing crowd. Taking a moment to judge the distance between us and the closest emergency exit, I take a step into Ever's space and warm apple scent billows around me.

"I dig the shiner." The concern on her face belies her words as she examines my blackened eye. "But try to remember to duck next time."

"I'll make a note of it, cutie," I say dryly, loving the fact that she doesn't press me for details. *No pasts. No futures.* Old habits die hard, I guess. I do my best to banish the bittersweet air floating between us by taking her hand. "Listen, I know I can dance better than that guy. You up for it?"

Her smile is like an adrenaline shot to the chest. "Hell yeah."

If God himself was on the turntables, the next song couldn't have been more perfect. It's the same track we danced to at the catering event—"My Type" by Saint Motel—and we trade *that* look. The one people trade when divine musical providence takes place and you're the *only* ones who understand. When I take Ever's hand, spin her one direction, then back the other, she has no idea what hit her. I'd held back a little at the Art League function because she'd been exhausted, but I'm going balls to the wall tonight. Her sparkle has been subdued by Bearded Wonder's lack of rhythm, but it blazes back to life now, her beautiful face glowing beneath the club lights. That shirt-dress she's wearing twists at the tops of her thighs—god*damn*—so I lean back and wolf whistle, letting her see my appreciation, sending her into a musical fit of laughter.

I don't give her much time to relax, though, before I turn her, pulling her back up against my chest. Trailing a hand down her hip, I grind once into her sweet ass, cursing my determination not to hit on her, then clasp her wrist and turn her in a circle, bringing her back to face me. We're close now, not touching, but a sheet of paper couldn't fit between us, either. Her expression is pure pleasure and I'm not going to lie, it gives me a kind of satisfaction I can't explain, seeing her have a good time. Knowing I made her happy instead of sad or confused for once.

"Charlie Burns, where did you learn how to dance?"

I settle a hand on her right hip, groaning deep in my throat at the rhythmic bump and sway. We're moving in perfect tandem, we always do, and it's a reminder of what I won't allow myself to have anymore, even though it's killing me. "I had a lot of babysitters growing up. My favorite was a police dispatcher named Malia." Ever's smile dips a little at the reminder I didn't have a mother around, but frankly, after days of thinking I would never see this girl again, there isn't much that can fuck up my mood. I saved her from a man who doesn't own a razor, she's letting me hold her, and I'm standing between her and any trouble that breaks out. It's a million miles from the shit show I was stewing in before I crashed into bed tonight. "She had a thing for young John Travolta. I think I've seen *Saturday Night Fever* sixty-eight times. But she mostly played the old soul stuff. She taught me."

Taking Ever's wrists, I bring them up over her head, sliding my palms down her arms, her sides, landing on her hips and twisting them right, left. *Hard*. Her breath catches on a bubbly laugh, her eyelids falling to half-mast. "God, Charlie, that's good."

"She'd say, let the woman know she's hot. Make her feel like the only person alive." I can hear the dispatcher's easy voice, echoing in my kitchen and tearing down the too-quiet, too-tense environment created by three driven males. "No need to remember those lessons when I'm dancing with you, Ever. It just is." *Way to keep it light and friendly, man.* Blowing out a breath, I let my attention drop to her lower body. "And damn, you're not so bad yourself, are you?"

"Yeah?" She gives me this adorable little boogie that no one would attempt sober and I'm smiling like a lunatic. "I'm just warming up."

Two weeks ago, I would have tugged her close, taken two handfuls of her ass and warmed *both* of us up, but if I do that now, it'll screw up this loose feeling we're sharing. No pressure. No chance that one of us won't feel right later on. We're just dancing. Talking. Bad as I want to take Ever home and coax her into bed, I've been gut sick for days knowing she felt used. By me. I'll never let her feel that way again, long as I'm living and breathing.

"Do you ever see Malia anymore?"

"Yeah. She still works for the department." Needing some form of contact, I rest my mouth against Ever's temple and move us with the beat. "She schedules prostate exams for my father and doesn't tell him until the day before. Everyone loves her for it."

Ever's chest vibrates against mine. "She's his work wife."

"Maybe. Maybe it works because she's part of the job, not a distraction from it." I try to be subtle about inhaling the scent of Ever's shampoo, regretting the fact that I never asked to shower at her place. "Where did *you* learn how to dance?"

"YouTube." We laugh and she winds her arms around my neck, like she's not really thinking about the action. It's just natural. It is. It feels that way. Her body against mine is the ninth wonder of the world—we fit together like puzzle pieces no matter which angle we're standing. "Jennifer Lopez music videos, to be specific. But I made the mistake of signing up for my middle school talent show before showing anyone my routine." Her expression is very serious as she tilts her head back to look at me. "I performed 'Jenny from the Block.' Solo. In a sequin top and a bandana."

"Christ, Ever." I drop my forehead to rest on top of hers. "Tell me you didn't."

"Stop. I'm still recovering." She sniffs. "That was the day I learned the meaning of smattering. As in, a smattering of applause."

I make a sympathetic noise, but I'm battling a

smile. "Speaking of YouTube, I bet your performance is on the Internet somewhere . . ."

"Assaulting a police officer is a felony, Charlie. Don't force my hand." There's no heart in her threat, especially because she's rolling our foreheads together, her fingers tangling in the ends of my hair. Does she realize what she's doing? I don't know, but I can no more stop her than I could screech the Earth's rotation to a halt. My dick is rock hard because, hello, Ever isn't wearing pants, but I've managed to keep my hips angled away, trying to keep this whole situation innocent. But she's gravitating toward me. Or maybe we're just being pulled like magnets, so I need to find a distraction soon.

"Hey." I nudge her forehead. "I'll buy you a drink if you show me some 'Jenny from the Block.' Right here, right now."

Her arms drop from around my neck, head tilting, a single eyebrow lifting. Sexy as all get out. A fantasy I should let go of, but doing so feels fucking impossible. *Feels wrong.* "Are you daring me, Officer?"

I cross my arms over the invisible gash in my chest. "Double dare." She gasps and my belt seems to tighten, so I drop a few lyrics from the song to get her moving, earning another laugh. "Let's go, fly girl. This is your moment."

She does some moves I recognize from the

music video . . . and it's glorious. People stop to watch her dance, chuckling into their drinks. Ever doesn't pay any of them a hint of attention, though, she's focused on me like we're sharing the world's greatest joke. We . . . *are*, aren't we? It hits me like a cab speeding toward a green light. Now that I've stopped trying to be her friend for the wrong reasons, we actually have a chance to be *real* friends. Not the kind I'd been angling for—friends with benefits—but buddies who laugh and talk about the past without judgment.

Only, there's not a chance in hell I could spend time with Ever like this. Not without wanting my mouth on every inch of her skin. Not without wanting her beneath me, moaning, telling me where it feels good.

And I can't have both. Not if the job comes first. She deserves to come first, no questions asked. I can't give that to her. I can't give her friendship, can't be her lover . . . I can't give her *anything*.

She stops dancing, looking at me funny. "Charlie?"

"Ever," I murmur, well aware that she can't hear me, but unable to raise my voice any higher. So I gesture for her to come closer, so I can disappoint her again. Will this be the last time? *Jesus.* "Cutie, I—"

That's when all hell breaks loose.

CHAPTER 19

Ever

Charlie is giving me the strangest look. I don't know what it means, but I'm positive it's going to pop this bubble we're floating in. Demolish it. When he walked out onto the dance floor, his presence was just a given. Of course he was there. I'd wanted it so badly, he'd just appeared. I've been short sighted and delusional, thinking I could go out for a girl's night and forget how much I miss him. Maybe we *could* be friends. Maybe it was worth the heartache of knowing he couldn't, wouldn't, give me more.

Because yeah, my heart? She is aching. Like a son-of-a-bitch.

In my entire life, there hadn't been a single person—not even my girlfriends—who made me comfortable enough to throw my arms around their neck. To just know they would welcome it. And they would feel great. So warm and eager to hold me back. Charlie is the person who demands holding, demands it from the very bottom of my soul and I can tell, I can tell by the way he's looking at me . . . it can't last. For some reason, he showed up here, but it wasn't to profess his feelings. Or tell me we could be more than friends. That much I know.

There's no time to examine his odd expression or what it means, though, because a commotion breaks out behind me. I have this cycle of déjà vu. As though I'd seen this moment play out, but my consciousness had stolen it away until the consequences were too late. It's Nina. I can hear her. She's yelling. A man is shouting back.

Charlie's expression goes from indiscernible to straight panic. He lunges forward, but I'm already whirling around, berating myself for forgetting Nina's ex was here. *Dammit, dammit, dammit.*

Someone pushes me from the left and I stumble a little, but the crowd is packed so tight, I bounce off another body in short order. People were dancing a moment ago, but the shouting has brought them to a standstill, their necks craning to catch the action. I hear a frantic Charlie calling my name behind me, but I keep weaving through the sweaty bodies, focused on making it to Nina.

I finally see her. The man she was dancing with before now stands between her and the ex-boyfriend, but he's laughing, like her distress is a game. She's crying, another girl is attempting to drag away Nina's ex. It's a scene and a half, and I need to get my friend out of there. Pronto. So we can wince over this at brunch tomorrow morning, none the worse for wear.

But when I've almost reached Nina, her ex reaches over the mediator's shoulder, shoving her back a step. Outrage makes everything in my line of vision bright, bright white. I shout my room-mate's name and I'm within reaching distance, when the mediator turns and two-hand pushes Nina's ex. Hard. He reels, falling back on his haunches before surging to his feet. Fists start flying and all at once, it's like everyone in the vicinity is fed a rage supplement. There's pushing on both sides of me. Yelling. The music stops. The lights come up.

An elbow hits me in the ribs and I stumble, the breath knocked from my lungs. An arm wraps around my waist, though, keeping me upright.

"Ever." Charlie's reassuring voice warms my ear, but it's laced with the same panic I saw douse his features moments earlier. *"Are you okay?"*

"Yeah." I nod, reaching out and grasping Nina's wrist, tugging her close. "I'm fine. Nina, are you all right?"

She turns wide eyes on the crowd, obviously shocked by the pushing, the mayhem growing worse by the second as people start to get nervous and rush for the exits. "Yeah, I think so. I don't know what happened—"

"*Hey.* I'm going to get you guys out of here. Now," Charlie interrupts, his voice calm, eyes focused on me. "Don't you dare run off on me like that. Not *ever* again."

His shaking voice leaves me no choice but to nod. And then we're moving. Fast. Charlie pulls me under one arm, Nina under the other and we skirt past the surging bodies, Charlie using his body to take the brunt of any flying fists. The closer we get to the emergency exit, I hear sirens and they grow louder, louder, until I realize there is a police presence in the hall, too. Everyone is scattering as a result, joints are being stomped out, people are calling the names of their friends, looking freaked out.

We burst through the emergency exit and hit the sidewalk, cool night air slapping my dewy skin, calming my buzzing nerves. Charlie steers us east, in the direction of our apartment. "What about your brother?" I ask him, my fingers curled in his shirt.

"Trust me. He can take care of himself." Letting Nina go, he keeps an arm around my shoulders and slants a look down at me. I get the distinct impression he hasn't quite forgiven me for running off on him. "He texted me to come find you because it wasn't a great situation. I'm sure he was prepared for the worst."

"He told me he was going to come to the apartment," Nina says, referring to her ex and sounding more than a little shell-shocked. "He said we need to talk . . . and he's coming over. Tonight." She meets my eyes behind Charlie's back. "I believe him. I've never seen him that angry."

"You can't let him in, Nina." I'm trying to sound firm and soothing all at once, but my voice is unnatural, thanks to the adrenaline. "He *pushed* you."

"What?" Charlie's back stiffens. "I didn't see. I was a little distracted."

Yeah, he's still ticked off at me. But his arm around my shoulders is tighter than ever, so I have no idea where we stand. That look in his eye before hell broke loose is still engraved on my mind.

"He has a key, Ever. Building *and* apartment," Nina says, slapping a hand over her eyes. "We always stayed at his place. I don't even think he's ever *used* them. But he could if he wanted."

"Yeah. Not *even* happening." Charlie's jaw is stiff as we turn the corner onto Second Avenue. "Call your super, ask him to come change the lock. I'll wait at your place until it's done." The laugh he lets out is so dark, I have to double check he's still my quick-witted, fun-guy cop in training. "Here's hoping he does show up, so he can push someone around his own size."

"You sound like an old-time movie actor." I bite my lip. "It's really cute."

"I concur," Nina mutters. "But there's one problem with your solution, Charlie. When we knock on our super's door, he just turns up the volume on Spike TV."

"She's right. We didn't have heat for two days last winter because they were having a Charles Bronson marathon."

Poor Charlie is getting more exasperated by the minute, but I'm too worried to appreciate how helpful he's being. I'd never considered Nina's ex a threat before, just an asshole, but that push brought things to another level. I want to make sure she's safe in our apartment.

Charlie is already pulling out his phone. "No big deal. I'll call a twenty-four-hour locksmith." He dips his shoulder and nudges Nina. "It's going to be fine, okay? No one is getting through me."

Nina nods, a relieved, hesitant smile playing on her lips.

And that's when I know. Without a doubt. I'm in love with Charlie Burns.

Charlie

I know Ever and Nina could have handled this on
their own. There's a chain lock and they know to
call the police, if necessary. Plus, they're a couple
of badasses that just escaped a riot and started
making jokes, without even missing a beat.

But I'm still mid-heart attack after watching Ever
run headfirst into a brawl, so I'm not budging.
Not a single inch. God help Nina's ex-boyfriend
if he does show up. I'm sitting on a kitchen stool,
arms crossed, staring at the door like a bull getting ready to charge. Static is bursting and siz-
zling in my veins, leftover from Ever being so
close to danger. I've got so much pent-up energy
inside me that if dipshit walks through that door,
it wouldn't even be a fair fight.

My sore eye tingles, as if reminding me of the
last fight I participated in. Hell, at this rate, I might
as well be training for the middleweight belt.

Ever disappeared into the bathroom a few minutes ago and I hear the water running, high heels
being kicked aside. She's probably naked. Definitely, probably *naked*. But I'm not here to find out.
Nope. I'm going to wait until the lock is changed,
kiss her on the cheek and leave. Tomorrow morning, I have a hell day, meaning Greer is running
drills. Plus I've signed on to train after hours with

the Emergency Services Unit—my father's not-so-subtle suggestion—to show the brass I'm serious about making up for the fight I instigated. The fist fight hurt my chances of making sergeant, and eventually lieutenant, on schedule, so I have a lot of ground to cover. I have no time to be playing Ever's boyfriend, even though it feels fucking incredible to be guarding her door, ready to take on anything and anyone who comes through.

She's looking for someone to take this job. Actively looking. I've seen the proof. There are dates scheduled. And I'm getting ready to leave for the final time. It's the right decision, even if it makes me ache. Makes me ill and dizzy and anxious.

Every muscle in my body jumps at once and I surge off the stool, going into the kitchen to make coffee, trying to occupy my frustrated energy. There are Tupperware containers all over the counter, packed with cookies and little yellow bars with white frosting. I pop one open but shut the lid like a guilty child when Ever walks out of the bathroom . . . and *ohhhhhh shit.*

"You can have one, Charlie." She twists her hair up in a big, floppy bun. "You can have anything you want."

The words, the way she says them, are completely bright and innocent. But nothing is occurring to my brain on an innocent level, with her in those shorts. They're like underwear, they're so tiny. So, so tiny and tight. Kind of like Ever.

Clearing my throat, I turn back around, blocking my lap from her view. "Are these, uh . . . lemon?"

Ever comes up beside me and Jesus, the shirt is worse. It's loose, with cut-off sleeves, because she's so cool, and her tits jiggle when she walks. "*Fresh* lemon. Made them this morning. They go great with coffee. Want some?"

"Sure."

She opens the fridge and bends down, showing off the beautiful curve of her ass, and my mouth literally drops open, hanging there. I'm the saddest, horniest man on the face of planet Earth. Look. Even her little ass cheeks are popping out the bottom of the material. It's so mean and hot. "You want cream?"

"What?" I rasp, my balls tightening.

Her toes wiggle beneath the fridge door. "Do you want cream in your coffee?"

"Yeah, sure." I brace myself on the counter, trying to pull my shit together. Christ, I've been inside this girl dozens of times and I've never been this desperate for her. It's because I can't see her anymore. It's because I watched her run away from me tonight and I'm still reeling. We're getting in too deep. This has to stop or we're going to get tangled up again.

She's going to get hurt, and I'll hate myself forever for it.

Nina walks out, wrapped in a robe. Her knowing gaze passes between me and Ever—and those shorts—putting a smirk on her face. But it vanishes when there's a loud bang on the door. Ever slams her head on one of the refrigerator shelves, and I stop to kiss the spot she's rubbing on my way to the door, natural as breathing, but my blood pressure is spiking like a football. "It's probably the locksmith, but stay in the kitchen. Just in case."

"*Nina!*"

"Just kidding, it's your ex." Both girls go wide-eyed. They're nervous in their own home, and that fact causes anger to belt me across the middle. At least until Ever pulls a knife out of the chopping block and batter's up, taking the bluntest edges off my rage. "Whoa. Good thought." I take her arm and lower it, unable to resist kissing her nose. "But let's see if we can handle this peacefully first."

Yeah. Right.

Giving them what I hope is a reassuring look, I cross to the door and glance through the peephole, long enough to determine the guy is drunk and talking to himself. He's also attempting to slide his key into the lock, which makes me really grateful I'm there—enough to make my knees feel like jelly for a few counts—because the chain on the door is weak at best, so he could've gotten in pretty easily. Before the cops had time to arrive. Quietly as possible, I disengage the flimsy chain, flip the deadbolt . . . and then I sneak attack the motherfucker.

My fists are twisted in his collar and we're across the hallway before he even knows the door is open. "Drop your keys. Do it now."

"What?" Metal hits the floor with a satisfying series of clanks. "Who are *you*?"

"I'm . . ." Ever's friend? Ever's boyfriend? Ever's nothing? "It's complicated." I strengthen my grip. "But let me explain to you what *isn't* complicated. This is your last time in this building." I let that sink in. "You're going to take your girl-pushing ass down the stairs, Uber back to 450 East Twentieth Street—that's right, I know your address—and never come near Ever or Nina again. Not even *once*. Or next time, I won't just send flowers while your new girlfriend is over, I'll send an army of strippers who all know you by name."

Spittle is rattling out the sides of his mouth. "That was you who sent the flowers?"

"Hell yeah, it was me." I examine him like he's a bug under a microscope. "I know your face now, too. And I don't fucking like it. How about you? Do you like it or should I rearrange it a little?"

"I-I like it."

"Guess that makes one of us." I release him with a shove in the direction of the staircase. "You've got ten seconds to hit the street before I change my mind about letting you off with a warning. One . . . two . . ."

He stands there looking dumbfounded for a few counts before throwing a final longing glance at the apartment door and taking off, calling me some pretty creative names under his breath. I scoop up the keys, tucking them into my pocket, and wait until I hear the downstairs door slam. To be honest, I'm disappointed he didn't protest a little more, because my blood is buzzing like a pissed-off swarm of bees.

It doesn't help when I walk back into the apartment, finding the girls crowded by the slightly open door. Nina looks relieved, patting me on the shoulder. But Ever . . .

She backs up a few feet, her face flushed, pupils dilated . . . and I know that look. I counted on that look for months. It says, *you're about to get laid so hard.* God, I want it. Want her. *Need* her. The need doesn't care that I'm supposed to be resisting her at all costs, though. And I have serious fucking doubts about my willpower to resist.

CHAPTER 20

Ever

Sweet Mother Mary.

I'm not into stroking men's egos. I am *not* a damsel in distress. Seriously, if Nina's ex had walked through the door and tried to hurt my friend, I would have shanked that fool. No hesitation. I don't need a man to fight my battles for me. But damn if my ovaries aren't lit up like the New York skyline on New Year's Eve. I'm not just burning up with lady fever because Charlie manhandled that jerk in the hallway and sent him running with his tail between his legs. No, it's a combination of *that*, his comforting manner with Nina and the way he rushed us out of Webster Hall tonight. Whether I like it or not, Charlie was a certified knight in shining armor, and I want to . . . reward him. I want to reward him good. From here until next Tuesday.

It's not wise. At all. I'm in love with Charlie Burns and he's made it clear, in so many ways, that he's not available. When we were dancing tonight, I felt him holding back. Trying to keep a separation between us. Even now, his gaze rakes over me, burning hot, but hesitant. Wary. I'm so lost here. I *need* him, I miss him, but I know I'll be continually devastated every time he leaves. When I told him I wanted something real, I meant it. Something real isn't possible with Charlie. But is something real possible with anyone else *but* him?

"I'm going to give you two a minute," Nina says, backing toward her bedroom. "I'll hear the lock-smith when he knocks."

"Yeah," Charlie responds, his voice like gravel as he digs out the keys from his pocket. He tosses them on the counter without looking. "Those are his keys, but let's get the cylinder changed, any-way, on the off chance he made a copy, all right?"

How dare he be this *capable*? I think that's how I'm staring at him. Like I'm pissed at him for be-ing so competent. "You okay, Nina?" I ask, sound-ing breathless.

"Oh, after that?" Her laugh follows her into the bedroom. "I'm walking on air."

When the door closes behind my roommate, it's

like a powder keg goes off between Charlie and me, sparks, smoke, internal *booms*. We edge closer on the balls of our feet, both of us breathing like we just ran up eight flights of stairs. "Ever." His voice is hoarse. "Stop looking at me like that."

I just want to hear him describe *anything* in that tone. "Like what?"

"Don't do this to me. It isn't fair to either of us." Expression agonized, he points to the kitchen counter. "I'm not leaving you like that again."

"Then stay." The words are out before I can put the kibosh on them. And I don't want to take them back, because this is it. I love this man and I have to take a shot. This is the moment I've been given, and I can't let it slip away without trying. "Stay one time. It probably won't work. Or maybe it won't be so bad."

An eyebrow lifts. "You ever think of going into sales?"

I don't answer. I just wait there, in that nonspace between the entry and the living room, which is fitting, since we are neither here nor there. Charlie rolls his tongue around his mouth, hands propped on his hips, like I just asked him to join me in a hot air balloon to China. He's going to say no. There's already a gaping wound in my stomach where his answer will settle, my intestines wrapping around it, welcoming it as a permanent part of my landscape. So I jump the gun, because I can't stand to hear him decline. What was I thinking, anyway? Bad idea. Such a *stupid* idea.

I force my mouth into a smile. "God, Charlie. You look like you're trapped in a nightmare." My throat is raw as I slip past him and open the door. "Thanks for everything tonight—you were truly heroic. I must really need some sleep or I wouldn't have asked you to—"

"Ever."

"We have a job tomorrow, which means vodka was probably a bad choice." I curve a hand around his elbow and attempt to guide him through the open door. "Good night, Charlie."

"You just asked me to stay the night, now you're throwing me out?" A line forms between his eyebrows, and he presses the door closed. "I just needed a minute to think."

"About what?"

Why am I whispering? I don't have time to consider it, because Charlie saunters into my space. Right up into my zone. Until the tips of his boots nudge my bare toes. "Making love to you. That's what I'm thinking about." He wraps a hand around the back of my neck and I swear, I almost faint. "Not fucking. Not this time. So when I leave in the morning, Ever, you'll know it's always been more with you."

"Oh." Still whispering. "Well . . . think away."

His lips twitch, then the room tilts, because Charlie is carrying me toward my bedroom. My bedroom. We're going inside for the first time. I don't even know if it's clean enough, but after a slight hesitation on the threshold, we walk inside and I'm relieved to see it's decent. Still holding me against his solid chest, Charlie turns in a circle, kicking the door shut behind him. His blue eyes seem to light on everything at once, cataloguing my knick-knacks, memorizing pictures and perfume bottles and the pictures of exotic vacation ideas pinned to my wall.

His attention lands back on me, dark and hot, as he allows me to slide to the floor. My breath hitches in and out as I pad over to the iPhone dock sitting in my windowsill and turn on some music. "Roses" by The Chainsmokers is the last song I listened to and the singer's voice drifts into the room now, dreamlike and smoky. In the window's reflection, I watch Charlie approach me from behind, dragging the T-shirt over his head, his gaze so focused on me, I can't imagine living in a time where he'd left. Or never been here at all.

His palms slide over my hips, thumbs digging in with delicious pressure, that mouth of his finding the Promised Land behind my ear. Making love. He said we're going to make love. That doesn't mean he *loves* me, though.

Charlie's tongue swirls at the back of my neck

and drags higher, up my nape. "What exactly does making love . . . entail?" I ask.

A puff of his breath inspires goosebumps all over my flesh. "We're going to have to find out together, cutie." His hands catch in the hem of my shirt, lifting it over my head, barely breaking in his relentless torture of my neck as he bares me from the waist up. "A lot of kissing, I think. Slowing down to catch our breath once in a while, instead of racing each other to the end." I feel his lips quirk in my hair. "Gazing into one another's eyes."

My ribs ache from trying to subdue my laughter. "That sounds horrible."

He palms my breasts, squeezing them lightly, then harder. "We'll figure out our own way." Finally, his lap pushes against my backside and we both moan, grinding our lower bodies together, slow, but firm. "Your little 'Jenny from the Block' dance made me stiff as a board tonight. Safe to say you redeemed yourself for that talent show."

I half laugh, half gasp, the muscles between my legs contracting, wetness dampening my thong. "Just because we're making love . . . does that mean I can't put you in my mouth?" I slide a hand back between our bodies, rubbing his erection through the rough denim. "Seems only fair, since it's my fault."

"Like I said," Charlie groans into my ear. "We'll figure out our own way."

The way we move, it's fluid and frantic, all at once. Charlie spins me around and I drop to my knees, both of us working on his zipper. I haven't given him head in weeks, but he's not the only one who has suffered the loss. Oh no. Charlie doesn't kick back and enjoy the show. He flat out loses his mind when I go down on him, like he's a virgin freshman getting sucked off by a high school senior. It's why I love doing it. Love licking his plump, smooth head and watching his thighs start to tremble, the way they're doing now. The veins on his lower abdomen grow prominent, his stomach heaving, choked noises falling out of his mouth. It's heaven.

"Put your hands on my head, Charlie," I murmur. "Hold tight."

He releases a string of gibberish, but does what I ask and holds his breath.

I rake my teeth up the inside of his strong, hairdusted thigh. "You have five minutes to do whatever you want with my mouth. Don't hold back."

A strangled laugh from above. "You think I can last five minutes in your mouth? That's pretty cute." Our eyes meet as I circle his tip with my tongue. "You've been watching too much porn, Ever?"

I know what he's thinking about, just from the way he tilts his head. As if he's issuing a reprimand. And oh boy, from down on my knees, it's *really* working for me.

"Yeah, I know what you watch when I'm not around." His right hand leaves my head, sliding around the base of his erection. Gripping. And everything south of my belly button clenches when he strokes, strokes, strokes. A feast right in front of my eyes. "Love that, don't you?" He grunts. "You said anything I want? Good. Wrap your little mouth around it and taste me jerking off."

As if I'm not diving forward to follow his instructions—which coincide perfectly with my fantasies—Charlie uses his hold on my hair to guide me, to hold me in place while he chokes his flesh, squeezing the root and dragging his grip toward my mouth. Faster, faster. Because this is Charlie, though, and Charlie can't maintain his composure while I'm pleasuring him from my knees, he lets go after a dozen strokes, in favor of thrusting into my mouth. He knows he can. Knows I love it.

His fingers tangle in my hair, a sheen of sweat beginning to form on his chest and abs, his flesh elongating and pulsing on my tongue. God, he's hotter than sin. I can't handle it. The seam of my shorts is drenched and I want them off, I want him inside me so bad, I'm moaning as he pushes deep into my throat, growling my name from above.

"Ever. *Ever.* Baby. Cutie. *Stopstopstopstopstop.*" He draws my mouth away, which makes a popping sound—another weakness of his—and he's helpless against sinking past my lips with a roll of his hips. His head falls back, chin dropping, thighs trembling, sweat rolling down his chest. "Little more, little more. *Fuuuuuuck.* Please don't let me come. It hurts. Lick my cock and taste how bad. Get a good taste of how you make it hurt. Need to fuck. Need to come."

Those words signal his breaking point. We trust one another not to push past that invisible marker, so I sit back, watching his wet inches strain against his thigh. Charlie scoops me up from beneath my arms, takes a few steps and throws me on the bed, which normally would have made me die laughing, but there's nothing funny about the way he stalks me. It's not just lust bathing his expression, either, it's something heavier, but elusive.

He kneels between my legs, and I only have a split second to appreciate his dewy muscles, the boy-next-door-who-got-in-a-fist-fight beauty, before the shorts are ripped down past my ankles. They remain hooked on one of Charlie's fingers as he holds them up, his expression the epitome of disapproval. "These are not an appropriate choice when a locksmith is coming over." He tosses them over his shoulder. "Save the sanity of the male population and start shopping in the big girl section, huh, cutie?"

CHAPTER 21
Charlie

Yeah. I barely got away with that one.

When a woman kneels and gives a man carte blanche with her mouth, it takes him a few minutes to come down, though, so sue me. Because she's Ever and she understands I'm not a complete asshole, she only gives me a lazy middle finger and stretches out on the bed like a cat. She throws her arms up over her head and arches her back, giving me the view of the century. Her pussy is barely covered by a peach-colored thong, with a little white bow on the super-low waistline. Those sugar-flavored tits are out. I could drag her under me, shove those pretty panties to one side and fuck her until she starts screaming for divine intervention. God knows my cock is begging for its usual rough, filthy, pounding session.

Whatever this feeling is inside me, though? This full, crowded, choking feeling? It's asking for something else.

It knows Ever needs more, so there's no option but to give it to her. Maybe it's danger that has me strangled right now by her beauty. Not just her body, which, let's face it, is an eleven. But it's the way she watches me, as if she's reading my thoughts and doesn't find fault with a single one. She knows not only me . . . but she knows *us*. She knows us together. That's the danger. I've found someone who could be my other half. I'm going to make love to her. And I have no idea what comes afterward anymore.

Ever pushes up on one elbow, blonde hair draping across one shoulder. "Charlie," she breathes, her eyes feverish. "I need you."

"Fuck, I need you, too," I say, all pretenses dropped. There's no place for them between Ever and me. Not here in the dark when we're in a bed together for the first time and my heart is tapping out Morse code at warp speed. I hook a finger in her thong and slide it down, down, licking my lips at the sight of her naked pussy, all slick and ready. Ready to take her man. There's a little freckle on her stomach I never noticed before and following instinct, I lean down to kiss it now, sliding my tongue into the hoop of her belly button ring for good measure. Tugging just a little. Listening to her gasp, while I roll the condom down to the root of my dick. "Christ." I shake my head, letting every thought in my head tumble out. "I can still see you running away from me tonight." It's there every time I close my eyes. The reminder has me looming over Ever, taking her arms and securing them above her head. "Someone bumped into you and you stumbled . . . and then I couldn't see you anymore."

"You were angry with me," she breathes, her toes sliding up and down my calves. "Maybe you shouldn't think about it right now, since you're supposed to be making love to me."

I lean down close and nip her bottom lip, making her gasp. "Maybe we make angry love."

"That doesn't sound like us."

Us. A wrench twists in my chest. Why do I keep seeing her disappearing into the crowd? Over and over. What if I'd never met her? Never became friends with her? No one would have texted me tonight. I wouldn't even have *known* she was in trouble. I'm setting myself up for a lifetime of not knowing what happens to Ever.

I shove my face into her neck and inhale, trying to break free of my dark thoughts, but they won't go. My frustration is manifesting itself in my bones, my throat, the dead center of my stomach. "No one is going to call me next time, goddammit, are they?" Not giving her a chance to answer, I bare my teeth against her lips and they open for me. The taste of her knocks me back into the light . . . until I realize I'm trying to get my fill. Get my fill of Ever. And that becomes my quest, in that moment. Store up enough of this insane way she makes me feel, so I can survive on the fumes as long as possible.

My body moves all on its own, dragging up and down her curves. We're synced flesh, rippling like an ocean current, her knees writhing like waves on either side of my hips. I'm not even inside her yet, and we're moving like I'm balls deep. *Yes*. It's not dry humping, because Jesus *fuck*, she's drenched and getting that wetness all over me.

"First time you let me bring you home, I couldn't believe you were real," I groan, my head tipped forward over her bouncing tits. "Still don't. Still can't. You know how I'm going to move before I get there. How do you do it?"

"M-me? I thought it was you." We breathe a laugh into one another's mouth . . . and ten tons of emotion slams into me. *I miss her.* How do I miss her when she's close as another human being can possibly get? I need an outlet, I need the *next thing*, or I'm going to swallow her whole. Gathering her legs up around my waist, I punch my hips and drive the full way into Ever's tight pussy with one thrust. *"Charlie."*

"God. God, Ever." I flex my ass, pushing, trying

to find a corner of her I haven't yet occupied, but I've got her crammed full. Every time I move, she whimpers and spreads her legs wider, my ultimate fantasy. Except every single moment we've been together like this, she's gotten better and my imagination can't compete anymore. It was laughable, this idea that we could make love. The base of my spine is splintering, spasming with the need to bury myself in her, again and again. A hard, slapping pace that we'll both race to keep up with.

No. No, I promised her something better. How, though. How? I don't know the first thing about making Ever feel special. Which is why I shouldn't have chased her in the first place, after she decided to move forward with her life. I was so goddamn selfish, but I couldn't help myself. She's . . . Ever.

Her fingers lace through my hair, her walls tighten around my cock and I'm drowning in the urge to claim her, while battling the responsibility to honor her in some way. The way I should have been doing all along. "Charlie." She shhh's against my mouth. "Everything is going to be fine. Just kiss me slow."

I'm not sure I can manage to feel her tongue and go anything but fast, but she opens her lips, squeezes my hair in two fists . . . and slants my head, directs me. She's saving me. A life preserver in a storm. I've been in this storm for days—I was barely surviving until now. But what about to-morrow?

"Ever . . ." I rasp, licking at her top lip. "More." My hips rear back and roll forward. "Give me more of that. Need more of everything you got."

Same way we do everything, what happens next is instinctual. Ever's hand puts pressure on my shoulder, but I'm already rolling onto my back, my spine curving like it's going to snap. She's never moved on top of me like this. Like she's riding a mechanical bull in slow motion. Tweaking her hips back until she's dancing on my tip, swiv-eling her hips on the way down, rubbing her clit on the thickest part of my root. I'm turned on out of my mind, because that place where we're joined is so fucking wet, I know she's hot for an orgasm. Needs it. But she wants the build.

Jesus, I want it too. I need her mouth. I want all of her against me, so I don't miss a single shudder or gasp or bead of sweat. Jackknifing into a sitting position, I band an arm around her waist, pump-ing my hips in that same deliberate, but filthy grind. "Put your hands on top of your head," I growl against her mouth. Her wet, swollen mouth. "Take all that hair and get it up. Let me see your neck. Need to see every part of you."

Her face tips up toward the ceiling on a moan, her body riding mine in long, hot glides. Those hands of hers shake as she gathers her blonde strands, making a mess of it on top of her head. "Charlie, it hurts," she whines. I *live* for that whine. "I can't last."

This is the other reason I wanted her hands on her head. Her nipples shake when she comes and now they're right there, swaying in front of my mouth like God's gift to man. We might be making love, but I still lap at her tits like a filthy beggar, sucking them deep into my mouth, batting them with my tongue. "Somewhere along the line, you became mine, didn't you, Ever? *Didn't you?*" My own release is building, snatching away any control I have over my mouth, my actions. "I've been writing my name on every part of you. Knew it and couldn't stop it. Couldn't help it since day one. Mine, mine, mine."

The muscles in my stomach start to contract, twisting and knitting into a pattern old as humankind, but new and fresh every time with this woman. Looking down, I watch her take my cock in and out, faster now. Faster. Her hands are still locked together on top of her head, making her look like a prisoner. My prisoner. Except, I'm *hers*. This whole time I thought our lack of commitment was setting me free, but in truth, she'd thrown away the key to my freedom the minute she opened her mouth. She didn't mean it, my Ever, but I'm imprisoned forever, just the same.

Her pussy tightens like a fist on me, telling

me the end is coming. I suck her nipple into my mouth the second tremors begin to rack her body, her hips pumping overtime, her lips busy on my face, in my hair. Kissing, gasping, kissing.

"Charlie." Her voice vibrates, catches. "Stay, stay, stay."

My heart hurtles into my throat and expands to eight times its normal size. "I'm not going anywhere." *Not tonight.* We grit one another's name as she bears down, working out the last drop of her climax—and then I'm on top again. Mindless. Living for my next thrust. "Pull me in tight. Help me get so deep. *Help me.*"

Ever's fingernails dig into the flesh of my ass, yanking me toward the wet goddamn paradise of her hot, little pussy. Our damp skin smacks together, both of us moaning loud enough to drown out the music, the groaning bedsprings. I can't keep my mouth off of her. It's sucking on her neck, attacking her lips, raking over her ear and whispering filthy words, praising words. A rushing sound is blaring in my head like static. I need to come. Need to come. But this could be the last time with Ever and I hear the sounds I'm making. Like a wounded animal. A desperate idiot.

I'm holding on until I can't anymore.

"You're disappearing into the crowd again, Ever," I say against her mouth, even though the words were meant to be contained in the whirling shit show inside my head. "You won't ever get hurt, as long as I'm breathing. I'll know if you're in trouble, won't I? I'll know and I'll come get you. You'll let me, won't you?" My lungs are drained, my body falling into the abyss, driving into my home, again, again, again. "Say yes, say yes, say yes. Don't take that away from me."

"Yes." Ever's thighs hug my waist, the miracle of her hands helping me grind out my peak. My hips are moving in a jagged, unpredictable rhythm, but Ever knows exactly when to lift, when to squeeze. When to lie still and let me pummel her with rough pushes of my draining cock. "Yes, Charlie," she cries into my shoulder. "*Yes.*"

But when I fall on top of her a moment later, sweat sliding off our skin into the bedclothes, I wrap my arms around her. I hold tight. And I swear, I can still feel her vanishing. *No.*

Ever must sense my struggle, because she finds a way to save the moment. Make it last forever. Lip caught between her teeth, she eases out from beneath me and flings a hand out to some nearby surface, bringing back her phone. Then she takes a picture of us together where we gasp, side by side, on the pillows. The picture I asked her for that day we kissed in the park hits my phone across the room a few seconds later. We meet eyes . . . and she's so beautiful, I never want to look away.

I'm not sure I can anymore.

CHAPTER 22

———— *Ever* ————

I've never experienced this floating feeling. It's not like the buzz that comes after one glass of wine, or the post-tequila shot fizzy lift. This post-sex, presleep period is a notch in the space-time continuum where everything outside the bed is just old *Friends* reruns and loathsome responsibilities. There's no reason to leave. Ever. Especially when Charlie's hand creeps across the bed and our fingers slide into a smooth, woven pattern, totally singular to us.

On the street outside my building, the sounds of Manhattan ensue. Metal gates being pulled down over storefronts. Hot dog carts lumbering down the sidewalk to whatever magical land they disappear to overnight. Cabs tapping their horns.

Inside, though, it's just breathing. Music still

drifts from my iPhone into the room's darkness, artificial light seeping in through my blinds to highlight the sheen of sweat cooling on our bodies. I've never felt closer or further away from anyone in my life as I do with Charlie right now. It's almost like we're on two different ships, both standing on the ends of a plank, facing one another. One of us need only take one step, climb onto the other's plank and be taken into the safety of the ship, but the tide keeps bobbing up and down, keeping the elusive something we're seeking *just* out of reach.

Here in reality, though, we're in my bed holding hands. And I'm trying really hard to be content with that. Something happened between us when Charlie was inside me. It's never been like that before. Intense, desperate, raw. He's still here, too, his fingers wrapped tightly around mine.

What happens next? Do we spoon? I can almost hear Charlie asking himself the same question in some discombobulated inner male dialogue. Truthfully, I would die to have Charlie pull me back against his chest, curving his warm body around mine. I would die to fall asleep with his deep breaths in my hair. Of course I want those things from the man I'm in love with. *Of course.*

Have I decided to be Charlie's friend with benefits? To attempt baby steps with him, like spending the night and holding hands . . . and hope for the best? No. I've made no decisions or devised any plans. I'm only living in the world of tonight. The world where Charlie spends the night in my bed and I don't have to say goodbye while my heart is still racing from sex. Maybe I'm just hoping the universe tilts and rights itself, doing me a solid, so I can continue having this man in my life without experiencing any of the pain.

"Ever," Charlie murmurs into the darkness. "Do you ever think back to when you were . . . I don't know, seventeen? And do you remember how positive you were at seventeen that you had everything sort of figured out? You thought there's no way I can speak to people better than I do now, or be more self-aware . . ."

"No way I can drive more efficiently or understand stand-up comedy better . . ."

His laugh drifts across the bed and curls up in my ear. "How did I know you would understand?" My heart squeezes, but I don't answer. "So even though we look back and know damn well at seventeen we were still learning, here we are at twenty-three, thinking the exact same way. We have it all figured out."

"And you wonder if, when we're thirty, we'll look back and shake our heads."

"Exactly."

"I know we will." I turn onto my side, yawning into the pillow. "The good news is, we never would have had this conversation when we were seventeen. We didn't have the hindsight yet. The fact that we have it now . . . that has to be progress. And admitting the problem is the first step, right?"

"Yeah." He rolls onto his side, too, bringing our faces mere inches apart. "Or . . . doing something again and again while expecting a different result is the definition of insanity. I guess it depends how you look at it."

"I like the progress version better than the we're insane version."

His lips tilt up, but his eyes are serious. "I don't want to turn thirty and wonder what the fuck was wrong with me at twenty-three." The muscles in his throat slide up and down, his hands tightening around mine. "You know what I mean, cutie?"

My body tenses, every pulse point ticking like a clock in hyper drive. What is he saying? That he wants to pursue an actual relationship, so he doesn't regret letting what we have fall by the wayside when he's older? *Or.* Or is he telling me he doesn't want to saddle himself with a girl, because he might regret it when he rounds the corner into his fourth decade? His eyes . . . it's hard to tell in the near dark, but I think they're apologetic. Oh God. Asking him to stay was a mistake. This is his exit strategy. "Y-yeah, I know what you mean." I try to take my hand back, but he holds tight, his brow furrowing. "It's scary to think decisions you make at twenty-three could . . . put you off course—"

"Right. I think. There's more than one course, though, right?" He goes up on an elbow, so he's staring down into my face. The intensity of his concentration momentarily steals my breath, so I can't dissect the doubts sprinting through my mind. "You can't focus so much on one course, you forget the one running alongside it. Through it." He gives a nervous laugh, but once again, his eyes are laser focused. "I'm not sure we're on the same page here, Ever."

"What page are you on?" I whisper, scared to find out. Relieved I'll finally know what he's thinking. Polarized by the possibility of change. Loss. All of the above.

The music cuts out as my phone starts to ring across the room.

Which is the shittiest timing on the planet.

Especially because Charlie is breathing heavily—so am I—and we're staring at one another in the darkness, like two people who left a costume party together and just removed our masks for the first time. I can barely move or blink, I'm so consumed by the way he's looking at me. But a memory from earlier today intrudes, and I have no choice but to go answer the phone.

"That's my mother's ringtone," I say, remembering how optimistic she'd looked today. Just for a hint of time. "I—she was going out tonight, and it was my idea. I just need to make sure she's all right."

Charlie nods, but I can see he's frustrated by the interruption. "That's fine. I'm not going anywhere."

"Okay." I let go of his hand and slip from the bed, stooping down to drag on my underwear and discarded shorts. By the time I reach the phone, it's ringing for the second time, causing panic to slither into my chest. *Crap.* What if something bad happened on her night out, setting her way back . . . and it was my idea. "Mother?" I answer. "Is everything okay?"

"Yes. *Better* than okay." Her enthusiasm, though restrained, reaches out and grabs me through the phone. "I did what we spoke about. I put on the green dress and went out to a singles mixer I overheard my coworkers babbling about. And it was awful. It was just *awful*."

In the window, I watch Charlie climb out of bed and approach me, his cock halfway to hard again, rebounding off his upper thigh with each step. A distraction for the freaking record books, but I command myself to focus on my mother's words, even as Charlie's hands settle on my hips, his lips pressing a kiss onto my shoulder. "If it was so awful . . ." I inhale through my nose, out through my mouth. "Why are you laughing?"

"Because it was *fun*, Ever." Her high heels hit the floor in the background. "Once I got over the tacky décor and the terrible music, I just . . . talked to the people around me. I even danced a little. With men *and* women."

A little sound bubbles up and out of my mouth, heat pressing behind my eyes. I've never heard my mother like this. Never heard excitement in her voice before. Not unless it was for show. The dazzle in her voice now is genuine. And we're sharing this moment together. "That's amazing, Mother. It was really brave of you."

"Oh, *pshh*. Enough about me." Clatters ping down the line, and I envision her removing bangles and earrings, setting them on her dresser. Charlie's tongue slides up my neck, clenching muscles I thought were retired for the night. I can see in the window, his eyes are shut tight, as if he's savoring the taste of me, though, and I'm prepared to lose as much sleep as necessary. But I do my best to focus on my mother as her upbeat flow of words continues in my ear. "I saw all these lovely people coupling up and thought, I hope my daughter can have that. Someone to come home to every night. Someone who will put her first and always be there." She laughs. "Even if it's just to listen to Adele and drink mediocre champagne."

Charlie's mouth stops moving. His eyes meet mine in the window, and I see devastation there. Just for a flash, but the impact is jarring, even if I'm uncertain what's behind it. "I, um . . ."

"Ever, we're so alike, you and I." A creaking in the background, like bedsprings. "Maybe you could have gone on happily following the rules. Being the second most important thing in a man's life, one month at a time. But I'm here to tell you, the happiness doesn't last. You'll slowly start to believe second place is where you belong." Her sigh finds my ear, just as Charlie's hands drop from my waist, his forehead landing in the crook of my neck. "I know it's early, but . . . well, have you met anyone worth gossiping about? Give me *something*. I just want to know you're trying and you weren't . . . affected by my example, Ever."

My breath catches when Charlie grinds his head into my neck, and I know he can hear every word of the conversation. What am I supposed to say? Yes, I met someone and fell in love, but I had to *convince* him to stay one single night? Isn't that the opposite of what she wanted for me? "I . . . uh . . ." Charlie's heat leaves me. With one last ravaged glance at me through the window, he turns his back and walks away. I'm left standing there, like a flag left out in the middle of a winter storm, rippling in turbulent gusts of wind. "I danced with some nice guys, Mother. Just like you." Invisible bolts turn on either side of my windpipe. "It was good. I'm going to keep trying, and I've got that date with the fireman—"

"Right." I can see her stilted nod. "As long as you're trying. You did so much to encourage me, and I just want to do the same. I've never been very supportive, and I'm so sorry. You . . . you really have no idea."

"It's okay, Mother," I manage. This is what I wanted. A reason to bond with my mother. Something to draw her interest and make her proud of me. It's everything I hoped for, isn't it? Yes. In a sense. We're chatting on the phone and she's apologizing to me, thanking me. I never actually thought it was possible. But I can't shake the feeling I just sacrificed Charlie. Which is ridiculous, right?

I'll know if you're in trouble, won't I? I'll know and I'll come get you. You'll let me, won't you? Didn't those words imply he won't be here with me, unless I needed him? God, part of me wants to cling to that promise and accept it, but it won't be enough. I wouldn't only be disappointing my mother, I would be letting myself down.

"I'm glad you had a good night." I turn to see

Charlie sitting on the edge of my bed, hands clasped between his legs. Staring at the floor. "I'll talk to you soon."

"Good night, Ever."

I disconnect the call and set down my phone. The room is dead silent, except for the gentle hum of traffic passing by outside and Nina opening the door for the locksmith. When Charlie holds out a hand to me, I go forward and take it. He pulls me down into the mess of bedclothes, fitting my butt against his lap. I swear to God, I don't hear him breathe once until we're wrapped up tight, my head using his right bicep as a pillow, his opposite arm tucking me close. So close, my eyes burn. And then he breathes. Long, winded, agonized. Final.

Without saying a word, he's just told me this is the first and last night he'll be spending in my bed.

Charlie

I just ran eight miles. Now I'm sitting in the deserted locker room beneath shower spray, letting it run down my face, my body. The gurgle of the drain is all I hear, but at least it's keeping me company. I appreciate the gurgle. It's helping to distract from the sound of Ever's apartment door clicking shut behind me when I left her Wednesday morning. She didn't wake up to see me out or give me a goodbye kiss. Or maybe she was feigning sleep. I don't know. I don't know anything anymore.

We had an advanced gun safety demonstration today, and it ended four hours ago. I'd needed exertion, though. More than that. I needed to deplete every store of energy inside me, so I wouldn't break down.

A humorless laugh leaves my mouth. I'm sitting on the nasty ass floor in the locker room and I have no idea how long I've been here. If this isn't a breakdown, I have no idea what the fuck one looks like.

I miss her. I miss her. I miss her. I miss her.

My hands fly up, forming a vise around my head. Like they can squeeze out the misery of walking away from Ever. Permanently? Yeah. It has to be this way. Or we're doomed to repeat the pattern set out in front of us. Lived by our parents. I won't neglect her. I won't let her be second place. She deserves the moon, the sun and stars. I could only give her late-night phone calls saying I'm going to be home late. Worry. Cancelled reservations. A cold side of the bed alongside her warm one. Anything less than one hundred percent focus on Ever and our relationship would be unacceptable. It's all I have to offer, though. Less than she deserves.

So she'll meet someone who recognizes he's hit the motherfucking lottery. And that guy will give her mornings in bed, trips out of town . . . fuck. FUCK. Children? I don't know. She's so young, but I can't imagine a man not begging to start a family with Ever. To see her reproduced in any way possible. I would have, wouldn't I? Yeah . . . hell yeah. Once I got stationed and Hot Damn started expanding, I could see it. Ever pursing her lips, reading the notecards stuck on the tree I gave her, a little belly peeking out the bottom of her shirt.

In my daydream, another man walks up behind her. Smiling. Asking what she's cooking. While she's reading my notecard tree.

My shout ricochets off the tile walls of the showers. I roll over onto my knees, pressing my face into the draining water. I'm probably catching malaria, and I don't even give a shit. Bring it on. Maybe it'll put me into a coma and I won't have to spend another minute wondering what I'm missing. What I'll be missing for the rest of my life.

Ever. Ever. Ever. Ever.

Why, God. Why did I spend the night? I would have been a pitiful excuse for a man, rolling around in piss germs, even if I'd left her apartment Tuesday night. But I wouldn't have the added mind fuck of knowing how she talks in her sleep. Talks *to me*. Sometime around three in the morning, she'd snuggled her face into my chest and murmured, *"Charlie, you were mean to farmers at the farmer's market. Bad Charlie."* Proving she was aware of me mad dogging the guy who'd sold her bok choy, but didn't even mention it. Proving she is the coolest, most incredible unicorn of all unicorns. And I'm without her now. I'm forever without Ever.

"Wow." Danika's voice in the men's locker room isn't even enough to bring my face off the ground. "He's going to need a tetanus shot."

"Jesus." Jack. "This is how you earn the title patient zero."

"Fuck off. Please." I roll onto my side and listen to the comforting gurgle. "I don't need you to tell me I'm a mess."

Danika retreats into the main locker room and returns with a towel. She wades into the shower on her tiptoes, shuts off the water and throws the white terrycloth over my lower half. "There," she says. "Not that you don't have a lovely dick, but I have rules against ogling another woman's property."

"Thanks." I still can't find it in me to move. Maybe I'll just stay here the rest of my life. "But I'm not her property anymore. She was never mine, either."

Jack makes this noise, like he's been silent too long and the suppression of his almighty opinion has taken its toll. It's the equivalent of a bear waking up and growling after a long winter of hibernation. "Look, you know I'm the last one to give relationship advice, but you've been dating Ever since the beginning. Doesn't matter what enlightened bullshit you were calling it."

"No. They *weren't* dating," Danika enunciates. "Dating means bingeing on Netflix together. Awkward nights out with each other's friends. Having a song."

"Wait." I finally find the wherewithal to sit up. The towel slips off and Danika throws up her hands, clearly disgusted, but she's the one raining on my pity party so she can just deal with my junk. "We do have a song. 'My Type' by Saint Motel. We danced to it at the art function and again at Webster Hall. Technically, she did meet you guys, too. And it was awkward enough, right?"

"Not that awkward," Danika says. "She barely batted an eyelash when she walked in and saw Jack arm wrestling shirtless. I liked her."

"Why wouldn't you?" I pound my head backward into the tile wall. "She's amazing."

"What are you upset about? This is great news." Jack rubs imaginary dirt off his hands. "You were dating all along. Show up with a Netflix password and some wine. Get this shit sorted out by the weekend."

"You don't understand." The pounding starts up again in my temples. "If I was dating her, I had no right to. As soon as I take the exam, I'm going to be working around the clock." I shove both hands through my hair. "I could only spare her an hour a day before. Once I graduate? That hour is going to shrink down to nothing. I watched it . . ." I swallow hard. "I was young, but I think I watched it happen with my parents. I'm starting to remember more . . . about how unhappy it made my mother. She was lonely."

Danika and Jack are silent a moment, then both of them are in the shower, sitting down beside me. In their clothes. Danika lays the towel over my lap and puts an arm around my shoulder.

Jack does the same, his expression more serious than I've ever seen it. "Real talk, Burns. Tomorrow, I'm going to deny saying any of this and I'll never repeat it, so listen well." He squints one eye, like he's looking into the bottom of a bottle. "You come from a long line of legends. It's true. Your father is already in the history books, and he's still alive and kicking. Your brother scares everyone shitless, and he'd run headfirst into a shoot-out. Fine. These are all true facts. But you have something we—" he cuts a hand between himself and

Danika "—value in the Kitchen, more than brass and medals. You've got heart. Okay? So maybe you're not cut out for forty-eight-hour shifts and going home to an empty apartment, content just to be respected. Maybe you need more. And you're a shit ton smarter than me, so don't look this way if you want the solution." He elbows me hard in the ribs. "You'll come up with it yourself."

My throat feels hot, so I clear it. "Christ, Jack. You wait until my dick is out to be this sincere?" Our laughter helps, but we're still not looking each other in the eye. "I don't know if it works that way for me, but thanks for saying so."

"I've never been so relieved to be a woman." Danika's voice is dry. "But one-half of this emotionally stunted duo is right. Look at you, man. You're sitting here in piss and mildew, and she's probably home thinking about you. Right now."

I snort. "Yeah. Thinking about what an asshole I am for leaving before she even woke up." I tilt my head back on a disgusted laugh. "She doesn't even know the half of what I've done since she started dating other people. Screwing with her dates, letting her think I'm some guy named Reve and agreeing to meet her—"

Danika rears back. "Come again?"

I hold up a hand. "Trust me, I don't deserve her. Not even a little."

"So, figure out how to change that," Danika says, getting pissed. "You can't just—"

"*Charlie.*"

At the sound of Greer's voice, all three of our spines snap straight, gazes shooting to the shower entrance, where my brother stands. Looking more disheveled and haunted than I've ever seen him. Without a command from my brain, I gain my feet, wrapping the towel around my waist. "What is it? What happened?"

Funny how tragedies have a way of putting what's most important into perspective.

Okay, not funny at all.

CHAPTER 23

Ever

There is a sliver of time between four fifty and five P.M. in Manhattan that signals the yellow cab shift change. Day shift ends, meaning those drivers are no longer taking fares. And the night shifters are coming on, but they're all being swallowed up by people dipping out of work and beginning the daily rush hour hustle. Uber hasn't solved the lack of available hired transportation, either, because there are literally eight million people trying to get home at once, while service industry folks—like me and Nina—are moving our asses, trying to make it to dinner shifts in bars and restaurants.

We tried to get a cab and failed. Uber wanted to charge triple the fare, and it wasn't in our budget for the night. Not to mention, traffic is gridlocked and cabs can't fly, anyway. So Nina and I are currently on the rush hour 5 train, holding four refrigerated bags full of pies, trying to get uptown and deliver them on time. To a cigar and pies rooftop party. Because why not?

Ask me if I'm in the mood for this. Go ahead.

Realizing that I'm glaring at innocent people on the train, I let my eyelids drop.

Well. I'm *not* in the mood. My skin is itchy under the straps of my overall skirt. I'm running on about eight cups of coffee because I slept past my alarm, then baked a trillion pies, two of them with kale, three with cardamom—by request—and I have no patience for another passenger's armpit in my face. I think . . . I think I'm overwrought. That's what this urge to cry and scream and bite a stranger is defined as, right?

Worse, I've had this awful knot in my stomach since I woke up alone Wednesday morning. No trace of Charlie, apart from the scent he'd left behind on the pillow. The smell is fading, though. Fading fast. I had to battle the urge to crawl into one of the refrigerated bags earlier and zip it shut. Sunlight is bothering me. Silence, too. All the things I used to love are missing an ingredient. Charlie. His smile. That endearing mixture of cockiness and vulnerability. The way he rests his tongue on the inside of his bottom lip when I'm talking. He does it when he's dancing, too, so I know it's a sign of concentration, and I miss that little gesture so much. *So much.* And I know I'll move on to something else about him soon, missing it just as bad. Like the bump on his nose. Or the fact that sometimes he wears old-school white undershirts.

Tonight is my date with Reve S. Guy. I have no idea how I'm going to manage it. After spending the night with Charlie, feeling him kiss my hair and neck when he thought I was sleeping, seeing another man feels wrong. Horribly wrong. I keep expecting him to text me or show up unannounced, admitting he misses me too, but he doesn't. He won't. Every minute that goes by feels like a bad dream.

"Why don't you blow off the date tonight?" Nina suggests quietly, leaning against the silver pole we're both wedged against. "I don't see it going well when you're still—"

"I'm going." I give her an apologetic look for being short. For every time I've been short with her all day, really. "If I cancel this one, I'll cancel the next one. And . . . it's over with Charlie." Swallowing is a feat. "I don't know why I asked him to stay over. It just made everything harder, you know?"

Nina sighs when someone bumps her from behind. "You asked him, because it was natural. He should have been staying every night. From the start." She shakes her head. "I'd never really seen you two together until the night we went to Webster Hall and . . . wow. I don't think you realize the way you behave together."

Don't take the bait. Don't ask. "What way is that?"

Nina's mouth turns down at the corners, her eyes sad. "Like you're each waiting for the other to say goodbye, so you can fall apart. And that's a damn good indication you shouldn't say goodbye at all." The loud speaker comes on, announcing the next stop, static and squealing breaks making the audio impossible to hear. "I mean, I had my doubts about him after . . ."

When Nina trails off, I give her a curious look. "After what?"

She chews her lip a moment. "There's something I have to tell you, Ever. I really hope it doesn't make everything worse, but it's been killing me—"

The train jolts to a halt, flinging us back a few steps. Having no choice but to postpone the odd conversation or risk missing our stop, Nina and I heave the refrigerated bags onto our shoulders and push through the sea of grumbling passengers, dodging new riders already trying to wade into the train. As we lug the heavy bags up the steps, my muscles groan, but I'm distracted by what Nina needs to tell me. God, I really can't take any more bad news right now. I just want to deliver these pies, go home, get ready for my date and face it head-on. As long as I keep my head down and move, maybe there's a chance tomorrow I'll miss Charlie a smidgen less.

Not likely. Especially considering I start looking for him the moment we step above ground onto the sidewalk. Didn't I run into him in this neighborhood after speed dating a few weeks ago? Maybe . . .

My phone buzzes in my pocket. No way am I answering it right now. We're mere blocks from the drop-off site, and I'm loaded down like a freaking pack mule. But as Nina and I cross the busy intersection, pedestrians bottlenecking around us, my cell vibrates again. And again.

I stop outside the address, carefully setting down the bags and massaging my aching shoulders, Nina doing the same. "Someone keeps calling me," I say, while at the same time, Nina mutters, "About what I was saying on the train . . ."

A quick check of my phone, though, and my pulse drowns out everything but the vicious hammering in my blood. "Charlie. Charlie is calling me."

Nina cocks an eyebrow. "Are you going to answer it?"

"He's called me six times," I say, mostly to myself, hitting the green button. "Hello?"

"Ever." His voice is like churning gravel and I'm

immediately on alert, my fingers going icy around the phone. "I'm sorry to call you like this. I know I shouldn't."

The street traffic is so loud, I cup my hand over the receiver and move into the doorway. "What's wrong?"

"My father is in intensive care." A door slams on the other end of the line, voices follow. "He had a heart attack. During a media briefing. And . . . fuck, can you come to me?" There's a short pause during which I think my heart explodes into a million pieces, with worry, relief, urgency. "I need you. Christ, I need to see your face so bad." My breath rockets out of my lungs, leaving them depleted, my knees turning to vapor. "Lenox Hill, Ever. Will you come?"

Charlie

There's a loose thread in the waiting room carpet. It's squiggly and beige, just to the right of my boot. And I wonder if it's the one squiggly, beige thread that has gotten the most attention in the world, from shell-shocked family members needing something to focus on besides the waiting room door. I wouldn't notice it any other day, but kind of like the gurgling drain back in the locker room, it's reminding me I'm awake. Whether or not being lucid is a good thing? That's debatable.

My father was brought into the emergency room at Lenox Hill in critical condition. Me, Greer, Jack and Danika had to push through a sea of reporters to reach the entrance, some of them recognizing my brother, although they hadn't gotten a single word out of him. Nor had I. After he'd ordered the waiting room television shut off, he'd sat down across from me, stone-faced and eerily silent, where he still remains. My friends have gone off in pursuit of coffee, which I'm grateful for, because I can feel them watching me helplessly, but can't form the right responses to let them know I'm all right. I'm *not* all right.

Chief Xavier Burns is supposed to be immortal. It never really crossed my mind that he was human. Children are supposed to grow out of that belief regarding their parents long before now, but none of them were raised by my father. I've never seen him show a weakness and yet—until Greer had demanded they shut off the evening news—they continued to replay the footage of him collapsing. His face paling, that iron fist clutching at his chest, legs giving way. I'm never going to get the image out of my mind.

And I'm never going to forget what occurred to me after the doctors confirmed our father was still alive, still fighting. I'd thought, *we will all die. I could die. I will die.* Maybe it'll be seventy years from today, but it's going to happen. All the achievements and commendations and records my father has earned? They didn't mean anything when the EMTs loaded him onto the stretcher. He hadn't asked for his medals or appointment book. According to my father's assistant, he'd asked for his sons.

And he'd begged for his wife, who of course, no one knew how to reach.

Because she was long gone.

Hearing that, I'd called Ever before I registered the shaking phone in my hand, my fingers punching the wrong buttons eighty times until I finally got it right. So that's where I'm at right now. In this cold, lonely, terrified place. I'm praying to every god of every religious denomination that Ever walks through the waiting room door, so I can lock her in my arms and throw away the key. I don't want to beg for her on my death bed. I want her now. Want her every day. And I'm terrified that it's too late. If she's only coming to the hospital to be a good friend, I would completely understand. I haven't been worthy, but if she shows up, I swear to all the gods, I will die making up for it.

The waiting room door opens, bringing Greer and me shooting to our feet. Jack walks in, followed by Danika, who says, "Found someone in the lobby."

It's Ever. It's Ever. I break the law of physics lunging across the room, dropping my face into her neck and breathing, breathing for the first time in hours. "You came." I look like such a pussy, leaning my entire body on this girl who I outweigh by several dozen pounds and I don't give a shit. "Thank you for coming."

She drops her purse on the ground, wrapping both arms around my waist. "Of course I came," she breathes near my ear. "Is there any news?"

"Not yet," I rasp. "Can you come with me for a minute? We need to talk, and it can't wait."

I glance over at Greer, wishing for the first time we were the kind of family who didn't shut down when something bad happened. Maybe I'll get the ball rolling. I have to, because it doesn't work for me anymore. "We'll be out in the hall. Come find me when the doctor comes?"

I wait for my brother's barely noticeable finger flick, then I take Ever's hand, leading her past the tense, busy nurses' station. A few of them watch us go by with interest, but I'm so focused on getting Ever alone, I barely manage a nod. As soon as we reach the dim side corridor, I pull Ever into my arms and we crash together against the wall. Urgency pumps in my veins, demanding I suck in great, greedy gulps of her. My mouth moves over her neck, into her hair, across her lips. Inhaling, retaining.

"Everything is going to be fine," she whispers, dragging me into the safety she began representing to me, somewhere along the line. "He's getting the best care, and everything is going to be okay, Charlie."

"But I'm not okay." I pull back, cupping the sides of her beautiful, singular face. The face I see in my dreams and while I'm awake. I never stop, and I was a fucking idiot to think I could let her go. "I'm not okay without you, Ever."

"Charlie." Her eyelids flicker as she looks down. "You're going through a difficult time right now, and you're not thinking straight. We should talk about this when your father is out of the woods."

"No." Oh God, this is what I was worried about, without being able to pinpoint it. I've been so goddamn elusive and unpredictable, coming in and out of her life, she isn't taking me seriously when I need it most. "No, you don't . . . just . . . *please*. Look me in the eye. Before we fell asleep in your bed, before your mother called, I started to ask you to be with me. All the time, cutie. *All the time*. But I panicked when I heard those things she said to you. About coming home to someone every night. Having someone you can depend on. And I didn't think I could deliver. I *knew* I couldn't." My heart has veered into a wild, never-ending drum solo, but I push. I *push*. Because I have no choice. This is do or die. It *has* been all along. I was just too stupid and short sighted to realize it. "But it took this fucked-up thing happening for me to understand. I understand now why I can look at you, Ever, and be happy and sad and horny and miserable and crazy and want to laugh—all at the same time. I'm in love with you. I love you so much. And you can depend on that. You can depend on *me* for the rest of your life. I won't let you go for anything. Just give me a chance to show you." I point in the general direction of my father's room. "This job? It can work around us. This *world* can work around me and the girl I love. Okay? This isn't a tragedy talking. This is what's inside me and I'm handing it all over, because you're the only one I trust to make sense of me. You make *sense* of me."

She's quiet for so long, I'm tempted to look for the closest window, so I can dive through it headfirst into traffic. But no. Even if she has to think about everything I said, I will keep coming at her. I'm not packing it in. I'm not giving up, so she can just—

"I knew you were a relationship guy all along." She sounds almost awestruck. "Ever since you failed the test and said you cried during the wrong scene in *Titanic*. I knew you were a relationship guy deep down, and I still went home with you."

My head is spinning. Is this good or bad? Do

I need a decoder ring in order to learn my fate? "What does that mean?"

"It means I love you, too, Charlie."

She looks a little shocked at having said the words out loud, but it does nothing to lessen the impact of total, blinding rapture. I don't even think my feet are touching the floor, but I manage to trap her against the wall, my hands flattened on the cinderblock above her head. "Get out of town."

"I do." Her laugh is gorgeous and watery, her eyes shining. "For a long time. Even before we tried to be friends—"

I shoot forward and snag her mouth in a kiss, but a dull note of panic starts to beat in my chest. I'm kissing her half because she loves me, half because the words *before we tried to be friends* just sent me screaming back into reality. The speed dating, the fire alarm at the tapas place, the lies I told. She knows none of it. Would she still love me if she knew? Or would she look at me as if I betrayed her? Did I?

Yeah. Jesus. I did.

As if I can erase the moronic things I did to ruin her noble plans, I press Ever back against the wall and give her everything I have to offer. Every ounce of feeling in my body, head to toe. Our mouths are the hungriest they've ever been, because there's no holding back when you love someone. When they know it. Feel it. These are things I'm learning on the fly, and I can't believe I was ever scared of this. Terror is being *without* this.

My tongue makes promises to her and she understands, responds with a whimper. I didn't even have a second to savor winning her back, before the prospect of losing her again hits me. Hits me hard, like a spike between the shoulder blades. But I'm a man who's scared of losing his woman, so I do what I'm driven toward. I try to distract from the oncoming pain with my body. To give her something to remember when she wants to murder me. I stroke her between the legs with my bulge, dragging it up and back, nudging her onto her toes. All the while, my lips pry apart her swollen, wet ones, giving her my breath, licks of my tongue.

"I love you." My mouth races along the underside of her chin, my hands climbing the backs of her thighs. "Oh God, I love you. Just try to be patient and understanding with me. Can you do that?"

She nods, her face glowing. But she has no idea what I'm talking about. Not yet. "You're going to come to my place when your father is better. You'll stay the night." Her eyes flicker. "We'll take it slow, but you'll stay, won't you?"

Jesus, I can't believe she still doubts me. "I don't

want to sleep without you. Ever again. And *fuck* taking it slow. I want to meet your mother. Want to charm her and explain that I'll be the one you count on, just like she hoped for. I want clothes and a toothbrush at your place. I want keys. And I want the people in your building to buzz me in when I forget my key, because they know I'm your boyfriend. I want to walk you home from concerts and dance to our song when it comes up on shuffle. You and me, Ever. I want it to be *you*. And *me*."

Her breath whooshes out against my lips. "Me, too. I want all those things. I feel like I've wanted them forever, but I didn't know until you said them."

I would love to go on standing there forever, making her promises. But there's no option but to tell her what I've done. To let her know I disregarded the importance of fulfilling her mother's wishes and tried to make her my fuck buddy. I hate myself right now. I do, so I try to bury it all inside her. Lifting her against the wall and molding our bodies together. There's a sliver of clarity left in my mind, so I know I can't take Ever in this hallway, but I can remind her we're so good together. Maybe it'll help. Maybe.

"*Charlie.*" She gasps when my teeth nip into her neck. "I know you're upset, but . . ." I squeeze her ass and she turns pliant, going limp between me and the wall. "I think we need to get back to the waiting room. I'm not going anywhere. *We're* not going anywhere. There's time for everything."

Now or never. I press my face into her hair. "Ever . . ."

"*Charlie.*" My brother's voice finds me from around the corner. "The doctor is coming out to speak with us. He's bringing us in to see Dad, too."

Worry for my father blasts back to the forefront, but revealing my treachery to Ever is there, too, clashing with it. Blackening my vision. She's there, though, stroking the sides of my face, kissing me hard on the mouth. Loving me, grounding me. "Hey, that sounds like good news. They wouldn't bring you in to see him if things were getting worse, right?" Another sweet kiss on my cheek. "Go. I'll be here when you come back."

I pull away, but I'm tempted to bring her with me. "Please be here."

"Why would I be anywhere else?" She covers her mouth a moment, then drops her hands to reveal an expression of pure, flushed happiness. "I love you."

Dear God, please let that love stay strong through what comes next.

CHAPTER 24

Ever

C harlie loves me. I love him back. We said the words. We meant them.

I'm floating on a cloud of purple smoke back to the waiting room, probably with eyes the shape of hearts. There is a lessening of tension at the nurses' station that bolsters my theory that Charlie's father is going to be okay. Thank God. I've never seen Charlie looking more haunted than the moment I arrived, like everything he knew had been shaken. I'm going to be there for him. He . . . needs me to be there. I still can't believe it. We started out as two people who didn't want anything serious and now, we want it all.

Before I push open the door, I stop to collect myself. I swear, my heart is lodged somewhere between my throat and breastbone, pounding out of control. This morning, I woke up thinking the man I love was lost to me. He wasn't, though. He came roaring back, and I realize now I should have had faith. I wouldn't love a man who could give me up so easily.

He didn't give me up at all, really, had he? No, he became my friend. He listened and understood why I wanted to find something serious. He'd confided in me, too. And now we are stronger for it. Lovers, friends . . . boyfriend and girlfriend. Maybe the attempt to strictly be friends had been a little far-fetched for two people who shared such a strong attraction, but Charlie had stuck with it. Showing up and supporting me, even though it couldn't have been easy to watch me try to date. *Try* being the operative word. I was never meant to spend a single minute in another man's company, though, and—

My hand flies up and smacks my forehead.

Reve. I forgot about the date.

I push through the waiting room doors and find my purse on a low, gray table, someone obviously having put it there after I dropped it. Danika sends me a slow wave, one corner of her mouth ticking up. "I assume from your smeared lipstick the *talk* went well," she says, flipping the page of her magazine. "Atta boy, Charlie."

Jack winks at me, but it's friendly, if a bit . . . roguish. "Looking forward to having you around more, Ever. Guess I'll have to start wearing pants around the apartment."

I laugh, sounding like a complete schoolgirl, because I'm still flying high over Charlie loving me. Loving Charlie back. "It'll be worth the leftovers I bring over."

Danika and Jack give each other a fist bump.

I cross the room and dig through my purse, taking out my phone. Looking at my torn reflection on the screen for a beat, I open the dating app, feeling obligated to message Reve and cancel the date. Shit, though. It's already seven forty. He's probably on the train riding to the restaurant. Or worse, he arrived early and is sitting at the table, waiting for me. Guilt sits heavy in my stomach. Maybe the man is nothing more than a casual online acquaintance, but I don't want to be the girl who stands him up. After the shit show that has been my foray into the dating scene and watching Nina deal with her breakup, I know how being treated without care or respect takes its toll.

It occurs to me how close we are to the restaurant. The hospital is only one avenue and six blocks from the Mexican food place where we'd planned to eat. I cast a glance toward the waiting room door, then back toward my cell phone clock. It would only take me twenty minutes to get to the restaurant, explain to Reve in person that I'm serious about someone else, but still appreciate him being so nice and giving up his evening to come meet me. I will probably be back before Charlie comes back out from meeting with the doctor and visiting his father.

Just do it. You'll feel better about it and save someone a blow to their self-esteem.

"You guys, I have to run somewhere really quick." I shoulder my purse, cell phone in hand, tapping it against my thigh. "Can you tell Charlie I'll be right back if he comes out before I return? I'm just nipping down the street."

They exchange a look and nod.

It's not until I'm dodging evening foot traffic on my way down the avenue that I realize Charlie's friends had looked . . . worried. Or something that wasn't on par with me running an errand they knew nothing about. A need to return to Charlie as soon as possible, to be there and comfort him, kicks my pace into a jog. I can't account for the yawning pit in my stomach, though. Almost like something is hovering just on the edge of my conscience, but isn't quite ready to be plucked free yet.

When I reach the restaurant, it's packed, people spilling out onto the sidewalk, debating whether or not to wait for a table. Knowing Reve made a reservation, I wade through the gathering of people to the hostess.

"Hi, I'm meeting someone. A table for two under Reve . . ."

"Yes." She runs a silver fingernail down the list. "He's not here yet. If you'd like to have a seat?"

Balancing on the balls of my feet, I battle the urge to charge back to the hospital and forget this whole mission to be a decent human being. But it's still only seven fifty-two. Reve won't be late for eight more minutes. Eight more minutes, then I could swing by a bakery, pick up some cookies and be back at the hospital in no time.

In the scheme of things, what's eight minutes?

Charlie and I are on an unlimited minutes plan now.

I squeeze into the red, leather booth with a smile on my face, ready to intercept Reve when he walks through the door.

Charlie

Even in sleep, my father looks pissed off.

He woke up a few minutes ago, nodding at Greer and me in turn, by way of actual words. He'd saved those up for the doctor, who was clearly already fed up with the surly police chief. Before they'd even admitted him to the ICU, he'd demanded to know when he could go home. Relief floated like helium in my gut, even if there was still a lingering uneasiness over having watched my father drop down to mortal status.

Greer stands beside the bed updating him on department news from the last few hours, while my father fusses with the nose tubes and frowns at the beeping machine. He hasn't brought up asking for our mother immediately following the heart attack, but there's a knowledge hanging in the air, all three of us aware it happened. If things remained status quo, we'll never discuss it. We'll pretend it never happened. But I'm tired of the norm. Living as though ignorance is preferable to confronting anything emotional? That almost lost me Ever. *Still* might, depending on the mercy of the woman I love with every bone in my body.

Greer finishes his gravelly spiel and silence settles in the room. I can tell my father expects us to leave. Just like that. As if he didn't almost die on the local news.

"I'm glad you're going to be okay," I start, two sets of eyes pinning me before the words have fully emerged.

My father tips his chin up. "Me, too. I need to get back on the clock."

"Yeah." I shove both hands into my pockets. "I meant I'm glad you're going to be okay, because you're my dad. Our dad." They're looking at me like I have sixteen heads. "Maybe work isn't the most important thing. Not always. Not every time."

"There's a girl," Greer says to my father, as if

three little words could adequately explain Ever. All the words in the world couldn't do her justice.

"There *is* a girl. Ever Carmichael. I'm going to try to keep her forever, if she'll let me." Christ, is my Adam's apple swelling up? "I almost let her go, though, for reasons that seemed really stupid with death on the line, you know?" No answer. "I was afraid of her leaving like Mom left us. I thought it would be inevitable, once I started working around the clock, the way I'm supposed to. The way I've been taught is the only way." I think of her out in the waiting room, fresh and flushed from kissing me. "When it comes time to take the lieutenant's exam, I'm opting out."

My father sits up straighter against the pillows. "What do you mean? Of course you aren't. We've been grooming you for this since you were in middle school."

"You've also drilled the importance of sacrifice into my head. We sacrifice, because it's our job. Sacrifice our lives, our safety." I jab the air with my finger. "I'm prepared to do those things. I'm going to be a damn good cop. But I'm making a sacrifice for her, because she's what makes me happy. Look me in the eye and tell me you don't wish, every once in a while, that you'd made some sacrifices for Mom. Tell me you don't have regrets. I know I do. I can't even remember saying thank you. Or I love you."

Greer's gaze snaps to mine, then over to my father. "For fuck sake, Charlie. Does this seem like a good time to get him upset?"

My father holds up a hand, tubes extending to the clear drip beside the bed. "I'm not upset." His sigh seems to take an hour escaping. "First of all, I remember you saying those things. She loved her children. I'm the reason she left."

Until I hear the words out loud, I don't realize how much I believed it was me who sent her packing. All me. Even against common sense, I thought I was the straw that broke the camel's back. The last ditch effort to save a marriage that wasn't working, but ended up only making it worse. There's no miraculous lessening of weight off my shoulders, though, because I see my father is carrying it. There's no winner here.

"The department makes me happy. My work makes me happy." His eyes lift to mine, shoot away. "But it doesn't love a man back. The job put me in this bed. This, my body, is my sacrifice. Your mother was a sacrifice, too. And I think I've done a lot of good for this city because of those sacrifices."

"No one is questioning that," Greer says quietly. I nod.

"I should have tried harder, though," my father surprises me by saying. "She was only asking for me to try a little harder. To be a husband, as well as a cop. I could have done it, but I was selfish. And then she was gone." His jaw flexes, his nostrils flaring on an inhale. "I'm . . . proud of you, Charlie. For recognizing happiness. I'm still not sure I know what it looks like."

"Happiness is a she. I can introduce you to her."

Greer groans. "Jesus, you fucking sap."

My father laughs as I punch Greer in the shoulder. "It's going to happen to you someday. Then we'll see who's a sap."

"Don't hold your breath. Someone has to pick up your slack, now that you've decided to play house." His shrug is stiff, but his lips are twitching. "I guess if you're signing up to be whipped by a woman, might as well make her a hot blonde."

"You did not just call my future wife hot right to my face."

"He did." My father is laughing, his big chest shaking. "I heard him."

The mood between the three of us is the lightest I've ever felt it. Incredible. I thought my decision would drive a wedge between the already stilted relationship with my father and brother, but somehow it had the opposite effect.

I can't wait to tell Ever. I can't wait to tell her everything in my head, for the rest of my life. Our life.

With the promise of her warmth making my blood zing, I slap Greer on the back a little harder than warranted—after all, he just called Ever hot to my face—then, I head back out to the waiting room, Greer already beginning to drone about department business before the door closes behind me. When I walk into the beige purgatory, however, I find only Jack and Danika.

"Hey." I scratch my head and turn in a circle, as if Ever will appear out of thin air. "My father is fine. They're going to keep him for a while, but he's out of the woods." They both visibly relax, Danika tossing her magazine onto the low, gray table. "Where's Ever?"

"Not sure." Jack clears his throat. "Said she was running out for a little while."

"But she'll be right back," Danika added quickly, giving me a curious look.

"Huh." I pace to the window and look down at the rushing lights of the city. As if I could pick her out among thousands of people from this height. "Where would she . . ."

Oh. Fuck.

CHAPTER 25

Ever

Well. Joke is on me. *I'm* the one being stood up.

At 8:01, I get a sympathetic look from the hostess and wave it off, smiling back. It doesn't matter. I'm actually relieved I don't have to explain to a virtual stranger that I'm in a relationship and I can't stay for dinner. For once, getting stood up makes things a lot easier. Impatient to get back to Charlie and find out how his father is doing, I head for the door—

Just as Charlie walks in, eyes wild. Sweat dots his upper lip and darkens the front of his T-shirt. His hands clench and loosen at his sides.

Despite his disheveled appearance, however, a thrill squeals through my body at the sight of him. His blue eyes pan through the waiting area and land on me, his stomach hollowing on a deep breath when he sees me. I know the feeling. My tummy is bottoming out just knowing I'll touch him soon. Talk to him.

That's my first reaction. It lasts a split second before dread settles in my chest.

"You went on the date, Ever?" Charlie croaks the words. "You *went*?"

"*No.*" His misconception must be the reason I'm nervous. But knowing I can clear it up with an easy explanation doesn't make me feel any better. The lighthearted joy I was feeling earlier in the night is being chafed by splinters. "No, I'm only here to cancel, and I was coming right back to the hospital. It was the right thing to do on short notice and . . . Charlie, you *know* I was coming right back." I go up on my toes and rub our noses together. "After all the dating nightmares over the last few weeks, I wanted to do someone else a solid. That's all. Look at me." More nose rubbing. "I love you."

His shoulders lose most of their tension, but the muscular lines of his body are still whip tight. "Yeah, I know. I know you were coming back to me." His eyelids fall shut. "Of course you would do something like this. It's why I love you, isn't it?"

Instead of being comforted by those words, words I'll never get accustomed to hearing, my dread amplifies. A horn blares right against my ear. "How . . . how did you know I would be here?"

When dudes in hazmat suits approach a suspicious package? That's how Charlie is looking at me right now. Like there's about to be a potential disaster. His Adam's apple drags up and down, thoughts racing behind his blue eyes. "Remember back in the hospital when I asked you to be patient with me?" I don't respond, but my heart does. It flies into a riot. "Is there any way that could take effect now?"

"Spit it out."

A rickety inhale. "I'm Reve." His lips barely move as he says the two words that make my skin burn. His must be burning, too, because it seems like he wants to crawl out of it. "Or there is no Reve. He's just the name on the profile I created."

Ice replaces the burning sensation on my arms, my neck. *"Why?"*

"Because I *missed* you. I needed to see your face. That was all it was supposed to be, but you messaged me and . . . cutie, then I was talking to you. And it felt like you were there with me. You were always *supposed* to be there with me." He drags a hand down his face. "I shouldn't have made this date, but you have to believe me. I was going to show up as Charlie and come clean. Unless . . ."

I'm afraid to ask. I've already been buried under

an avalanche, but I need to know. I need to hear everything. "Unless what?"

Misery slashes across his face. "Unless I could convince you to come back to me before tonight ever happened."

"Come back to you?" My voice is high-pitched and unnatural, but I can't help it. There's an earthquake taking place inside me. "We weren't even together until tonight."

His eyelids lift and all I see is shame. Shame. And it terrifies me. "When I created Reve, I still wanted things to go back to how they were. When we were just . . ."

"Hooking up," I whisper through numb lips.

The blood drains from my face, scenes beginning to play on a screen inside my head. The speed dating fiasco, the fire alarm going off in the restaurant. And then the scenes that made tears burn in my eyes. Charlie showing up after speed dating and taking me for a drink, opening up to me about pressure at the academy, listening to me speak about my mother. Charlie showing up with the notecard tree, taking me to the farmer's market. Taking me to the memorial after my disastrous date. "Oh God, Charlie, what did you do?" I clutch my throat, preventing it from ripping open. "Don't tell me you've been sabotaging me. Not after I told you how important it was to try for my mother."

"I'm sorry. I'm so fucking sorry."

He's trying to yank me into his arms, but I'd rather die. At this point, I would rather dive out of an airplane than let him comfort me. He's the reason I need comfort in the first place, and I'm reeling. I'm *reeling* so hard I'm dizzy, the room twisting around me. "You wanted to go back to just hooking up," I state. "When did that change? Did you ever really want to be my friend? Or was that all bullshit?"

"Ever." There's a tremor in his voice. Like he already knows I won't appreciate his answer. "I fooled myself into thinking it was bullshit, but cutie, you have to *believe* me. I was in love with you the whole time. I was running all over town trying to make sure someone didn't steal you away from me." His fingers rake through his hair. "I was a goddamn idiot for believing I would do that unless there was something real here. And we're the realest thing out there, Ever. You *know* we are."

"How can you say that when you've been lying to me? Disregarding something you knew was *important* to me." My voice has been reduced to a whisper. All I can see is Charlie's earnest face, acting surprised to see me after I'd been humiliated at speed dating. The firmness of his handshake when we decided to be friends. The words he'd said when we had sex on the couch. *No one moves like us, Ever. No one talks to each other without words like us. Don't you* know *that?* "All you wanted was to get me back into bed."

"No." His face is white as a sheet. "*No,* I thought that's all I wanted. Ever—"

"I have to get away from you." And I really do. I've dropped from the highest high into a lake of razors. I need to go somewhere dark and sort through what I know. To judge the extent of the damage. There's one fact that is unshakeable, though, and it's that Charlie has made me a complete fool. "Who do you think you are? Messing with my life like that? How dare you, Charlie? How *dare* you?" Tears roll down my cheeks and he sucks in a breath, watching them travel down, down. "Did you think it was funny? Ruining my dates so I would come running back for the no-strings sex?"

"It was never funny being without you. Not for a second." He's talking very slowly, very quietly, as if he's mere seconds from losing his sanity. "Ever, please don't leave me. You can't leave me when I love you so much. Please. I'm begging you to comb through this with me, second by second, so I can tell you what I was thinking. I need to make you understand."

"I don't trust you to be honest. I don't think I'll ever believe you again."

The words burst out of me and pop in the

air. Bright red fireworks. Charlie falls back and bumps into someone, but doesn't seem aware of it. And I take that opportunity to push out of the restaurant and run for the train, my heart dragging behind me on the filthy sidewalk.

CHAPTER 26

— *Ever* —

I'm sitting in the living room with Nina and my mother watching *The Dog Whisperer*, eating cheese Danishes. Perhaps not conventional break-up remedies, but we're working with what we've got. Nina apparently retrieved my mother's phone number from my cell while I was indulging my-self in a crying jag under my pillow, because she arrived in a perfumed flurry an hour ago, bakery box in hand. My hair is wet from the shower they forced me to take against my will, and I'm let-ting it drip all over the couch cushions in protest. Weirdly, that tiny rebellion is making me feel less shitty. But I'm nowhere near better.

It's Tuesday afternoon, and I'm still in this weird bubble. A bubble filled with fog. After the scene with Charlie, I dived into a yellow cab, floated up the stairs to my apartment in a blur and crawled under my comforter. My cell phone went absolutely bonkers at first—guess who—so I shut it off. An hour later, my apartment buzzer started going off nonstop, so I did the mature thing and disconnected it from the wall with a butter knife and scissors. Really short sighted, considering my super will probably take six months to repair it. Something tells me he won't be thrilled with the excuse, "I needed to have a think-cry and the noise was distracting."

Charlie could have easily gotten into the building—by charming a female neighbor or flat out breaking the door down—but I think he knows I would deck him if he didn't respect my free will, while I'm contemplating murdering him over that very same thing.

Here's the thing. I *know* Charlie meant it when he said he loves me. I sure as shooting meant it, too. My dilemma is whether or not I'm still willing to form a relationship with someone who acted so selfishly. Someone who hurt me, whether or not it was intentional. After my mother's revelation about loneliness, I was *scared*. I confided in Charlie the importance of following through on my promise to my mother, and he still tried to ruin my chance at a committed relationship.

On top of everything, I'm embarrassed. So *very* embarrassed. I cringe every time I think of my

wide-eyed optimism the night he saved the catering event. Or how I shook his hand after the speed
dating debacle and agreed to try to be buddies.
Maybe he really does want to be my friend, I'd thought
both times. Was I really so stupid and naïve?

*I fooled myself into thinking it was bullshit, but cutie,
you have to believe me. I was in love with you the whole
time.*

My heart lurches and tears spring to my eyes.
Dammit, I miss him so much my bones ache. Can
I believe him when he says he loved me the whole
time? After all the lies of omission and letting me
think he was someone else?

Every time I think about him pretending to
be Reve, I growl. And right now is no exception.
Nina's and my mother's gazes bounce between me
and the television, obviously not sure if the sound
came from me or one of Cesar Millan's dogs.

"Is that a sign you're ready to talk, dear?" My
mother nibbles at her Danish. "I could be doing
something productive, you know. Like watching
this exact same program in the break room at
work."

My mom makes jokes now. Bad timing, though,
because I don't feel much like laughing. However,
she did make the effort to leave her job and come
see me, an effort that would have shocked me a
month ago, so I attempt wordage. "Charlie . . .
pulled the fire alarm while I was on a date." My

tone is bemused because it's one of the four emotions inside my bubble. Anger, humiliation, sadness and bemusement. "Like, he's going to be a *police officer* and he pulled an *illegal* stunt, soaked at least a hundred people . . . and then he called me on my phone to go *meet up*." I shove a bite of Danish into my mouth. "I'm trying to decide if that makes him deranged or—"

"Desperately in love?"

I'm left sputtering over my mother's comment, which gives Nina the unfortunate opportunity to jump in. "You should see the way he looks at her. All big, blue puppy dog eyes. Like he just wants to flop down in front of Ever and have his belly scratched."

My mother turns to me. "Why didn't you tell me about him?"

It's meant as a reproof, but I can hear the hurt in her tone and it makes me feel guilty. "He didn't want anything serious. It's why we started . . . hanging out—"

"Fucking? You can say the word in front of me, Ever, I'm an ex-mistress."

Nina buries her face in a pillow, her sides shaking with laughter.

"Okay, yeah. What you said. The F-word." I'm not ready to drop bad language in front of my mother yet. Maybe someday. "You asked me to try dating seriously, so I broke it off with Charlie."

My mother frowns. "Did you *want* to break it off?"

"No," I say honestly, remembering how hard it had been to watch him go. How I'd lived in a black cloud until I'd seen him again. "We'd been seeing each other for thirty-one days when I ended things."

Nina doesn't pick up on the importance of the number, because she doesn't know the rules my mother and I lived by for so long. My mother, however, knows what it means. I broke the rules for Charlie. In our world, it might as well be an admission of love. Nina seems to sense the need for the two of us to be alone, because she hops up from the couch, snagging her keys off the coffee table. "I'm going to go grab the mail. Be back in a while."

As soon as the door closes behind my roommate, my mother gracefully turns, pointing her pressed-together knees in my direction. "Ever, I wanted you to find someone so *you* could be happy." She wets her lips. "It sounds like you were doing it for me."

"I was." My voice cracks, but I don't feel like I need to appear strong in front of my mother anymore, when I'm on shaky ground. I can just be honest. "I was, and it worked and you're here now. I've seen you more in the last couple weeks than I have in years. The dating gave us something to . . ."

"Have in common?" Her eyes are troubled. "I

think what we have in common is the desire to see you happy. And if this Charlie made you happy, I'm sorry I steered you away from him."

"Don't be. Things between us weren't right back then." An image of him dancing at Webster Hall flies through my head. Followed by him kneeling at the police memorial, hugging me in the bar, guarding my door from Nina's ex-boyfriend. "I didn't even know him until I broke it off," I murmur. "Until we became friends."

"And you are friends, aren't you?"

I nod, because I'm finding it hard to speak around the lump in my throat. Whatever ill-conceived notions were behind Charlie becoming my friend in the first place, the truth is, we got there. We got there and it was glorious. Would he go to such extremes to be around me if he only wanted sex? No. No, that's not Charlie. He might have made some huge mistakes, but he's gold on the inside. I think of him watching my cab drive away after our talk at the memorial and it hits me, it hits me so hard that he was dying in that moment. He was considering chasing the cab, wasn't he?

"Yeah." I swallow hard. "We're friends."

Will we end up more, though?

Nina walks back into the apartment, and I do a double take when I see the stack of identical envelopes she's holding. "Uh." She drops them beside me on the couch. "You've got mail."

There are at least a dozen letters . . . and they're all from Charlie.

Trading a surprised glance with my mother—who is literally bouncing with excitement—I open the letter marked "READ ME FIRST" in all caps.

> *Reve = Ever spelled backward*
> *Reve S. Guy = Ever's Guy*
> *Always have been. Always will be.*
> *I love you so much. I'm sorry. Take me back.*

With tears in my eyes, I do some quick math. He called himself my guy right at the beginning of our friendship. That had to mean he felt more for me than attraction, even then. Didn't it? Swiping at the moisture on my cheeks, I open the next letter. And the next . . . and the next . . .

CHAPTER 27
Charlie

S leep is for the weak. Or for better men than
me. Men who don't make the love of their life
cry. Men who don't dig themselves into such an
awful, disgusting hole that experts haven't even
invented a tool yet for digging them out.

You can bet your ass I'm going to try, though.
I'm going to claw my way toward the sunlight, because I've felt it on my face. And I don't know how
to live any other way now. Give me Ever, or give
me death.

Death, coincidentally, is pretty much synony-
mous with my condition.

When it became obvious I wouldn't be reaching Ever with modern technology or face-to-face,
I started writing the letters. A *week* ago. I haven't
seen or touched or smelled my girl in a fucking

week. After what happened with my father, the academy gave me time off and it's a good thing, too, because maintaining my usual sparkling hygiene has been a challenge. Also eating. I don't eat anymore. Flat out cut it from my daily schedule, and apart from visiting my father in the hospital, I've been doing nothing but writing letters. And mailing them to Ever.

My hand gets stiff, I shake it out and dive back in. I'm documenting every single moment I've spent with Ever—this requires a good deal of math, a calendar and some estimating—and there isn't anyone or anything that can stop me. Except for a straitjacket.

Minute eight: the day we met.

I almost didn't approach you at all. Jesus. How scary is that? You were/are/always will be the most beautiful woman I've ever laid eyes on. But before you even opened your mouth, I knew you were going to change me. Change my life. So it took me an extra eight minutes to get brave enough to come closer. I had to prepare for whatever you threw at me. And Ever, if you had told me, right there in the glow of the Knicks game, that you only did serious relationships, I know now that I still would have kissed you. Still would have brought you home, fucked up, tried again, fought to keep you, lost you, won you back. All of it. I would have done it all, even if I spent the whole time fooling myself into thinking I wanted casual and easy. Nothing is easy without you. And nothing is casual about the way I love you. I miss you so much. I'm sorry.

Minute thirty-two (roughly): the night of the day we met.

The second time we kissed was in the back of an Uber. It was raining, and we were stopped at a red light on Broadway—do you remember? The driver was listening to talk radio in his language, and it was the least romantic setting ever. But it wasn't. It wasn't. Because there were raindrops in your eyelashes, and you were freezing from the air conditioner after getting wet while running to the car. You were smiling and blowing into your hands. And you were so real. You were everything real and beautiful and I thought, maybe I should drop her off and leave, instead of coming inside like you'd invited me to do. Because I couldn't imagine keeping my distance from you. I couldn't imagine being casual. So maybe cutting it short was a good idea. But the idea of that bothered me so much, I kissed you instead. I tugged you close with the strap of your overalls and kissed your incredible mouth.

I should have known then we were forever. You tasted like forever. I'm sorry, Ever. I'm so sorry. Come back to me.

Minute seventeen hundred and three: a Wednesday afternoon.

On my way to your place, I saw you through your window. From the street. Since I'd observed the layout of your apartment—I'm a cop in training, remember?—I knew you were at the kitchen sink. But you weren't washing anything. You were just staring out at the neighborhood or the sky, looking a little sad. When I got to your door, though, you were smiling. You flirted with me, dragged me inside and let me take you against the door. There wasn't a single trace of that sadness. And I knew you'd hidden it from me. There was so much more of you to know, and I couldn't pretend I didn't see it anymore. From that point on, it got harder and harder pretending I wasn't dying to know every tiny iota of thought and feeling that makes up Ever. I ignored how wrong it felt to leave you each day. I forced myself to focus on seeing you the next time, the next time. So when you broke it off with me, I panicked. There wasn't going to be a next time to focus on. So I fucked up beyond any apology I can offer, *but please know that being without you hijacked my common sense. I'm the world's biggest idiot and I miss you. I miss you. I miss you. I miss you. I miss you.*

Minute three thousand and eighty: the day I knew something was wrong.

I offered to fix your leaky pipes on this day, Ever. You really should have given me more shit about that, because it was about as smooth as a pothole. I saw you slipping away from me that day. Saw it in your eyes, the way you clammed up on me. You know how scary that was, when I never really had you at all? I had no foothold, no leverage. Nothing. And this scared asshole you hooked up with decided the best foothold would be friendship. To get you back. Becoming your friend was the greatest decision I ever made. The worst decision I ever made was lying to you, lying to myself, pretending the never-ending drive to be around you was all about sex. It wasn't. It was about Ever and Charlie. And the fact that I'm so in love with you, your heart, your soul, your thoughts and words, that I can't even breathe right while I'm writing this (day five of being without you . . . kill me now). Please take me back, cutie. Please.

Minute three thousand and six hundred: the day I joined DateMate.

I'd spent hours touching you, looking at your gorgeous face, licking your skin. Seeing you through the eyes of a billion other men was Armageddon for my sanity. They could have you now. I'd blown it. You stood in your kitchen and told me you wanted something serious . . . and I didn't jump all over it. What was wrong with me, Ever? Jesus Christ. When you messaged Reve, I should have told you I was Charlie. We could have saved so much time and you wouldn't have been hurt, if I'd just been honest and said, "This is Charlie, I'm talking to your pictures, I'm miserable, can I come over and apologize for the rest of my life?" Instead, I did something stupid. Something that hurt your feelings, when that's the last thing I ever want to do in this life. I'm sorry. I'm so fucking sorry. P.S. Do you still have the pink bikini? I'm not saying you'll definitely take me back (please take me back) but I'm just curious. If you still have it. Laying around.

AND SO ON. In total, I think I've written ninety letters. Every time I finish one, I put a stamp in the corner, walk down to the blue post box on the corner of my block and drop it in. Looking like a fucking homeless mental patient in my grease-stained sweatpants. Jack and Danika have taken turns trying to haul my ass into the shower or convince me to go see Ever in person. But they don't know my plan.

You would think I never wanted to form another plan as long as I live, right? Well this one is different. The letters are only phase one. I want her to open her mailbox and have it stuffed full of my heart on paper, every day. I want her to read them and think about them. To understand that I'm a fuckup, but I'm a fuckup with good intentions that loves her beyond reason.

Once I've convinced her of that? I'll roll out phase two.

You don't want to miss it.

Ever

Maybe I'm a pushover. I don't know. But dammit if Charlie didn't have me back with the fourth letter I opened. Sue me.

He'd engaged in some really backhanded business, though, so I'm letting him sweat. I need to be sure he won't try to deceive me ever again. He may have won me back with the perfect honesty of those letters, but I'm still a touch angry. It would be impossible for me to get over lies and humiliation at the drop of a hat. But I can't pretend my heart hasn't spent the last two weeks with Charlie, uptown at the hospital. I miss him so much, my chest feels like an oversized, crushed aluminum can.

I engaged in a little cyber research myself and found Danika on Facebook, allowing myself to check in once per day to make sure Charlie's father is still doing fine. If something awful happened and there was a turn for the worse, I would be in a cab uptown without stopping to put on shoes. Charlie is my guy. Right now, I'd like to sock him in the stomach and give him the silent treatment for about a year, but I love him.

I love him more with every letter.

The one that won be back should have been the worst letter of all. Seriously. How could I not catch on to his game, when he'd been standing two blocks away after my speed dating fiasco? *I should have hugged you on the sidewalk that night*, his letter said. *You were waiting for me to hug you, but I didn't realize it until I knew you better. Now I look back and see things I missed and I never want to miss them again. Thank God I know you better now. I went about doing it the wrong way, cutie, but knowing you is my life's greatest accomplishment. Better than passing the lieutenant exam could ever feel. Which is why I'm not taking it. If gaining something causes me to lose you, it's not a gain at all. It's a loss of the best thing I've ever had.*

Oh, Charlie is taking the exam. If I have to drug him and cart him there in a wheelbarrow, he will be there to pass it with flying colors. We will find a way to make time for one another when his job becomes hectic. It's his good fortune he wound up with a girl who likes to spend a fair bit of time alone. And it's *my* good fortune that I ended up with a guy who is willing to set aside his life's ambition to make me happy. I'll be happier if he achieves it, though, and I will make sure Charlie knows it.

As soon as he stopped sending letters and came to see me.

Although, speaking of alone time, I haven't had much of it lately. After coming clean about pointing Charlie in the direction of my speed dating event, my roommate has been extra sweet, cooking meals and letting me have control of the DVR. I've forgiven her, too, but I'm waiting to reassure her until I make it through season five of *Supernatural*.

As for my mother, we're getting closer every day. Especially since we had our talk about my love life and how I'd dated to bring us closer together. My happiness can't be designed around capturing a feeling I didn't have growing up. It has to grow with the future. We'll find things in common, she and I, but this is my life and there's only one way I want to live it. With Charlie. Hard or easy. Confusing or clear. Shouting or silent. Likely, all of the above.

Speaking of Charlie . . . what is taking him so lo—

Sirens go off outside my kitchen window—
police car sirens—and it's so unexpected, I
scream at the top of my lungs, but the sirens are
so loud, you can't even hear me. Oh my God. Oh
my God. There has been like, an explosion or a
crane collapse and I'm going to die. I'm going to
die, and I didn't even tell Charlie I forgive him
yet. I'm only wearing a towel, but I run barefoot
through the living room, straight to the kitchen
window and frantically scan the street below.

Dozens of police cars cram into my block, all of
them flashing their lights and blaring their death
sirens. But I can't figure out where the crisis is
taking place. Which probably means it's in my
building. Great. I shimmy forward onto the sink,
craning my neck to look down at a hundred uni-
formed officers, maybe more and . . . and there's
Charlie. Standing on the hood of a police car.

He lifts a hand and the sirens cut out. Just like
that.

While I stare dumbfounded, he lifts a bullhorn
to his mouth. "Hey, cutie."

I'm in total shock, but his voice is muffled
through the closed window, so my hand works
frantically to disengage the lock and push it open.
"Charlie," I call, sounding like I swallowed a frog.
"What is this?"

"It's your last letter." How dare he look at me with

his heart in his eyes when I'm three floors away from him? "Do you, uh . . . want to go get dressed? I doubt anyone down here is complaining—myself included—but I'm a little sensitive about people telling me how hot you are. That's going to be unavoidable if you're naked."

Blood rushes to my cheeks and I look down. The towel. It snagged on the sink when I was looking out the window. I'm literally showing the entire avenue my rack. "*Shit!*" I hurtle myself backward off the sink onto the kitchen floor. After taking a moment to die a small death, I wrap the towel around me—securely this time—and gain my feet once again, making sure it stays in place as I lean out the window. "I'm decent."

Charlie gives me that slow smile, like we're in on a secret together, and my embarrassment evaporates like mist. He looks awful. On the surface, he's as sexy as ever, in his academy uniform and bristly cheeks, muscles for days, but I can see he's been sleeping about as well as I have. As in, not well at all. I just want him to end whatever production he has planned and come upstairs, so I can stuff him full of leftovers and take him to bed, but he lifts the bullhorn again before I can make the request.

"I love you, Ever. I love you so much." There's definitely some male groans happening around him, but he doesn't even flinch. "There won't be a day in my career where someone doesn't call me Romeo or Casanova because of this—and you know what? If you forgive me right now for what I did, I'll smile every single time I hear those nicknames. Because I'll know it was worth it. It would have been worth it every day for a hundred years. And I'll know I'm the lucky bastard who gets to come home to you every night." The bullhorn drops down to his thigh. "Please, Ever," he shouts. "I'm miserable."

My eyes are like sprinklers. Tears are actually squirting from my ducts and all the while, I'm laughing. I'm laughing because this man is so incredible. "Who goes around ruining someone's dates, Charlie? Who *does* that?"

"I don't know." He covers his face with the bullhorn a moment, then he's speaking into the mouthpiece once more. "Probably someone who'd do something like this . . ."

A song pipes up from one of the police car stereos, amplified through the speakers on top of the vehicle. As soon as I recognize it, the crying-laughing jag starts up again. All I can do is watch as officers climb out of their cars, their expressions totally deadpan as they sing "My Type" by Saint Motel.

Halfway through the song, Charlie calls to me again. "Take a good look at all these cars, Ever. I'll be washing them for a year to pay for this."

My heart is going to expire from happiness. I'm clutching at my chest, laughing, tears spilling onto my arms, rolling into the seam of my mouth. All I can think about is getting Charlie upstairs, into my arms, so I make a blind grab for the keys on my kitchen counter, dangling them out the window a moment, before dropping them into Charlie's waiting hand.

A cheer goes up. Sirens go off again. Charlie is off the hood of the car so fast, his form blurs on its way toward the building. Mine probably does, too, as I make a mad dash to the door, throwing open deadbolts and twisting locks. The door opens immediately . . .

And there's Charlie. All haunted eyes, stubbled cheeks and twisting hands. I launch myself at him, not caring one bit about the towel any longer. His strong arms are heaven around me. Perfect, unbreakable, never-letting-go heaven. The sound he breathes into my neck as I'm lifted off the ground is relief in its purest form.

"God, Charlie. *God*." I'm sobbing and holding on to him for dear life. "Look what happens when you harness your powers for good instead of evil." His laugh is hoarse and it vibrates my neck. "That was amazing. You're amazing."

"No, I'm a moron. I'm a desperate, exhausted moron who can't spend another second without his girlfriend." His blue eyes find mine, tired, but intense. "I have you back, Ever?" His voice is choked, beautiful. So, so beautiful. "Do I have you back?"

"You've had me back for days," I whisper, my knees shaking. My stomach. "If you'd come to find me, you would have known."

He grips my shoulders, stroking them up to my face. Cupping my cheeks. "I wanted to show you how hard I'll work. To make you happy. To correct myself when I screw up." His mouth hovers over mine and we moan. We moan, because it's been too long since we kissed. "I needed you to see. I'll keep you loving me. I won't take it for granted. I'll treat you, and this love, like the gift it is. You trust me, Ever?"

"Yes." I wind my fists in his shirt and tug him close, close as possible. "Will you trust me to know what I can handle? When I'm missing you or you're gone too long, I'll tell you and we'll work it out. But you're taking that exam, Charlie. What's important to you is important to me."

"Of course I trust you, cutie." His laugh is gruff and disbelieving. "And of course you wouldn't let me back out of the exam. I should have known." He shakes his head slowly. "At some point, I'll stop forgetting I fell in love with the most incredible girl on the planet, I swear."

"Anyway, someone who can juggle the police academy and execute sabotage at the same time can handle being a lieutenant and still keep his girlfriend happy."

"That's cute," he breathes, walking me backward toward the bedroom, his expression awed. "Real cute. Thinking you won't be my wife by the time I make lieutenant. You haven't learned how determined I can be by now?"

We fall backward onto the bed, my towel a thing of the past. Charlie's lips are just above mine, brushing them together. I watch as he notices my bed is covered in the letters he's been sending. Every single one of them kept me company as I tried to sleep. And his eyes take on a damp quality, his jaw flexing.

"I'll make you a deal." He reaches between us, unfastening his pants, both of us laboring to breathe within seconds. "When I pass the exam, you let me put a ring on your finger. Vows in your mouth."

"Done," I gasp as he thrusts into me, my back arching off the bed. "I love you so damn much, Charlie Burns."

He releases a ragged groan into my neck. "I love you more than life, Ever Carmichael."

EPILOGUE
Charlie

Life is . . . good? That's a massive understatement. Let's go with incredible. In fact, they haven't even invented a word yet for how fucking wow my life is right now. Sure, I only got Ever back yesterday, but we danced to James Brown this morning in her kitchen while she cooked me eggs, so . . . *wow*. Compared to the low point I hit when I lost her, this isn't just heaven. I'm on cloud nine, baby. And it's only going to get better from here.

I'm lying between Jack and Danika on a mat inside the gym. Greer just handed us our asses and we're in recovery mode. Out of the dozens of zombies in academy uniforms sprawled around us, though, I'm the only one smiling like a crazy person.

"Ever is spending the night at our place tonight." I squint one eye and check the clock, still grinning at the thought of seeing her in my bed for the first time. Holding her there. Listening to her talk in the darkness. "I need to wash my sheets."

Danika's nose wrinkles. "When is the last time that happened?"

"No clue."

She groans. "Some Febreze wouldn't go amiss, either." Her elbow meets Jack's ribs. "That goes for you, too, Garrett."

"And yet the complaint department has been totally silent." He stretches his arms over his head and yawns. "Does Ever staying the night mean we should invest in some ear plugs, Charlie boy, you dirty dog, you?"

Sure does. I can't think about what Ever did for me last night without tenting my uniform pants, so I better not. But it involved her mouth and a lot of moaning. All right, now I'm thinking about it anyway, might as well continue.

Ever broke out the pink bikini.

There goes my cock, rising like baked bread in the oven. Turning onto my side, I untuck my shirt to hide it.

I took her out to dinner last night, because you don't surprise your girl with a flash mob, then order sushi. No, I took her out for Italian, like a good New York boy. Wine and everything. And I think the wine is what gave her the pink bikini idea, so I'm looking into buying nineteen cases of the stuff. She sauntered out of her closet in the strips of pink and I proposed. Again. Since we already agreed she would become my wife after I aced the lieutenant's exam, she only laughed. Before proceeding to rock my world.

She stripped off the tiny, little bottoms—real slow, like she wanted to drive me insane—and hung them on that down low part of me she owns. Maybe that's what she was trying to signal. Well, guess what? She didn't need to. I'm hers. Until the end of time. I'll wear a sandwich board that says Ever's Guy on it if she asks me to.

Her knees found the floor in front of me after that. Tightening the pink material around the base of my erection, she dipped her mouth closer, closer . . . That's when the moaning—mine— started. I don't mind saying hers was even louder ten minutes later.

Ideas are already forming on how to make them glass-shattering tonight.

Honest to God, I'm looking forward to our conversation in the dark afterward just as much as the sex. We were up until the middle of the night last night, talking about everything from movies to recipe ideas to memories from our childhoods. Damn, I feel like I've only scratched the surface of her. Thankfully she's giving me all the time in the world to get right to her center. Right where I want to live forever.

"You all right over there, Charlie boy?" Jack asks with a knowing look.

"Oh, uh . . . yeah. Yes, I would look into ear plugs." My sigh is one of pure satisfaction. "Because we're going to be doin' it."

"Thanks for the clarification," Danika says dryly. "Do you want to give me the birds and the bees talk, too?"

Jack goes up on an elbow, beaming that 40-watt pirate smile. "Well, you see, honey. When a man and a woman have established a mutual respect for one another—"

"Stop." Danika is laughing as she claps both hands over her ears. "Make it stop."

Two things happen next that start my cop sense tingling. Jack begins tickling Danika, which isn't unusual. It's clearly nothing more than two childhood friends playing around and mild compared to the roughhousing that goes on in the gym every day. But when my brother, Greer, walks in, he takes in the scene and stiffens, eyes flaring.

"Keep your damn hands to yourself, Garrett," my brother snaps.

Danika shoots to her feet and stands like we're getting ready for daily inspection, although she looks irritated at herself for reacting that way. Jack doesn't budge, but the smile he sends Greer is lazy and patronizing as hell.

That smile vanishes a second later when a redheaded girl walks into the gym behind my brother, carrying a clipboard. Jack sits up slowly, following her progress around the room with nothing short of fascination. And maybe . . . yeah, even a glimmer of recognition. Like he's seen her somewhere before.

"Listen up, recruits," Greer shouts, his annoyance still written on his features, especially when he slants a glance at Danika. "This is your new arms instructor, Katie McCoy."

Jack's mouth drops open. "Fuck. Me."

Are you already dying to read
Jack Garrett's story? Well, you're in luck!
Read on for a sneak peek at

INDECENT EXPOSURE

Coming early 2018 from Avon Books!

CHAPTER 1
Jack

Growing up in the brothel where my mother worked had a couple of drawbacks. Here is the main one: I know way more about women than any man should.

For instance, sometimes when they say they're fine? They're actually fine and you should stop asking and shut the fuck up. I learned my lesson the hard way, as one does when sharing a bathroom with a rotating door of females, not to mention a best friend with the almighty X chromosome. Those lessons have served me well, though, haven't they? Knowing when to retreat carefully, push forward, or backpedal like a motherfucker during a conversation with a girl means I never go home alone.

Alone is a funny word, though, isn't it?

Sometimes I'm the most alone when surrounded by women. And that situation happens a lot more often for ol' Jack than it does for most guys. Is that a brag? Damn right. When women see me coming, their hormones whisper my name. I'm a demon in the sack. And most importantly, I treat girls with respect. Why shouldn't they want to go home with me at the end of the night? A couple hours in my bed means laughs, some patented sweet talk, a few orgasms, and cab fare. They could definitely do worse.

It's not their fault that I'm barely there when it's happening. That I'm watching myself touch them from above like a creepy, naked angel and wondering how long the mild queasiness will last. But like I said, that's not the girl's fault, is it? Women get blamed for enough without me adding to their plate. I'm there to give them a safe, shameless, satisfying ride and send them off with a smile.

Jack Garrett. Superhero. Protecting New York City's women from two-pump chumps one night at a time.

Look. I've witnessed the way men can disregard women as garbage once they've had their fun, so this calling of mine is not such a joke. Am I arrogant to think my dick is making a difference in the world of women? Yes. Am I apologizing? Hell no. Did I mention the orgasms and cab fare?

I've just come from a visit with my mother,

who now works as a pet groomer's receptionist—
thank Christ—and, as always, I marvel over
how my old neighborhood of Hell's Kitchen has
changed. They're calling it Clinton now but I don't
have time for that nonsense. It's the Kitchen to me
and it always will be. Doesn't matter how many
gastropubs and yoga studios pop up, I can still
see the grit beneath the glitter. I pass the doorway
where I finally got a hand up Melissa Sizemore's
shirt when I was thirteen, only to find out she'd
been wearing a Wonder bra the whole time we'd
been dating—and that's when I spot the redhead.

There is a lot of new blood in the Kitchen. Mid-
twenties millennials, like myself, trying to make
it in the city, while crammed into an apartment
with three roommates. Right now I'm calling the
East Side neighborhood of Kips Bay my home
while I train to be a cop under the annoyingly
watchful eyes of my NYPD instructors, but someday I'll come back to the Kitchen.

And if this sexy redhead is an indication of what
awaits me, it'll be sooner rather than later.

What the hell is she up to, though? She's on her
tiptoes, peering through the window of a dive bar
I know too well. In her hand is a shiny pink camera. She's snapping away with a look of total awe
on her face. A face I can only see in profile, but
that's enough to peg her as . . . cute. Cute as a button, even. Huge eyes, full cheeks, the kind of red,

puffy lips that stop traffic. At least when I'm at the wheel.

When it comes to women, I don't have a type. Tall, short, curvy, freckled, pierced, black, white, etcetera. All applications are accepted and approved. This redhead, though . . . I can't quite put a name on what pulls me toward her on the sidewalk. Is it her smile? The wobbly tip toe dance she's doing to make up for her lack of height? I've established she's adorable, but she's probably not looking for a hook up. Yet. Although, I never pursue women outside of bars, where I spend a lot of my time. If you ask my best friend, Danika, way too much time. But the alcohol makes it a shit ton easier to say yes. Yes to the girl, yes to what my body wants right now, but will regret later.

I push the troubling thought aside and focus on the redhead.

Coming to a stop beside her at the window, I get a nice whiff of mint and wonder if it's courtesy of lotion or direct from the herb. "Need a boost?"

She drops back onto flat feet and flicks me a glance. "I'm grand, thanks."

Irish girl. Her accent loops around in the air, but doesn't distract me from her huge blue eyes. Nothing could. They're the color of pale denim, outlined by a crowd of black lashes.

Hot. *Damn.*

Those twin beacons scan my face in slow motion, like a couple of barcode readers . . . and go right back to spying in the window. Huh. Disinterest from a girl is definitely new, but then again, this is why meeting women on a night out works so well. There's no mystery. For all I know, this girl is waiting for her husband to exit the dive where I had my first beer. No ring on her finger, but maybe they're traveling from Ireland and she left it home to be safe.

My mouth screws up in disgust when I realize I'm performing detective work involuntarily. Freaking academy is actually working.

"What are we looking at?" I ask, trying again.

"You're looking at me. I'm looking at this historical landmark."

"O'Keefe's?" I wave at the familiar bartender through the window. "Are you sure you didn't confuse this for the Empire State Building? Easy mistake. Happens to everyone."

One end of her incredible lips gives an upward tug. "I know what I'm at. Could you get lost now?"

"You're asking me to leave when I just made you smile?"

"I imagine it's not difficult for you to make a girl smile. What else you got?"

My chest vibrates with a laugh. "What else do you want?"

Thoughts skitter across her face like a blown dandelion. "I won't know until I see it."

I prop my shoulder against the building and wink at her. "Look no further."

She peers up at me and I swear to God, she's not even seeing what I've got on the surface. She's digging deeper, deeper . . . looking for *more*. When is the last time that happened? Never. Not that I can remember. She's not playing a game with me. She seems to be *truthing* me. Being totally honest.

Who *does* that?

"I'll decide when I'm done looking." With a jolt, she goes back to looking through the window. "But I think that's enough for now."

I'm not even offended. I'm more fascinated than anything else. It's not that I've never been turned down before—it has probably happened at least once—and I should really walk away now. No means no. Zero excuses. I'm just finding it pretty difficult to walk away and never hear the tilting notes in her voice again. To forfeit a chance to look into those unmatchable eyes at least one more time. And damn, she was searching for something below my surface and I'm kind of bothered that she hasn't found it yet. Hell, I'm not even sure what's there. But the fact that she tried at all makes me want to stick around. "I'll make you a deal. Just tell me why you're out here like a peeping tom and I'll go. Just satisfy my curiosity, would ya, honey?"

The twin patches of pink on the girl's cheeks tell me she's not totally unaware that I'm attractive. The cajoling did it. Women like it when I beg, whether or not it's only for show. This time doesn't feel like it's for show.

When she drops back onto her heels, humor is dancing in her expression. "Once I tell you, getting rid of you will be easy enough, I suppose."

Now that I finally have her undivided attention, I just want to hold on to it. Even though she wants to get rid of me. Maybe the lighting on the street is bad and my face is hidden by shadows. Or the sun is blinding her. That has to be it. "Let me be the judge of that."

Lips pursed, she tugs a book out of her back pocket. It's titled *The Ultimate Guide to Famous New York City Mob Hits*. She gestures toward the window with the book spine. "In there is where Whitey Kavanaugh was whacked during the mob wars of eighty-seven." Her eyebrows give a mischievous waggle. "You're kind of interrupting my murder tour here, good looking."

Katie

In Dublin, we have a word for this kind of man: a ride.

I'm fighting the temptation to peek over his shoulder and see if he walked off a movie set. Honest to God, he's a dream. A taller version of James Dean, charisma gliding off him in lazy, rolling plumes of smoke. His smile is its own story altogether, the way it crinkles the corners of his eyes and creates dents in his cheeks. I wouldn't call them dimples, because they're more like twin, side-by-side dips on both ends. Like his mouth is in quotation marks.

All manner of things are happening here. The dead center cleft in his chin. His stubbled cheeks and jaw. Dark, sweeping eyebrows over green eyes. His hair is in a crew cut, but I can see it's black and if it were long, would probably flip just perfectly over his forehead, framing his gorgeous face. Tall. He had to be tall and fit, as well? Really? It seems an awful gluttony of five star qualities on a single person. God should have spread them around his other creations a bit.

I could have used a few inches of height myself. My neck is already beginning to protest being craned so long to look into the face of such flawlessness.

Good thing he'll be moving on soon. No one sticks around for a girl who has a long-standing fascination with organized crime. At least, I don't think so. I've never voiced this interest of mine out loud to a man. I barely speak to men at all, although I have plans to change that while I'm visiting New York. As soon as this completely unrealistic, possibly CGI creature stops trying to knock me into a coma with his physical charms, I'll be off to the races.

"Good looking, huh?" Of course, he focuses on the name I called him. "And yet you're so impatient for me to leave."

"Oh, em . . ." When his smile sags a touch, I realize I've been outright rude. But I'm too embarrassed to explain why. That I thought he was just having a laugh at my expense on his way into the pub . . . and couldn't possibly be interested in me. I mean, I'm only after getting off the plane at JFK, no shower or hairstyle to speak of. My jeans and tank top are rumpled from traveling and will probably have to be burned. What could possibly have drawn this man in my direction? "I apologize. I just assumed you had somewhere else to be and I was . . . giving you leave. To go there."

He tilts his head, interested. "Where do you think I'm headed?"

"Hmm." I lean back and size him up. When I reach his eyes, one thing is obvious. He already thinks he knows my answer. "Piano fingers."

Shock transforms his expression and the digits in question twitch at his side. "What about them?"

"Maybe you're a piano teacher? On the way to a lesson?" Why is he so quiet all of a sudden? "Am I that far off?"

"No, but . . ." He shifts. "You look at me and think I could be a piano teacher?"

"What do you *want* me to see?" His lack of response jumbles my nerves. "Wherever you're headed, I was just trying to be polite and give you an easy send off. I didn't mean to sound eager or anything."

He gives a quick shake of his head. "You don't need a reason for wanting me gone." He seems intent on impressing this important point upon me. "It's your decision and I should have listened the first time."

I'm suspicious by nature. "Are you being this agreeable now because I'm murder sightseeing and you're trying to get away from me?"

"No, actually I think murder sightseeing is pretty fucking cool."

"Is that why you're still here?"

"Yeah. And the fact that you're beautiful." He arches an eyebrow when all I can do is sputter. "If you've changed your mind about ditching me, I'll bring you inside to get a decent picture. Do you know which chair Whitey was sitting in when—"

"Third from the end."

"Had a feeling you would know." With a half-smile, he offers me his arm, which is wrapped in the soft cotton of a black hoodie. "Come on. I'll kick whoever is in it out."

"I don't go into bars. That's why I'm out here probably looking like a bloody lunatic." The reasoning behind my no bar rule is personal—too personal to tell a stranger—so my gaze automatically evades him. Otherwise he might see the hurt and I don't share that with anyone. It's mine. But I feel him watching closely as I tuck my camera back into its case and replace it in the pocket of my backpack. "Thank you for the offer . . ."

"Jack." His throat sounds crowded when he answers me, along with his eyes. "And you're . . ."

"Katie." I sling my backpack on over my shoulders, trying to remember if I thanked him for calling me beautiful. Or if I should even call attention to the fact he did, because he might repeat the word and I'm not sure I can handle hearing it twice in one day. Not without giggling and making a complete arse out of myself.

The last four years of my life have been spent training for the Olympics non-stop. Grueling hours of practice that meant zero time for the opposite sex. Now, at the first sign of freedom, I'm thrown right into the arena with James Dean's great-grandson. When I decided to sandwich in a torrid love affair during my business trip to New York, I had someone more approachable in mind. Like a nerdy desk clerk. Or a portly crossing guard. "Listen, I'm not judging or anything. About the bar. Really. You can go on in—"

"There you go, trying to ditch me again." His thousand-watt smile turns back on and steals the breath straight out of my lungs. "Are there any other famous mob-hit locations in the neighborhood, or is this your last stop?"

"There's one more," I hear myself say. Shite. How am I supposed to relax when he's smiling at me like that? If he concentrated the full power of that smile on a stick of butter, it would be a gooey puddle in seconds. Needing a distraction from his face, I consult my mob hit guide. "McCaffrey Park. Is that close?"

"Right down the street." He ticks his head in that direction. "Ready?"

No, I'm not ready. For one thing, he's a stranger in an unfamiliar city and might be planning to harvest my organs. Two, he's fresh and stunning, while I'm in ratty trainers and wearing a purple backpack like an oversized toddler. And three . . . I just have a feeling mysterious Jack is going to be bad news for me. Call it a sixth sense or common sense or what have you, but this ride with the bad boy smile has trouble oozing out of his pores.

This should be a no-brainer. When a stranger shows an unlikely interest in me, it's probably for the best to avoid walking with him to a dark park where mob hits have taken place. Just as a rule.

I've been expected to act beyond reproach my entire *life*, though. I barely survived a strict Catholic upbringing before being thrust under the Olympic microscope. Every day of my life has been scheduled and executed without fail.

This man is not on my agenda.

Then again, I did promise myself adventure during this two-week trip. Swore to myself I would fulfil a vow to someone I love, by living without constraint. After being under my father's thumb so long, I'm so light. So without responsibilities, I didn't even take the time to clean up after my flight, throwing on my runners and bursting out of the hotel. Could Jack be part of my adventure?

No, it's impossible. Surely he's filming a romantic comedy down the street and he's method acting right now. Then again, those piano fingers . . . the way he acted so surprised that I would point them out has me reluctantly intrigued.

His green eyes cloud with disappointment the longer I take to answer him, though. His smile winds down in degrees until his mouth is nothing more than a grim line. I'm about to turn him down for the walk to the park, when he says, "No hard feelings, Katie. Huh?" He winks, but it's a sad one. "Even if it is going to take me a damn long while to forget those eyes."

My heart is in my mouth when he goes. His hands shovel into his pockets and he walks backward a few paces, keeping me in his sights, before turning and strolling down the block. It's insane, the anxious bubbles that begin to pop in my belly. My hands tighten into fists at my sides and the backpack starts to feel heavy. "Wait," I shout. Then I cringe. Because everyone on the sidewalk, including Jack, turns to look at me. "Ah . . . sure go on. Just the walk, then?"

Even from a distance, Jack's mouth spreading into a slow smile is breathtaking.

As I walk toward him, my feet on the warm concrete seem to be chanting one word.

Trouble, trouble, trouble.

Next month, don't miss these exciting
new love stories only from
Avon Books

The Duke by Katharine Ashe
Six years ago, when Lady Amarantha Vale was an
innocent in a foreign land and Gabriel Hume was a
young naval officer, they met . . . and played with fire.
Now Gabriel is known to society as the Devil's Duke, a
notorious recluse hidden away in a Highlands castle.
Only Amarantha knows the truth about him, and she
won't be intimidated . . .

Such a Pretty Girl by Tess Diamond
As the FBI's top profiler, Grace Sinclair knows that real
life is rarely as straightforward as the bestselling
mysteries she writes. But her new case isn't just brutal—
it's personal. And the FBI special agent assigned to her
team is trouble of another kind. Two years ago, she and
Gavin Walker shared one earth-shattering night before
she vanished from his life.

Tangled Up in Tinsel by Candis Terry
As if the holidays weren't stressful enough, Parker
Kincade has a restaurant to open. The fact that his
Groomzilla brother wants the place for his perfect
Christmas wedding doesn't help. Then there's the
stunning woman who appoints herself his new chef
before he's ready to hire one. But one look at Gabriella
Montani has Parker reassessing everything. And that's
before he tastes what she has to offer . . .

Discover great authors, exclusive offers,
and more at hc.com.

REL 0917

NEW YORK TIMES BESTSELLING AUTHOR

JENNIFER RYAN

THE MONTANA MEN NOVELS

AT WOLF RANCH
978-0-06-233489-3

WHEN IT'S RIGHT
978-0-06-233493-0

HER LUCKY COWBOY
978-0-06-233495-4

STONE COLD COWBOY
978-0-06-243532-3

HER RENEGADE RANCHER
978-0-06-243535-4

HIS COWBOY HEART
978-0-06-243540-8

Discover great authors, exclusive offers,
and more at hc.com.

JRY 0717

NEW YORK TIMES BESTSELLING AUTHOR

SUSAN ELIZABETH PHILLIPS

CALL ME IRRESISTIBLE
978-0-06-135153-2

Meg Koranda knows breaking up her best friend Lucy
Jorik's wedding to Mr. Irresistible—Ted Beaudine— is the
right thing to do, but no one else agrees. Now Meg's stuck
with a dead car, an empty wallet, and a very angry bridegroom. But she'll survive—after all, what's the worst that
could happen? She'll lose her heart to Mr. Irresistible? Not
likely. Not likely at all.

THE GREAT ESCAPE
978-0-06-210608-7

Instead of saying "I do" to the most perfect man she's ever
known, Lucy flees the church and hitches a ride on the back
of a beat-up motorcycle with a rough-looking stranger who
couldn't be more foreign to her privileged existence. But
as the hot summer days unfold amid scented breezes and
sudden storms, she discovers a passion that could change
her life forever.

HEROES ARE MY WEAKNESS
978-0-06-210609-4

Annie Hewitt has been forced to return to an isolated island
off the coast of Maine, a place she hasn't visited since a disastrous summer when she was a teen. She couldn't be more
ill-prepared for who she finds on the island: Theo Harp,
the boy who betrayed her in a way she can never forgive. Is
he the villain she remembers, or has he changed? Her heart
says yes, but the wrong decision could cost her everything.

**Discover great authors, exclusive offers,
and more at hc.com.**

SEP4 0317

Funny, poignant, sexy and totally outrageous fiction from
New York Times bestselling author
_____

SUSAN ELIZABETH PHILLIPS

Just Imagine

978-0-380-80830-4

Kit Weston has come to post-Civil War New York City
to confront the Yankee who stands between
her and her beloved South Carolina home.

First Lady

978-0-380-80807-6

How does the most famous woman in the world hide in plain sight?
The beautiful young widow of the President of the United States
thought she was free of the White House, but circumstances
have forced her back into the role of First Lady.

Lady Be Good

978-0-380-79448-5

Lady Emma Wells-Finch, the oh-so-proper headmistress of
England's St. Gertrude's School for Girls knows only one thing
will save her from losing everything she holds dear:
complete and utter disgrace! So she arrives in Texas on a mission:
She has two weeks to lose her reputation.

Kiss An Angel

978-0-380-78233-8

How did pretty, flighty Daisy Deveraux find herself in this fix?
She can either go to jail or marry the mystery man her father
has chosen for her. Alex Markov, however, has no intention of
playing the loving bridegroom to a spoiled little featherhead.

_____

**Discover great authors, exclusive offers,
and more at hc.com.**

SEP3 0317

At Avon Books, we know your passion for romance—once you finish one of our novels, you find yourself wanting more.

May we tempt you with . . .

- **Excerpts** from our upcoming releases.

- Entertaining **extras**, including authors' personal photo albums and book lists.

- Behind-the-scenes **scoop** on your favorite characters and series.

- **Sweepstakes** for the chance to win free books, romantic getaways, and other fun prizes.

- Writing **tips** from our authors and editors.

- **Blog** with our authors and find out why they love to write romance.

- **Exclusive content** that's not contained within the pages of our novels.

Join us at
www.avonbooks.com

AVON *An Imprint of* HarperCollins*Publishers*
www.avonromance.com

Available wherever books are sold or please call 1-800-331-3761 to order.

*G*ive in to your Impulses!

These unforgettable stories only take a second to buy and give you hours of reading pleasure!

Go to *www.AvonImpulse.com* and see what we have to offer.

Available wherever e-books are sold.

AVONIMPULSE

IMP 0811